More from Lauren Baratz-Logsted

Johnny Smith Novels
Isn't It Bro-Mantic?

Jane Taylor Novels
The Thin Pink Line
Crossing the Line

Diversion Books
A Division of Diversion Publishing Corp.
443 Park Avenue South, Suite 1008
New York, New York 10016
www.DiversionBooks.com

This is a work of fiction. Names, characters, places and incidents either are the
product of the author's imagination or are used fictitiously. Any resemblance
to actual persons, living or dead, events or locales is entirely coincidental.

For more information, email info@diversionbooks.com

First Diversion Books edition February 2015.
Print ISBN: 978-1-62681-760-9
eBook ISBN: 978-1-62681-605-3

the bro-
magnet

LAUREN BARATZ-LOGSTED

DIVERSIONBOOKS

I Am Born

(and I begin as life intends me to go on)

Right from the start, I've been a disappointment to women.

Here's me at my own birth:

On January 1, 1977, after thirty-two hours, fourteen minutes and fifty-three seconds of labor, most of it during a heat wave so bad there are citywide power outages—a heat wave that would have been perfectly normal in Florida, but in New England, not so much—my mother, Francesca Smith, gives birth to me at home at exactly 2:19 P.M.

She insisted on the home birth because she said it would be more natural.

Alfresca Tivoli, Francesca's sister, is present as Francesca's birthing coach because my father, John Smith, says it's women's work. Plus, he's scared shitless.

As I emerge from between my mother's legs—all thirteen pounds, eight ounces of me—Alfresca catches me. Then I do the usual baby stuff: I get my cord cut, I'm slapped, I cry, I get weighed and measured, someone wipes the cheesy stuff off my hairy head, and finally I get handed off to my mother.

"Oh," Francesca says, gently parting the swaddling to examine my body further, "it's a boy. This wasn't what I was expecting at all. I was so sure, all along, I was going to have a girl."

Then, she dies.

"If you'd been a girl," Alfresca says, taking me from my dead mother's arms as the midwife tries in vain to resuscitate my disappointed mother, "this never would have happened."

I know all this, not because I was born with some kind of precocious baby-genius capability to instantly understand language, but rather, because Aunt Alfresca has spent the last thirty-three years reminding me, at fairly regular intervals but with surprisingly little malice, that I killed her sister.

As I said, right from the start, I've been a disappointment to women.

Some people would tell you it couldn't happen to a nicer guy. All of those people would be men.

Here I am in grade school:

You'd think my father would hate me for, you know, killing his wife, but such was not the case.

Occasionally, feeling guilty about my part in my mother's death, I'd say that it sure would be nice to have a woman around the house; you know, someone other than Aunt Alfresca.

"But we can tell fart jokes as much as we want to," he'd say back. "Hell, we can fart as much as we want to! Drink orange juice straight from the carton, burritos every night, leave the seat up in the toilet, no need to pick up our dirty clothes from the floor, sports on the TV all weekend long, scratch our balls without embarrassment—now, *this* is living!"

Don't get me wrong. He'd loved his wife, still keeps their wedding picture on his night table to this day so he can kiss her goodnight last thing before going to bed and greet her first thing in the morning, but he also loved us being just-two-guys-together-in-this-thing-called-life, which was pretty much what we were all the time. Well, except for whenever Aunt Alfresca came for a visit.

"Go outside and play, Johnny," Aunt Alfresca directs me. "After killing your mother, it's the least you can do."

I'm called Johnny because my mother had intended to call the baby that was supposed to be a girl Johnesca to honor my father. Since there was already one John in the family, to honor her wishes my father put Johnny on my birth certificate, restyling himself Big John.

Not wanting to make Aunt Alfresca any madder than she always is, I go outside.

It's not hard for me to get other kids in our Danbury neighborhood together for a game of kickball. At least, it's not hard to get other boys to play. Tall for my age and lean, despite the thirteen and a half pounds at birth, at eight years old I have the athletic prowess of a far older kid. Every boy likes to play with me, especially if they get picked to be on my team. So before long, I've got six boys who are eager to play.

"We need one more," says Drew Bailey, "so sides'll be even."

But we don't have one more boy on our street.

"I'll go ask Alice," I say, referring to the girl who lives right next door to me.

"Aw, don't do that," Billy Keller whines his disgust. "We don't need her. You're so good, you could count as two people on your team."

But I'm already at her door.

Knock, knock. Press my thumb on the bell until someone answers.

And there's Alice—Alice who is eight, like me, and damn cute.

"Um, you wanna come play kickball with us?" I shuffle my feet. "We kinda need one more player so sides'll be even."

"Nice way to ask, Smith," she says with a toss of her chestnut hair and a glare of her chocolate eyes. "'We kinda need one more,'" she mimics me, and does an incredible job of imitating my voice I might add. Then she sneers, "You don't want me, specifically. You just want your stupid sides to be even."

"Go outside and play," I hear Mrs. Knox yell from within the house. "It's a beautiful day. The exercise will do you good."

Alice narrows her eyes at me. "Thanks a lot." Then she comes outside, slamming the door behind her.

After we join the others, it's decided that me and Billy Keller will be captains. I win the shoot-out to see who picks first—natch—and I'm about to pick Drew, who's the third best after me and Billy, when I get a brilliant idea.

Alice, for all her cuteness, sucks at sports. Alice, therefore, whether in the neighborhood or at school, is always picked last. As my finger's about to point at Drew, it occurs to me how lousy that must feel. And I, who have never been picked last at sports in my entire life, have my first real flash of human empathy. No wonder Alice never wants to play with us! No wonder she'll only do it if her mother makes her.

I decide right then to make her day.

Today, Alice will be *first*.

As Drew stands there looking smug, expecting to be tagged first, as the other four guys around him strain their arms in my direction—"Pick me! Pick me!"—I point my thumb at Alice before jerking it over my shoulder. And so there's no mistaking who I'm picking, I specify, "Alice. My team."

I don't know what I was expecting. A kiss on the cheek? An enthusiastic hug? No, probably neither of those, certainly not with everyone else watching. But some form of gratitude. Home-baked cookies, maybe just a sweet smile...

As Alice trudges to take her place behind me, Drew thrusts his arms out, palms up, as if to ask, "What the fuck, dude?"

And as Billy immediately moves to tap Drew for his team, Alice leans forward to whisper in my ear.

"You suck, Smith. Way to make me look bad. Everyone knows you only picked me first because you felt sorry for me. Now—whoop-de-doo—I get to be the weakest link on your team."

Even though Alice doesn't get to base once, even though she never catches one ball or throws another player out, even though she gets hit in the head and later knocked over by a teammate trying to make a catch, we still win 18-7. Like Billy says, I'm as good as having two players.

"You suck, Smith."

No. Definitely not gratitude.

• • • •

Here's me in middle school, just barely middle school, so sixth grade to be exact:

I'm in the cafeteria with Billy and Drew and the rest, waiting in line to get my orange tray. Mm, sloppy joes…I'm not even kidding about that mm—I *love* those things!

Standing right in front of me is, yeah, Alice Knox. It's the first day this year with a real promise of spring in the air and, like a lot of the other girls, she's dressed as though it's the middle of summer, instead of, you know, fifty-three degrees. She has on a pink tank top, not loose in the slightest I might add, and in the past four years since that kickball game her figure has, um, changed.

Alice Knox has the nicest breasts of any girl in our class. Hell, the nicest breasts of any girl in the whole school—throw in seventh and eighth grades, because those are some amazing world-class breasts!

Which is why, as she receives her tray with a salad on it and I reach for my own orange tray with one hand, I reach out the other hand, place one finger under the suddenly blinding white bra strap that's peeking out from beneath her pink tank and snap it.

Snap.

Which is almost immediately followed by…

Slap.

Oh yeah, and that's almost immediately followed by Alice dumping her tray over my head.

And that *is* immediately followed by Alice seething, "I hate you, Smith," before helping herself to a fresh tray.

You'd think the guys would laugh at my humiliation, being covered with no-calorie, fat-free Italian salad dressing and all, never mind the lettuce leaves and shredded carrots on my shoulders, but such is not the case. Instead, there's high-fives and choruses of "Awesome, dude!" all around. At least from the guys.

Now here's the thing: I do know that was a colossally rude thing to do to Alice, but, in the moment, I couldn't help myself. Something came over me. And it's not like I did anything borderline illegal like, say, reach out and actually grab one of her breasts, which you can't blame a guy for wanting to do since, in the entire history of the world and if God really did create the human body, *nothing* has ever been invented yet to rival the beautiful glory of the female breast. (And if you're about to psychoanalyze that sentence, maybe try to tie it in to the fact that my mother died on the date of my birth and therefore was never able to breastfeed me, well, don't.) But I would never do that. I would never disrespect Alice in that way. As a matter of fact, respect was exactly what I'd been trying to show her. Just like if Billy stole second base, I might give him a pat on the butt to signify, "Yo, nice job," with nothing sexual about it at all, I was simply trying to give Alice a similar compliment; you know, something along the lines of, "Yo, Alice, nice job—great work on those breasts!"

OK, so maybe that does sound sexual, but that's not how I meant it to come across. I swear.

Now here's the other thing: The guys may think it's hysterical – like, pretty much every guy in the whole school hears about it by the end of the day – but the girls don't. From that day forward, the girls christen me The Snapper and mostly they stay far away from me.

Senior prom:

I'd be lying if I said I'd had no female contact since The Snapper incident six years ago, but I'd also be lying if I said any of it could be categorized as something more than cursory, fumbling, brief or "before the girl in question found out I was The Snapper."

The theme song for prom is Elton John's "Can You Feel the Love Tonight?"

No, Elton, I'm sorry to say, I really can't.

I can't feel it because I'm going to senior prom with seven other guys in a limo I rented for the night with some of the money I've saved helping my dad out in his painting business. It used to be called John Smith's Painting, Interiors and Exteriors, but after Mom died he renamed it simply Big John's.

It's not like I wouldn't like to be taking a girl to the prom; actually, one girl in particular. There was only ever one girl in that school I'd buy a corsage for. But as I walked up to her in front of her locker about three weeks before the big day, getting up my nerve to ask, I could hear the response already: "You suck, Smith." So, not really wanting to hear those words directed at me yet again, I asked to borrow a pencil instead.

"Really, Smith?" Alice said. "What—am I the only person in this school who might have a spare writing implement? Do I *look* like a pencil factory to you?"

So that's as close to inviting a girl to prom as I ever got.

Oh, and when word got out that I was going, but going stag, and seven of my buddies decided to go stag with me because they figured it would be more fun? Pretty much every dateless girl in school decided they hated my guts for taking seven guys off the prom market.

Anyway, it's the big night and I'm wearing a regular black tux with white shirt because my dad always says that any color other than black, like something trendy, you regret later in life when you look back at the pictures. He should know. In the wedding photo he's got on his night table, he's wearing an all-white tux with wide lapels, with lots of big gold chains and medallions dangling down from his neck.

In the pocket of my black tux, I've got the condom Dad slipped me on the way out the door.

"You know," he said awkwardly as we shared our big bonding moment, "just in case."

As if.

Then he reached out, smoothed my lapel with one hand while he crushed his beer can with the other. "Your mother would be so proud."

Really, Dad? Mom would be proud of her dateless son? I'm thinking no.

I'm still thinking that as I climb into the limo and later as we pick each of my seven friends up at their houses.

"Hey," Mike II says when he climbs into the limo, the last

to be picked up, "look what my dad gave me." I'm thinking he's going to pull out a beer and, whoop-de-doo, we'll share it eight ways for a whopping one-point-five ounces each. But instead he pulls out a condom. And before you know it, all the rest are excitedly pulling out condoms too, all courtesy of their dads.

What are the dads in this town, like, the most optimistic guys in the world ever? Do they really think that eight stag guys are going to somehow magically pick up eight dateless girls at prom and somehow score?

As my friends high-five each other over their new prophylactic prowess, I'm figuring by dawn we'll be using these to throw water balloons at each other.

As we make our big entrance at prom, I can tell the other guys still think it's so cool we're going stag together, and I can tell that even a lot of the guys who have dates wish they were us, free to do whatever we want all night instead of having to pretend we like to dance or that we care about corsages.

Secretly, I'd love to dance with a girl. I'd even love to get stabbed by the pin of some stupid corsage I bought a girl if it means I get to slow dance with her.

And the girl I'd really like to dance with most just walked in on the arm of Mark Leblanc: Alice Knox, who's wearing a simple long white sheath dress, shoulderless on one side and not at all like the elaborate dresses all the other girls have on, the kind they'll regret later in life when they see themselves in pictures. Alice's chestnut hair is gathered into a high ponytail, the tresses flowing beautifully, and around the crown of her head is a narrow sparkling circlet thing that looks just perfect and proves to be prophetic when later on she and Mark win King and Queen of the Prom.

I'd be jealous right now, but I just can't be as they dance to Prince's "The Most Beautiful Girl in the World," because she deserves this. She is the most beautiful girl in the world and she's nice, even if she's always telling me she hates me and that I suck. And while I'd really like to hate Mark, I can't do that either, because he's like the definition of nice and I know he's good to her and that he'd, you know, never snap her bra in public. Hey, wait a second: Did Mark's dad give him a condom too?

I shake that thought away.

And I realize then that I might as well give up on girls, at least for the night, that my dad's condom-in-the sky dreams for me aren't going to come true at prom and even though I'd been secretly hoping to at least get *some* girl to dance with me once, I decide to do what Luther Vandross says in his remake and "Love the One You're With."

Unfortunately, in my case that means Billy, Drew, Pete, Mike I, Mike II, Steve and Matt, the latter of whose long hair I hold away from his face as he pukes out the window of the limo a few hours later. As some puke flies back onto my tux sleeve, I'm thinking all those dateless girls should be thanking me for taking Matt off the prom-date market.

"You're my best friend, man," Matt says, eyes closed as he collapses back against the seat.

Why is it, I wonder now, that I'm so good at so many things (even if I'm the one saying so) and admired by so many (well, it's not immodesty when, *obviously*, all guys admire me), but I have no luck with girls? This is beginning to bother me.

"No," Billy says to Matt, "he's my best friend."

"No," Drew starts to say, but never finishes because right then Mike II stands up, sticks his head out the sunroof of the limo, waves his bottle of J.D. at the city of Danbury and shouts, "This limo rocks!"

And now I'm thinking that the theme for my own personal senior prom should be Seal's "Prayer for the Dying."

That's right. Oh, and by the way? Fuck you, Elton John.

College graduation:

Yup. Still got that rubber in my pocket.

Outside of murder, there's a statute of limitations on most things in life, so by the time I got to college, even though some girls from my high school showed up at the same college, all The Snapper talk had pretty much died down. Besides, in college there were guys doing a lot worse things than snapping bra straps.

But not me.

Still, it wasn't like I was able to reinvent myself there, at least not as I'd hoped to. Somehow, when you get treated a certain way for X amount of years, like the kind of testosterone-heavy Neanderthal who's only worthy of having girls say "You suck, Smith" to him, you begin to internalize it.

So, not long after starting freshman year I finally gave up and decided to go with the flow. I began belching at the dinner table. I was always the first one at a party to do a keg handstand. At football games, I yelled the loudest. Guys loved me. I mean, *all* guys loved me. Even the gay ones. They might act like I was crude on the outside, but I saw those secret smiles. Girls, however? Not so much.

The thing is, it's not like I'm ugly or anything. In fact, most people would say I'm pretty damn good looking! But it's never gained me any advantages in life.

Anyway, once I pretty much gave up on girls, I was free to study, which is why I managed to graduate Magna Cum Laude. My major was Poli Sci and I'd been figuring on maybe going to law school, but then right after the graduation ceremony, the mortarboard still on my head, Dad says:

"You want to be a lawyer? But that's crazy talk. Lawyers are miserable, they hate what they do, plus they make everyone else miserable too."

"But it's a profession, Dad. I'd be a professional."

I'd been thinking he'd be happy. I was the first in the family to graduate from college. Wasn't the point of all this to wind up with a high-paying, well-respected profession?

"Professional, schmofessional," Aunt Alfresca says. Leave it to her to make up a new word. "If you hadn't killed your mother, and she'd gotten used to you not being a girl, she'd have never wanted you to be a lawyer."

This was news to me: the idea that Mom might have had specific plans for me, if I wasn't a girl.

"What would she want?"

"She'd want you to go into business with me," Dad says,

like he's as sure of this as he's ever been of anything in his life. He raises his arm and slowly moves his open palm as though he's picturing skywriting against the heavens of a blue June day as he intones, "Big John and Johnny," and then "Paint: It never lets you down."

Which is exactly what was the motto of first John Smith's Painting, Interiors and Exteriors and then Big John's.

So that's what I wind up doing with my college degree.

I become a house painter.

And here's me now, age thirty-three, the same age, may I point out, that Jesus was when he got crucified. I'm the Best Man, about to give the toast at Billy Keller's wedding. Let's see if my life has changed in the past eleven years since graduating college.

You be the judge.

Always a Groomsman

Billy was so determined to make his bride happy that he refused to heed my advice about traditional wedding attire which means it's kind of hard for me to get psyched about standing up in front of one hundred and seventy-three people while wearing a white tux with purple bowtie and matching cummerbund, not to mention the white patent-leather penny loafers and white socks, but I give it my best shot, delivering the speech I rehearsed in the shower first thing in the morning.

I hold my champagne glass out toward Billy and his bride, hand steady.

"A man's life is composed of circles," I begin. "First, there's the circle of the entire world, which a man keeps in contact with through reading the papers and watching the news. Or not." I pause, give a wry smile. "The world can be a pretty depressing place."

I pause again, wait for the laugh.

It comes.

"Then, if the man is like Billy and me and he chooses to stay in the same town he grew up in all his life, there's that town. It may not be much but," I raise my glass a little higher, "go, Danbury!"

Some more laughter, a few answering calls of "Go, Danbury!"—the latter mostly from locals who hit the open bar early and hard and a few out-of-towners trying to fit in and be supportive.

"Then comes the circle of a man's acquaintances: friends of friends, coworkers, the guy with the little hot dog cart outside the library who overcharges like crazy but makes the best dogs in town. What's that guy's secret?"

Only a polite chuckle for that one. I detest polite chuckles.

When it comes to laughter, a person should be all in or all out.

"And then comes a very small circle: the circle of a man's dearest friends, his best friends"—I give a nod to the groom, Billy—"and family." I tilt my glass at Big John in his wheelchair—MS. "I love you, Dad."

I pause again, not waiting for the laugh this time—there won't be any laughter for the rest of this speech—but rather to get control of my emotions, the tear in my eye mirroring the tear in Big John's.

Tearing my gaze away from my father, I let my eyes sweep the entire audience.

"Now if you've been paying attention, you'll have noticed something. The circles I've been describing have been steadily decreasing in size while at the same time increasing in importance. And so now, finally, we come to the last circle, the smallest circle. If a man is extremely lucky, if he's the luckiest man in the world, he finds the right person to share his life with, to form that smallest circle of two with, and that is exactly what my friend Billy has done."

And now I raise my glass one last time toward Billy and his bride.

"To Billy and Alice: May the two of you always be a perfect circle together, as symbolized by the rings you exchanged just a short time ago."

That's right. Billy Keller—the fucker—somehow managed to snag Alice Knox. Go figure. Neither of us sees her for about a dozen or more years, then she moves back to the area, he runs into her in the cereal aisle of Super Stop & Shop, they debate the relative merits of steel-cut Irish oatmeal versus regular, then they date for a year, he drops to one knee and asks her to marry him right after she catches the bouquet at Drew's wedding, and the rest is wedding-album history. Billy farts sometimes when he laughs too hard, he belches after he eats and his feet smell. So I was surprised when they started dating, amazed when they got serious and shocked when they got engaged. If I told you I haven't spent this entire day wondering "Why him and not me?" I'd be lying. But he's my friend, one of my best friends, so I have to wish him well.

"To Billy and Alice!" the calls come from all corners of the room.

I'd like to say that there's not a dry eye in the house, but that would only be half true.

The guys all have tears in their eyes—"That was beautiful, man"; "If I ever get married again, I want you to be my Best Man and give that exact same speech"; "I'm Best Man for my brother next month and don't have a clue what to say—could you write that down for me?"

The women? Not so much.

The chicken's been eaten, the groom has danced with the bride, the bride has danced with her father and now it's the whole wedding party's turn to mix it up. All of the ushers and bridesmaids head straight out for the dance floor but Billy's talking head-to-head with Alice, who sits at the head table between us—you know, girl-boy/girl-boy seating—with Alice's maid of honor, who's some out-of-town cousin, on the other side of Billy. The cousin's looking a little bit three-sheets-to-the-wind and I'm thinking maybe I can sit this one out, so I get up to get another beer. But then, halfway to the bar, I get some kind of weird tingling sensation that makes me look back. That's when I see Three-Sheets Cousin teeter to her feet and hold her hand out to Billy. Her being the maid of honor, how can Billy refuse? It would be so ungentlemanly. So he follows her out to the dance floor, leaving Alice alone at the head table.

I shrug, turn back to the bar, start to walk toward it again and something stops me again.

I turn back to the head table. Alice is still there. Alone. A bride alone on her wedding day.

This isn't right.

Which is how I finally wind up dancing with Alice Keller nee Knox fourteen years after prom to "Can You Feel the Love Tonight?"

Fuck the DJ for thinking show tunes were a good idea.

"You make a beautiful bride," I say, one hand lightly on Alice's waist, the other primly on her shoulder, as many inches as possible while still slow dancing separating our bodies so mine doesn't even think about getting an erection. Or, if it betrays me and goes ahead anyway, hopefully she'll never know.

"Thanks," she says, but she doesn't look happy with the compliment. "I can't believe you did a retread at my wedding."

"A retread?" What's she talking about? Retreads are tires.

"A retread." Now she's exasperated at my stupidity. "You gave that same exact 'circle of friends' speech at Drew's wedding."

Oh. See? This is what I meant earlier about the guys getting tears in their eyes on account of my speech while the women present did not. It's because the guys always hit the open bar so early and so hard at these things, they don't remember that maybe they've heard that speech before. But the women? Except for the diehard alcoholics they're smarter. They drink slower in the beginning and therefore, they tend to remember pesky little details.

"I can't believe," Alice continues when I fail to say anything in my own defense, "you gave a wedding toast you'd already given once before."

Actually, I've given that speech not just once but seven times before, this being my eighth stint as Best Man—hey, when you've got a crowd-pleasing event-appropriate speech in the can that is loved by at least half your audience, why mess with a good thing? But Alice was out of town all those years and therefore missed the other six times I gave the 'circle of a man's life' speech, and hey, I'm not going to be the one to clue her in.

Anyway, it's not like I've given the *exact* same speech eight times. Used to be, when I'd near the end I'd say, "If a man is extremely lucky, if he's the luckiest man in the world, he finds the right woman to share his life with," but then I was Best Man at a gay wedding so I had to swap "woman" out in favor of "person" and ever since then it's just stuck. Hey, gotta be PC, gotta move with the times.

"I'm sorry, Alice," I say, contrite. Then I brighten. "But hey, your uncle Paul seemed to like it. I don't think I've ever seen a grown man cry so hard. And the way he hugged me!"

"Oh," she shakes her head in disgust, "he's an alcoholic. He cries when he watches *Wipeout* too. Believe me, Uncle Paul crying is no endorsement."

Perhaps it's time to change the subject.

"So," I say, "now that you and Billy are husband and wife, I guess you and I'll be seeing more of one another?"

"God, I hope not," she says. "I don't know what Billy sees in you."

What do I even say to something like that?

Thank God I don't have to say anything, because just then I see a pretty feminine hand tap on Alice's shoulder—*tap, tap, tap*—and there's Three Sheets, cutting in on Alice so she can dance with me.

"What's your cousin's name again?" I whisper in Alice's ear as we switch partners and I take Three Sheets in my arms.

I don't know why I can't remember the cousin's name—you'd think I'd be able to after the engagement party, rehearsal, rehearsal dinner etcetera—but it's a wedding thing, like this mental block. I know I'll never see this person after a certain point, that point in time being in just a few hours, so why waste the limited storage capacity of my brain by committing her name to memory?

Another look of disgust from Alice—"You're kidding me, right?" she says—and then Billy's whirling her away like he's a taller, bulkier Fred Astaire. Huh. Those pre-wedding ballroom dancing lessons he took are really paying off.

I look down at Three Sheets wishing I had the balls to ask her name but that would be too embarrassing. For her, I mean. She'd probably get depressed, thinking herself so unremarkable, she's not even worthy of someone she's been in a wedding party with remembering her name. Me, I'm used to being embarrassed. Honestly, most of the time I don't even notice anymore when it happens. I just keep going.

"So," I say, going for a reliable conversation starter, "some wedding, huh?"

Three Sheets tilts her head up at me and for the first time it registers that she's pretty. Sure, she's packing an extra fifteen to twenty pounds – wedding-party dresses can be so unkind, particularly purple – but I've never minded a little bulk on a woman. Her hair is dark blond and thick, even if it does look a little too retro in that maid of honor updo, and her baby blues are kind if a little bleary.

"It's great," she says, giving me an admiring look, "and that 'circle of friends' speech—I can't remember the last time anything moved me so much. How did you ever come up with exactly the perfect thing to say about Alice and Billy?"

Ah, the advantages of out-of-town wedding guests. Three Sheets is probably the only woman in the whole room who thinks that was a custom-made speech – even the wait staff in this place have heard it more than once!

The cake is cut, dessert is eaten—I love it when the bride eschews tradition and goes for the chocolate—then Billy throws the garter and I catch it (my eighth but I never try; they just always somehow land in my possession) and Alice throws the bouquet and Three Sheets catches it.

So there I am, sliding the garter up Three Sheets's stockings-clad leg. I don't have much experience taking garters off women but I'm something of a pro, after seven previous times, putting them on women. The trick is to make it look sexy enough to keep the boozy crowd happy but without defiling the garter recipient's reputation in any way, which can be a challenge if the recipient is drunk and proves almost impossible in the case of Three Sheets.

She's got her legs crossed demurely at the knee but as soon as that garter goes past her ankle, she spreads that top leg straight out wide and hikes up her dress to make my job easier. She does such a good job of spreading and hiking, I find myself confronted with the fact that underneath that maid of honor dress, her own stockings are held up by garters and she's, um, traveling commando.

Holy shit!

I'm hoping that the fact that everyone's consumed a lot of alcohol, coupled with the fact that my kneeling body is right in front of her, will prevent the crowd from seeing what I just saw, which includes London, France and Three Sheets's lack of underpants. Maybe they only caught a flash and will think that dark thatch I'm seeing up close is some part of her hiked purple dress?

Quickly, I deposit the garter somewhere below her knee and immediately pull her dress down so everything's all modest again.

As the guests groan—"Couldn't you get it up?" (very funny) "Couldn't you get it any higher?"—and the garter falls back down around her ankle, Three Sheets leans forward in her chair and now I'm getting a big serving of cleavage.

"You're cute, Mr. Speechmaker," she says, placing hands on either side of my face for a squeeze and in the process reminding me a little too much of Aunt Alfresca the few times she's ever felt warmly toward me. "Meet me in my room at the hotel next door? I'm staying in 213."

I'm about to say no—you know, the Aunt Alfresca thing, but then I shake that off. Hey, you always hear about guys getting lucky at weddings. Why shouldn't it be me? It *should* be me. Holy crap, it *is* me! Plus, she called me Mr. Speechmaker. So chances are she doesn't remember my name either, making it perfectly OK for me to bang a girl whose name I don't know.

"Sure thing," I tell Three Sheets. "But let's wait for a bit. It wouldn't be right to duck out of the wedding before the bride and groom."

Earlier, Alice said she didn't see what Billy saw in me as a friend. Well, I think, as we all wave them off, maybe Billy will tell her now while they make the short journey from the reception to the hotel right next door. See, as part of my wedding present to the two of them, in addition to a check—people love getting money, right?—I sprang for two nights in the honeymoon suite so they wouldn't have to get on a plane the very next day.

"But we want to get to Bermuda as quickly as we can!" Billy objected when presented with my idea.

"No, you do not," I said. "Don't you remember what happened to Drew and Stacy?"

Drew and Stacy's flight left first thing in the morning the day after they got married. They were both still pretty much well drunk from the day before, so Stacy barely made it on the plane because she was too busy puking in the airport bathroom, then on top of that she picked up a parasite in the Dominican Republic, which she could have avoided if she hadn't needed to have a drink as soon as she got there for a little hair of the dog and misjudged and drank something with ice cubes in it. So then she ended up sick the whole time they were there, leaving Drew to spend much of their honeymoon playing pool volleyball with a bunch of Germans, and she wound up having to go to the hospital when they got back.

Frankly, none of us think the marriage will ever recover. Now, if they'd only thought to let an extra day pass before getting on that plane...

Tell a story that uses the word "puke" enough times and you can persuade almost anyone of anything, which is how I convinced Billy to accept the two nights in the hotel, thereby no doubt saving the future of his marriage.

Me? I know everything about how to do a wedding up right.

"Ready, Mr. Speechmaker?" Three Sheets says, sidling up to me.

The bride and groom are gone. It's a wedding. I could do worse.

"Ready as I'll ever be," I say and put my arm around her. "Let's hit it."

Perhaps not as nice as the honeymoon suite, still, Room 213 will do.

There's a big bed, out the window there's a view of the highway in the distance, in the room there's a mini-bar – all the comforts of home.

"So, um, what did you say you do for a living?" I ask.

I'm crouched down checking out the mini-bar selection, figuring I'll just give Three Sheets some cash before I go to cover whatever I take, when—oof!—something crashes into me from behind. I'm not quite sure what Three Sheets was trying to accomplish, whether she was making an amorous move on me or if she simply tripped on her way over to those travel-sized bottles of liquor. But whatever. The results are the same. I'm sprawled on the floor, half on my side, and she's sprawled on top of me. Before I was thinking maybe we'd have a drink and then maybe kiss for a while first, maybe even finally learn each other's names, but as she rearranges me so that I'm flat on my back and leans over me with all that purple-encased cleavage, I'm thinking: Yeah, this could work.

And then Three Sheets is kissing me, she's got her tongue down my throat, I'm a little taken aback by the suddenness yet somehow manage to respond in kind, then she's sliding my white tux jacket off, ripping off my purple bowtie, undoing the buttons on my shirt. The cummerbund confuses her for a bit, but then, don't cummerbunds confuse everybody?

And now I'm playing catch-up here, sliding that ridiculous purple dress off Three Sheet's creamy shoulders and—wow!—she's got no bra on underneath to go along with the no panties underneath I glimpsed earlier. This is so easy. It's almost too easy. Now she undoes my belt, tugs my white pants down over my hips so that they're bunched up around my ankles. Wait! Don't I have to get this stupid tux back by five? Oh, that's right, I still have until tomorrow night. My white patent-leather penny loafers still on my feet, I'm tenting my boxers but she relieves me of that restraint too and then takes a quick dive, her breasts are bobbing in rhythm with her head, and I'm thinking this is great, this is really great, this is the best wedding I've ever been to, this is so good. And that's when I gently shift a little away from her mouth, gently push her away from me because I don't want to just come and make her have to wait for me to get hard again, and I find my pants and I'm reaching in my pants pockets—Do I have a condom? Of course I have a condom. I'm a thirty-three-year-old single man. I've always got a condom, and no, it's not the same one I kept from senior prom through college—and now I'm sliding it on, and it keeps rolling back from the base like condoms sometimes annoyingly do, and the annoying rolling gives me a moment to look at the woman who's supposed to be the object of my desire, at least right at this moment, and she's slouched on the ground, her naked back barely propped up by the side of the bed, her updo's somehow become a downdo, a thick hank of hair stuck to her cheek by what looks unpleasantly like drool, her eyes are at half-mast and she's starting to nod, and I'm thinking, *NO! Do not pass out! Please, do not pass out! I want to get laid! I may not be a virgin, but it has been a very long dry spell!* I don't say this out loud, of course I don't, but I'm patting her on the cheeks, trying to get my date to be more, um, alert. And now she is alert! And she's saying, "Don't worry, I still want to do this. That speech, my God, that speech," except that she's really slurring now, even worse than before, so it sounds more like "Don ree, ill wanna da-dis. Thaspee, mygah, thaspee," which I'm only able to decipher because I flunked Spanish but I do speak Drunk, and I'm going to go for it anyway when it suddenly hits me: No, this really is too easy.

Why is it that it's just the somehow-impaired ones who ever go for me?

Three Sheets is too drunk, reminding me of another girl in another place and time. She may think she wants to do this but she's not capable of making a decision right now.

And that's when I force myself away from her.

"But—" she says.

"You don't even know my name," I say.

"But—" she says again.

But I will brook no buts. I hike myself back into my boxers and pants, then help her up and onto the bed. Somehow I get the covers down and her underneath them, tuck the blankets up under her chin. By now she's snoring quietly, so I tiptoe around as I locate an empty champagne bucket to put near the bed in case she needs to puke and I liberate a water bottle from the mini-bar and put it on the night table along with one of the trial packets of aspirin I always keep on me just in case—she'll need both when she wakes up—and finally money to cover the charge for the water bottle when it appears on her hotel bill.

Unaccountably, I'm still horny so I go into the bathroom and jerk off into the toilet, remembering to wipe the seat and put down the seat and flush—Aunt Alfresca's training—before exiting Room 213.

No sooner do I close the door behind me and begin adjusting my tie than a door far down the hallway opens and who should it be but the newly minted Mrs. Billy Keller.

Alice startles when she sees me.

"What are you doing here?" she asks, puzzled. Then her expression darkens into a scowl as she sees the number on the door behind me. "Oh you did not just bang my cousin, did you?"

I say no, just for form and to protect her cousin's reputation, but I know she doesn't believe me.

I go back to the reception, figuring to snag a recovery beer before heading on home. The place is mostly empty now, just a few stragglers left.

Big John wheels himself over to me.

"You did good by Billy today," he says. "Your mother would be proud. *You* should be proud."

"Thanks, Dad."

"And that 'circles of a man's life' speech"—he pounds his fist against his heart—"no matter how many times I hear it, it never gets old."

I love my dad. Almost everyone else, they always refer to it as the 'circle of friends' speech. Big John is the only one here who gets it, who knows to call it what it is: the circles of a man's life speech.

"Thanks, Dad," I say again.

"I only hope I'm still alive someday to hear someone give as good a speech at your own wedding."

You and me both, Dad, I think but don't say.

Just then our male-bonding moment is interrupted by some guy who looks as though he spent the day going drink for drink with Three Sheets.

His thick tie's so loose it's just a gentle tug away from becoming a scarf and his hair looks like someone messed it up so he'd resemble a young Einstein.

"Hey, man." He places his hand on my shoulder. Usually I'm not crazy about strangers touching me but he's weaving back and forth so much, I'm happy to provide ballast. Better that than have him crash to the floor and need me to take him to the hospital to check for a concussion. "That speech... You know, I'm getting married in six months. I already asked my brother to be my Best Man, but now I'm thinking maybe I could swap for you? George'll only wind up saying something lame for the toast. You, on the other hand, if you could just give that speech..."

God, what is wrong with these guys?

I shake off his hand, disgusted.

"Do I even know you?"

My BFF

By the time I arrive home from the reception, it's full dark out.

When I slip my key in the lock and turn it there's no resistance and I realize that the door's unlocked. No, I didn't leave it that way. Aunt Alfresca trained me well: safety first.

Fucking Sam.

I push the door open and, yup, there's Sam sprawled out on my living room couch, a bottle of Sierra Nevada Pale Ale open on the table along with four bottle caps and a half-dozen takeout cartons of Chinese food, a pair of chopsticks poking out of one of them—Sam can eat, and drink—and the TV on. The digital display reads 63, which is MSNBC, and I immediately recognize the show as being one of those things the station runs every weekend about hardened criminals and incredible crimes. Sam loves those things. Me, not so much, although I do occasionally watch with Sam for a while because I like to see if I can come up with loopholes that, if I were the lawyer, I'd use to get the criminals off. Not that I want more criminals on the streets or anything, but I like solving puzzles and working on finding a loophole is like getting one big brain massage.

Sam doesn't even visually acknowledge my presence as I enter my own home, toss my keys on the table by the door.

"Can you believe the tats on that guy?" Sam says, eyes glued to the criminal on the screen. Then, Sam burps.

"The tits?" I say. "Well, he does look like he's spent too much time in the prison gym."

"Not the *tits*." Sam is disgusted, not an uncommon occurrence. "The *tats*. The tats all over his body."

"No, I can't," I say, taking a seat on the ottoman. "He's like one big tat, which, when you think about it, is probably

28

preferable to being one big tit. Not that there's anything wrong with tits." I squint at the TV. "Does he even have any eyes?"

"I don't think so."

"Did you and Renee have another fight?"

"What do you think?"

"It's Sunday night, you're here instead of next door. I'm thinking chances are good."

Every time Sam and Renee fight, Sam comes over here, using the spare key if I'm not home. Sam and Renee have been together for about a year, and I doubt they'll last another, but finding Sam on my couch has been going on a lot longer than that. Sam just likes my place better than the one next door, says the paint job here is better for promoting good feelings. No duh. Paint—it never lets you down. Paint—it's what I do.

Sam's been using that key for a good six years now, ever since I moved into this complex; Aunt Alfresca scoffed when I bought the condo, said a house would be a better investment, but it turned out that for once I was right, what with condos holding their value a lot better than houses in the current economic climate. When I moved in Sam'd already been here a while, we met the first day, instantly bonded, Sam helped me and Billy and Drew unload all my stuff from the U-Haul, we exchanged keys in case of emergency, and have been BFFs ever since. I realize the BFF designation is somewhat girly, but Sam says that's what we are and I've learned not to argue with Sam.

I kick off my white patent-leather shoes. Geez, my dogs are tired.

The shoes make thunking sounds as they hit the floor and Sam tears her gaze away from the TV long enough to see where the thunks came from.

"What the hell are those things?" she says. Then, for the first time, she looks at me. "Oh my god, what are you wearing?"

I look back at her. Sam is five feet ten inches of perfectly formed woman. She has longish honey-colored hair, perfect skin and green eyes behind black-framed rectangular glasses that make her look intelligent in a very sexy way. Right now she's wearing short-shorts, even though it's a pretty cold February evening, and a bikini top like they might reopen the pool down by the clubhouse any second. Sam also loves the Mets, the Jets, the Lakers, beer, poker, buddy movies and *Morning Joe* on MSNBC—all the things I love. Honestly, if she weren't a lesbian and my BFF, I'd date her.

As if a non-lesbian Sam would ever have me. As if.

"Did you forget I was going to a wedding today?"

I'm feeling miffed. I have no problem keeping track of everything going on in Sam's life, on *her* schedule. You'd think she'd be able to remember something as significant as me being Best Man in the wedding of one of my oldest friends and the girl I had a major crush on for a ridiculous amount of years.

"Sorry," she says, with a half-apologetic shrug. "You're in so many weddings. And what with all the Renee drama today and all…"

She trails off, no doubt expecting that by the time she finishes trailing, I'll stop being miffed.

"*God*, you look like a dork dressed like that."

Thanks, Sam. Like that's going to help me get over it.

"Oh, yeah?" I counter. "Well, you look like you're going to the pool."

"Aw, don't be mad." Here Sam pays me her highest compliment: she picks up the remote and shuts off the TV. "I want to hear all about it," she says eagerly, "every detail of what it was like being Best Man at the wedding of Bobby and Alex."

"Billy and Alice," I correct, not for the first time. The Alice/Alex part is fairly new but Sam's been calling Billy by the wrong name off and on pretty much since they met that first day in the back of the U-Haul. Billy and Sam don't exactly love each other. Billy, figuring he's my best friend because he's known me longer than anyone else, gets kind of jealous of any competition for first place, hence his not inviting Sam to his wedding even though they're both in my weekly poker game. And Sam, well, Sam may know she's my BFF but she's got her own jealousy issues where I'm concerned.

"Hey, I was close with the names! But wait. I'm going to get another beer. Don't start until I get back."

Like I was going to? Like I was going to just tell myself the story out loud? Fucking crazy Sam.

A moment later, her voice comes to me from the kitchen. "Hey, you want one?"

I love it when she offers me my own beer like it's her fridge.

My buzz from the reception is entirely gone. Might as well start work on curing the hangover. Or start on the next buzz. Besides, it's still early. "Sure," I holler back.

By the time Sam returns with two beers and a bottle opener, I've shed my tux jacket and scooted over from the ottoman to the prime spot on the couch in the right-hand corner.

"Hey!" Sam's outraged. "You stole my seat!"

I raise an eyebrow that I hope conveys the message: *My* couch. *My* seat.

"Asshole," Sam mutters, pushing past me, but there's no malice in any of it.

I cross my legs, so my right ankle is resting on my left knee.

"Nice socks," Sam says.

I study my white socks, shrug. "It was either that or purple. You think I should have gone for the purple?"

She pops the caps on the beers, hands one over and sits down a foot away, tucking one leg under her bottom as she faces me.

"So. The big wedding. Spill."

I take a swig of my beer and do as instructed.

I take her through the whole wedding ceremony, the cocktail hour, my speech – "I love the 'circles of a man's life' speech!" she says – and finally the dance with Alice.

"What was that like, finally getting to dance with Alma after all these years?"

This time, I don't correct her on the name.

"It was great," I say. "Well, maybe not great. More like incredibly awkward, especially when she gave me a hard time about my speech."

"What's wrong with that woman? How could anyone give you a hard time about the 'circles of a man's life' speech? Leave it to Barney to marry someone with an attitude problem and no taste. Everyone loves that speech. It's a crowd-pleaser."

"I know, right? But I guess for some reason brides don't like to be toasted with the same toast they've already heard at another wedding."

"Huh." Sam's puzzled. "Go figure."

"I know." I swig more beer. "You're telling me? But that's brides for you. They can be particular about little stuff. And they can *really* be particular if they catch you exiting their cousin's hotel room after the reception."

"Hold on a second. Back up."

So I do. I back up to the reception and Three Sheets, her loving my speech because she's the only woman there who hadn't heard it all before, the garter belt, her squeezing my face ala Aunt Alfresca and everything else.

"You're kidding me, right?" Sam says when I'm finished.

"I don't know," I say, trying to think what in all of that a guy would want to make up. "Which part?"

"You were right there with Three Sheets, practically doing it, and you just stopped because she was shit-faced?"

See? This is one of the reasons Sam's my BFF. No one puts things the way she does.

"Well, yeah."

"But why? Was it that she was so drunk that she was sloppy and you got turned off?"

"Well, no. I mean, she was sloppy but not excessively so. Well, not until she nearly passed out."

"Why then? Why would you get so close and then stop? If there's a guy who needs to get laid, it's you."

Gee, thanks, *BFF*.

I feel myself blush, a rare thing.

"I wanted to, but it just didn't seem right. It felt too much like—"

Sam practically spits her last swig of beer out, she's so worked up right now as she points her bottle at me. "Oh, you are *not* going to finish that sentence by saying 'The Night'."

I feel the blush deepen. Thank God I don't have to look at me right now. If there were a mirror in front of me, I'd be so embarrassed by my own embarrassment.

"It's true," I say. "Suddenly it felt exactly like—"

"*The Night*," she cuts me off, flops backward, her head hitting the couch like she's a lousy actor who's just been shot in a Western. "Jesus, Johnny."

I have no idea what she's talking about. "What?"

Sam pops back up again. "You are not going to compare this to the night you were going to lose your virginity and then didn't."

She's talking about when I was twenty-one, junior year of college. Sam didn't know me back then, but she does know my stories, knows more of my stories than anyone else. And the story she's referring to now, the one known as The Night, is about the time Marcy Bonano and me hooked up at a kegger, got really drunk together, confessed our mutual virginity and then decided to do something about it, got more drunk before the actual doing, and then right before, I stopped myself because it didn't feel right. I didn't want Marcy Bonano's first time to be something she wouldn't even remember. It seemed too much like something other people could call rape, something *I* would call rape.

Of course I did eventually lose my virginity, but still.

"I'm not?" I say. "I'm not going to compare it? How come?"

"Because there's no comparison!"

"Why not?"

"Because the legendary Marcy Banana—"

"Bonano."

"Whatever. She was, what, seventeen?"

"Sixteen," I correct. "She was smart and a super-early admission. Plus, you know, she looked a lot older."

I've always felt uncomfortable about the five-year age different between me and Marcy Banana—shit, now Sam's got me doing it—but really, we were only two grades apart, so it didn't feel like that big a deal at the time.

"And Three Sheets was how old?"

"I don't know." I shrug. "We're adults. It's not like being a kid where the first things you ask when you meet someone new are 'How old are you?' and 'What grade are you in?' and 'Do your parents let you stay up til eleven on weeknights?'" I shrug again. "Probably my age or thereabouts."

"See? It's nothing like The Night."

"It's not?"

"No, not even remotely. We're talking about a woman who's *of age*, who's old enough to know how much she's drinking and makes a conscious decision at least until she's almost unconscious to do so, who shows you London and France and the fact she's not wearing any underpants"—I did tell her that part, including the rhyme which I was pretty proud of—"who practically shoves her boobs in your face, gives you a cheek squeeze, invites you back to her hotel room, throws herself at you. No, Johnny, it's not the same thing."

"What—you're telling me you would have gone ahead and done her?"

"Was she cute?"

I think about Three Sheets and her extra fifteen to twenty pounds, her mussed-up hair and her bleary eyes. Still, she was cute, even with the awful purple maid of honor dress. Hell, I think all women in all their various colors and shapes and sizes are cute or pretty or gorgeous or handsome or attractive. Women: they're a beautiful thing. But scary too. Very scary.

"Yeah," I say, "she was cute."

"If I wasn't already living with Renee? Um, *yeah*, I would have done her then," Sam says. "Cute and *she's* throwing *herself* at *me*? Definitely."

"And the drunk thing wouldn't bother you?"

"Not for a second. Do you think, if the shoe was on the other foot, you were the drunk one and you came on to her, do you think *she'd* feel guilty about doing you?"

"But isn't there a law or something?" You'd think I'd know this one but I don't. "Isn't it illegal to have sex with someone who's incapacitated like that, like some form of rape?"

"Still wouldn't bother me. She's the one who offered."

"Do lesbians even have rape?" I say.

"Of course we can get raped." Sam looks at me like I'm an

idiot. "If some guy—"

"No, I mean by another girl. Do lesbians rape each other?"

Sam shrugs. "Well, it's not something you hear about on TV every day."

Suddenly I feel thunderstruck—not by the idea of lesbian rape but by everything else.

"You mean I could have gotten laid today?"

Sam nods.

"And I wouldn't have even had to feel guilty about it?"

Sam nods again, doesn't say anything but I know what she's thinking: Asshole. I know she's thinking that because I'm thinking it too.

I clasp my hands to my head. "I am *such* an idiot!"

"Hey, I didn't say it."

We sit like that for a while. Sometimes I can't get over how dense I can be about, well, pretty much everything. I need a non sequitur to help me get out of feeling so stupid.

So I grab her bare foot, study the nails.

"You need me to paint your toenails for you?"

She fingers the big toe. There's a tiny chip in the green lacquer. "Nah." She shrugs. "I'm good."

I let the foot go.

"So what was today's fight about?" I ask.

"Renee says I'm insensitive to the feelings of others. Can you believe that? Me, insensitive?" She moves from outraged to insecure. "I'm not insensitive...am I?"

I study my BFF, think about her treating my home like it's hers, commandeering the remote, drinking all my beer, forgetting things like me being Best Man at Billy and Alice's wedding.

"You?" I say. "Insensitive? Never."

"Damn straight."

I wish other girls—you know, straight ones—could be like Sam. Hell, I wish I could be with other girls the way I am when I'm with Sam.

"Love sucks," she says, curling up next to me on the couch and snuggling in close, one arm going across my midsection.

I kiss her on the top of her head lightly. Her hair smells like roses and rainwater.

"I suppose," I say. "I wouldn't know."

"You want any of this food?" she says, gesturing at all those Chinese takeout cartons. "I got plenty."

I ate a lot at the wedding but now that seems like so long ago.

"Sure." I shrug. "I could eat."

I find one with shrimp in it, figuring to stay away from the chicken and the beef. Outside of weddings, ballgames and hot dog stands, I've been trying to be a pescatarian lately.

She leans over to the coffee table, picks up the remote.

"So," I say, "you working tomorrow?"

"Who we got?"

"Steve Miller. His wife wants the dining room done again. Aqua this time."

"Aqua's a good color." Sam wants to be a novelist but I guess that's a difficult job to come by. So while waiting for that to happen, she takes in freelance writing and copy edit work. When that's slow, which is almost always, she works with me. "I'm in."

She clicks on the TV, yawns.

We watch for a bit.

"Can you believe this guy thought he could get away with that?" Sam says.

When I don't answer, she yawns again, tears her gaze away from the screen long enough to glance over to the corner of the living room.

"So," she says, "how long are you going to keep that tree up?"

Yes, it's the middle of February. Yes, I still have my Christmas tree up. But hey, it makes my home look more cheerful, particularly when it's all lit up like that, which Sam must have done herself tonight even though she always teases me about my tree.

"Until something good happens," I finally say. "Until something good happens."

Interlude I:
Goes to Character

How does a guy become a *man's man?*

Damned if I know. It's not exactly like it's something I ever aspired to be in life. I mean, sure, I'm glad that guys like me, want to spend time with me—what guy doesn't want that?—but it's not something I've ever deliberately cultivated with that intent in mind. It's just the way things are and have always been.

But how did I get here?

How did I get to be the guy that men all gravitate toward but that women, except for lesbians, mostly shun?

As stated, I'm good looking. I know I'm the only one who's said that here so far, but you'll just have to trust me that independent witnesses have corroborated that fact over the years, and not all of those witnesses go by the name Big John, although he's certainly said it many times. As shown, I can be considerate and sensitive to the reputations and sensibilities of women: witness my restraint with both Marcy Bonano *and* Three Sheets, and me putting that seat down in the bathroom (although I must confess, despite Aunt Alfresca's training, I do not always remember about the seat). Add to all that, I'm a fairly intelligent guy.

So you would think I would fare better with the fairer sex, would you not?

All I can do, constituting my lack of any real defense, is to offer up the following. I present to you, the jury, the following exhibits, all of which could easily fall under the ominous heading of Things I've Done That Guys Love And Women Don't:

Exhibit 1: The One with All the Cars: Between the ages of sixteen and twenty-two, I owned a total of twenty-five cars. Not all at once and sometimes not even all by myself; a few of those cars I owned jointly with Billy Keller. See, the thing is, I couldn't see the point in driving anything new or even remotely new. I excel at understanding what's going on under the hood and I loved the challenge of finding the clunkiest clunker I could find—more than one of those cars was discovered in *The Penny-Saver*—and then doing the necessary work to get that baby on the road. Put in a little more work, and not only were those cars drivable but also profitable when I'd turn around and resell them. My proudest acquisition? A VW that Billy and I purchased jointly for twenty-five dollars. It's *amazing* what a little duct tape and a few strategically placed rubber bands can do for a car!

The thing those twenty-five cars all had in common was that no matter how much work I put in, no matter how good a mechanic I was and still am, they all each would break down at least once, often at inopportune times, like say on dates.

Guys' Verdict: "How cool! You get to tool around town in a different car every few months. You avoid the high costs of buying new or good used, thereby having more money to spend on partying or prime tickets to ballgames. You beat the system by never having to pay high insurance or taxes on your vehicles. Coolest. Guy. Ever."

Women's Verdict: "Asshole."

Apparently, women prefer reliable transportation over variety and savings.

Exhibit 2: The One with the Distributor Cap: So there I am, age twenty-two, on my last clunker, clunkers being something I gave up when I went into business with Big John. I'm on my way to see the Mets play. In the car are Billy, Drew, Mike II—who we still all call Mike II even though Mike I has since moved to Maine—and one guy I've never met before. This new guy is a co-worker of Drew's. Let's call this new guy Fred.

It's obvious from looking and listening to Fred—the way

he dresses, the way he talks—that he doesn't think much of preppies. And it's further obvious that he thinks I'm a preppy. Ridiculous—I know, right? But the thing is, on this night, I'm kind of dressed like a preppy. Reason being, I've just come from a job interview. Wanting to do something to supplement my income from Big John's, so I can afford my own place faster, I've applied for a nighttime job as a bartender. This means that instead of my usual game uniform of jeans, T-shirt, work boots and Mets cap, I'm wearing khaki slacks, a collared polo shirt, and my hair's trimmed neatly and parted on the side, no baseball cap. Aunt Alfresca's doing. She said if I wanted the job I shouldn't apply looking like a bum on my way to the ballpark.

And for once Alfresca is right. I did get the job.

But now I'm driving my last clunker to the ballpark and I can feel Fred's eyes boring into the back of my skull right through the headrest, and I can hear exactly what he's thinking: *Preppy asshole.*

It's vaguely annoying.

But it stops being vaguely annoying when my last clunker starts to overheat like crazy and I'm forced to pull over into the nearest gas station.

I hop out of the car, grab a rag I keep under the driver's seat for just this very purpose, pop the hood, use the rag to remove the distributor cap—see, instinctively I know exactly what's wrong with the car—and stand there laughing as filthy sludge shoots up like a winning geyser in Texas, drenching my preppy clothes and spraying so high it splatters the American flag waving over the gas station.

Sorry, Old Glory.

Now all the guys in the clunker are laughing too, even Fred, and from the open back window I hear Fred say to Billy, "Your friend is seriously cool."

I know, right? Me, I could have told him that.

Guys' Verdict: "Johnny is seriously cool."
Women's Verdict: "Asshole."

Exhibit 3: The One with the Fight: Several months after I get the job bartending nights, it's St. Patrick's Day and my manager asks if I can work the day shift instead. Big John says it's OK. By the time I finish my shift, what with customers buying me green beer and shots all day and everything, I'm pretty hammered.

That's the condition I'm in, hammered, when I leave the bar where I work to do my own partying at another bar. Hey, you don't shit where you eat—Aunt Alfresca's training.

So there I am, getting even more hammered. I'm sitting by myself at the bar because even though I was supposed to hook up with Billy and Drew after my shift, I seem to have forgotten in my hammeredness just which bar I said I'd meet them at.

Or maybe I'm just hoping it'll be easier to pick up women if it doesn't look like I'm part of a cabal.

Anyway, as I'm sitting at the bar, just minding my own business, two big guys come in, belly up to the bar, one each on either side of me. Immediately, drunk as I am, I sense negative vibes surrounding me.

Let me interject here that this is the only instance I can recall in my life of guys not instantly liking me. The reason for their dislike will make itself manifest imminently.

Guy #1: "It's the guy!"

Guy #2: "Yeah, you owe us two hundred bucks!"

And then Guy #2 pokes me in the shoulder.

Two things I know: 1) no guy likes being poked with a finger, and that includes naturally even-tempered me; 2) I don't owe anyone two hundred bucks.

Oh, and one other thing I know: I've never laid eyes on either of these guys in my life.

But apparently they think differently because they keep going on about the money I owe them, how it's wrong to be a mooch and a leech—like I don't know that—all the while keeping up with a steady stream of finger pokes, trying to provoke me into a fight. It also becomes apparent that they think I'm some guy named Bob.

Me, I'm just trying to mind my own business. Me, I don't want any trouble. Me, I keep telling them calmly that my name isn't Bob; it's Johnny Smith.

But they don't believe me, they keep it up with the finger poking, so I finally whip out my wallet and show them my ID.

"See?" I say. "Can you guys read? It says Johnny Smith, doesn't it? *Not Bob.*"

They instantly look sheepish, start backing away from me, palms up, apologetic.

Fuck that shit. They've been finger poking me for like an hour here. Suddenly, I *do* want trouble.

"Screw that 'I'm sorry' shit," I say. "We are so fighting now."

I don't care that they're big and there's two of them to just one of me. They've spoiled my pleasant night.

I come out swinging—Big John's training this time, with a healthy helping of Aunt Alfresca; the woman can box—and in the ensuing bar brawl I give as good as I get. It's the only brawl of my life and, obviously, I could have avoided it, but what the heck.

When the fighting's over, they introduce themselves, apologize once more, buy me a few rounds of drinks.

To this day, we still exchange holiday cards.

Guys' Verdict: "Only you, Johnny."

Women's Verdict: "Asshole."

Bonus Exhibit: I'm at Shea Stadium, back when it was still called Shea Stadium. My team's just actually won a game after a horrendous dry spell and I do something I've always wanted to do, my whole life. I wait until the stadium's nearly all cleared out and when there's practically no one left but the cleanup crew, I vault down the field and run the bases.

The cop—of course, there has to be a cop—tries to stop me as I near home plate, but since this has been a lifelong dream, I circle around him and tag home before letting him cuff me.

Just in case you don't know this, it's against the law to do what I just did.

But as I'm standing there in cuffs, the cop and me get to talking, one thing leads to another, turns out we have a lot in common, he's always longed to run the bases at Shea too, plus he laughs again when he recalls that as I ran the bases I used a running style that, let's just say I always refer to it as The Funny Run.

The cop tells me that normally he hauls people in for doing what I just did, that he should haul *me* in. But then he just uncuffs me instead.

"That run." He chuckles again. "And hey, it's just me here and the grounds crew. We're all overworked and underpaid and we almost never get anything to laugh at, not like that."

The Funny Run is a crowd-pleaser.

There's just one problem. While the cop might think I'm funny enough to let go, while the cleanup and grounds crew might think I'm hysterical, my date does not find my running the bases and nearly getting arrested to be humorous at all.

That's right. I did all this while on a date.

Guy's Verdict:

Never mind. I think you get the picture by now. We don't even need to get into Bonus Exhibit 2, the one in which I commandeer one of those construction caterpillars on Halloween while wearing a vampire costume, driving it down the center of the Merritt Parkway with my black cape flying behind me.

Suffice it to say that in a world where the average masculine aspiration could be summed up as, "Women want me, men want to be me"—an aspiration I might share if I felt I had any control over such things—what I've managed to achieve instead is more like, "Women don't want me, men want to be with me."

And that, Dear Jury, all of the above, would fall under the heading of Nature.

Apparently it's just my nature to be a man's man.

They say one of the definitions of insanity is doing the same exact thing over and over again, hoping to get a different result. I've spent my whole life doing the same thing over and over again, which is essentially to be myself—you know how everyone always says to "just be yourself"—hoping that *this* time it'll work out with some girl even though it never has in the past.

Just being myself and hoping for a different outcome, over and over again—could this mean I'm insane?

Men at Work

I step out my front door the same time as Sam steps out of hers. There's a light snow falling that should stop as soon as the temperature rises a bit, and Sam pulls the fur-trimmed parka hood over her head as we trudge side by side to the work truck. It still says Big John's on the side even though it's my business now. I don't have the heart to change it. Neither of us says a word until we're buckled in and I turn the radio on to my favorite station, The Wave, which is "All Sports All The Time," as the saying goes.

"You and Renee make up yet?" I say.

"Pfft."

"I'll take that as a no. Ready to hit it?"

"Ah, Mondays," Sam says in response.

A lot of people I know who do work on houses—construction, window washing, masons, other house painters—like to get to work as early as possible. Me, I tell customers nine-thirty but it's always more like ten, ten-thirty by the time I arrive. My intentions are good, but it's a long drive from Danbury to most of my jobs in the wealthier part of Fairfield County, plus there's traffic to consider and always a bunch of stops to make before really getting going.

First stop: the paint supply store to get some tape and other supplies. Sam loves to tease me about this.

"It's crazy," she's pointed out to me more than once. "Why don't you buy in bulk? You run your business like you could be quitting and going on to do something else any second."

"Well," I like to say back, "you never know," even though

I've been doing this for eleven years now and will likely do it until I'm too decrepit to stand on a ladder anymore. It's the principle of the thing. And sure, I guess I could buy a few things in bulk at the colossal hardware store, but it's good to support the little guy. Seeing me come in every day helps Pete believe his business is still going strong.

After the paint supply store, it's time for Leo's Coffee Shop right next door.

"You coming?" I ask Sam as I hop out of the truck.

"Nah," she says. "Just get me the usual."

"OK," I say, leaning in and putting the key back in the ignition, giving it a turn. "I'll leave the heat on for you," I say against the sound of The Wave surging back as the engine turns back on.

Leo's Coffee Shop is so old—this is where, if I were a stand-up comic, the crowd would shout back, "How old is it?" But the truth is, I got no punch line. It's just really old. Like Leo.

There're two people waiting in line at the counter and another two at a table in the corner. Add me, and that makes five simultaneous customers. Business, for Leo's, is booming. Leo must be stoked.

As I wait my turn I pick up a copy of the *Post*, turn it over to the sports pages.

"What can I do you for?" Leo asks when it's finally my turn.

"The usual," I say and he pours me a large cup of black. I survey the room. "You're busy."

"Yeah," he says, "it's a regular rush hour in here. It's been like this all morning. A few more days like this, and I'll give those idiots a run for their money."

By "those idiots," he means the national chain with their designer coffees that set up shop down the street when I was still in high school, stealing most of Leo's customers. I could go there too, but I don't like designer coffee and I do like Leo.

"That's right," I say. "You'll get 'em yet. It's just a matter of time."

"That's what I'm thinking." Leo nods emphatically. "The girl with you today?"

"Oh, right. I almost forgot. Yeah, give me another large, but don't forget to add extra sugar and extra cream. Oh, and if you've got any chocolate syrup kicking around—"

"I know, I know." Leo moves to make Sam's coffee. Leo refuses to put any kind of syrup in his customers' coffee— "Syrup is for sundaes," he likes to say—but he'll do it for Sam.

"Oh, and I need something to go with that," I say.

"Like what?"

"I don't know. Something sugary. Whatever you've got that's got a ton of frosting on it."

Whenever Sam drinks, which is often, she likes something sweet the next day. She says it doesn't really help with the hangover. It just makes her happier.

Leo brings me Sam's coffee and puts it in a bag along with a carrot cake muffin that's got about an inch of frosting on top. He nods his head at the newspaper. "So what do you think of the Mets' chances this year?"

"Oh, geez," I say. "Spring training hasn't even started yet and already there's this nonsense, all this fuss they're making about Beltran's unauthorized off-season operation. Do they really think this'll help matters any?"

"I know, right? But what do you think of their chances?"

"Well, a guy can always dream—"

"But they'll still break your heart. It's the Brooklyn Dodgers all over again."

Minus the part about Beltran, Leo and I have this same conversation, almost word for word, every morning.

I hear a polite cough behind me and I turn to see that another customer's come in.

"Oops, sorry," I say to Leo. "Better get out of your way. Looks like you've got another rush."

"Don't do anything I wouldn't do!" Leo calls after me, his daily warning.

"I wouldn't even dream of trying!" I call back. I'm not even sure what that means exactly, in this context. It's just what I always say to Leo. Every day.

Back in the truck, it's nice and toasty now, but…

"What the fuck, Sam?" In my absence, she's slipped a CD on. "I leave you alone for five minutes and you switch off The Wave in favor of some chick music?"

"What did you expect me to do? Sit here listening to *your* stupid sports station while I freeze my butt off?"

"But you love sports."

"I know but I love to *watch* sports. I don't need to hear people talk about it every second."

"Here's your stuff." I hand her the bag.

She peeks inside. "Ooh! Frosting!"

"You're welcome." I key the ignition, pull out of the parking lot, wonder how long I have to listen to this music before I can switch it off and turn The Wave back on.

Actually, the music's not too bad.

"Who is that?"

"Allison Iraheta."

"You say that like it should mean something to me."

"She came in fourth on *American Idol* last season."

"Hey, wasn't that CD you slipped in last week by someone else who came in fourth on a previous season?"

"So?"

"What's with you and people who come in fourth?"

"Four is my numerology number."

"Oh. Of course."

"Plus, I like losers." I glance over. She's got frosting on the tip of her nose and she's giving me a meaningful look. "Sometimes, in their own way, they wind up winning."

"Deep, Sam. Really deep."

We've been at the job for about a half hour, just taping so far. I've got my earbuds in, listening to The Wave. They're still talking about the Beltran thing, but now they're taking callers. I expect to hear some guy going on about the Mets but it's a woman caller.

Huh. The Wave almost never gets women callers. It's not like there's a written law or anything but...

"They did it without Washington and Jenkins," she says and immediately I know she's talking about the Jets, not the Mets. I also immediately know that she has a sexy voice. "Can you imagine what they'll do under Ryan next season?"

I can. And like Sexy Caller, I'm excited about the Jets' prospects too. No one expected anything from them last season – rookie coach, rookie quarterback, plus, you know, they're the Jets, they're supposed to break your heart even worse than the Mets. You have to learn to like the pain of defeat or you'll go crazy. But sometime last fall, something changed. Even though everyone still expected the Jets to lose every week, they kept winning to the point where it felt like it wouldn't matter if they lost a game. They'd already won.

"Actually," Stanley, one of the co-hosts of The Wave cuts off Sexy Caller, "we were focusing on the Mets this morning."

But Sexy Caller's not having any. "I remember how you laughed at Ryan last fall," she goes on. "What did you call his color-coding system again? 'Football for Preschoolers'? I just think you should man up and admit—"

But I never learn what she wants Stanley to admit because there's a tap on my shoulder.

Fucking Sam. She's probably interrupting The Wave to have me listen to some Allison Iraheta song.

But when I turn around, it's not Sam. It's Steve Miller and he's standing there in his bathrobe, holding a big mug of coffee, dark hair disheveled, dark eyes looking like he had a rough night. This is not the first time I've seen him in his bathrobe looking like this.

"Oh, Mr. Miller." I take out my earbuds. "Hi."

"It's Steve. How many times are you going to paint my dining room before I convince you to call me Steve?"

"Steve. Right."

This first-name basis thing is both good and bad. It's good because I'm pretty sure he's a year or two younger than me, so it always feels weird calling him Mister. But it's weird calling him Steve because, well, he's a lawyer and I'm doing work in his house. I don't really care about the lawyer thing so much—after all, I could have been one if I hadn't agreed to go into business with my dad—but one thing Big John always instilled in me is that it's important not to get too familiar with customers so as to maintain a more professional business relationship. Of course, some of my customers don't make this too easy.

"Katie let you in all right?" he asks, referring to his wife, who I've never seen looking rumpled in a bathrobe and who always gets off to work on time.

"Yup," I say, self-evidently, "we're here."

"And she got off to work OK?" Before I can even nod, he adds, "Good, good." He gestures at my earbuds with his mug. "What are you listening to?"

"The Wave."

His eyes light up. "I *love* that show! What are they saying about the Mets' chances this year?"

"Oh, you know," I say, and I launch into pretty much everything I said to Leo back at the coffee shop, including the stuff about Beltran.

"That sucks," he says, very unlawyerly. Then be brightens. "Hey, Johnny, you should come to Opening Day with me. My firm has season tickets."

Before I can answer, I hear a snort from the other side of the room.

I look over Steve's shoulder and open my arms in a "What the fuck?" that I direct at Sam. But she just shakes her head and smirks, putting her own earbuds in before going back to taping.

"What was that all about?" Steve asks.

I don't know and I'll have to wait until later to find out, but in the meantime I figure I'll fix Sam's wagon.

Laying my finger next to one nostril, in a hushed voice I confide, "Major coke problem."

I can't believe I said that, just to get back at Sam. What kind of employer would say such a thing about an employee? Big John would never say that to a customer about me. But Steve doesn't seem bothered by my indiscretion.

"Oh, that's sad," he says. "Such a pretty girl. Beautiful, really." A thoughtful look crosses his face. "You two ever…"

It takes me a while to realize what he's getting at here, and when I do...

"*Sam?*" I shake my head vehemently. "God no. She hits for the other team."

"Oh," he says wisely. "What? Red Sox fan?"

"No," I say. "Lesbian."

"Oh!" Enlightenment dawns. "Oh." Disappointment. Then: "Well, that's a shame."

"Not really," I say.

"How do you figure?"

"Well, if I worked with her and she liked guys but I never got with her, that could be depressing—you know, picturing her doing stuff with guys other than me. But this way..."

A light dawns in Steve's eyes. "Free fantasy!"

"You got it," I say. "Exactly. Like, if I picture her with some other girl, who am I hurting? Not even me."

"I like the way you think, Johnny. Now about those season tickets. The Yankees? Opening Day?"

"Oh geez, you didn't say it was for the Yankees," I say, feeling relieved. Do I really want to go to any game with Steve Miller? "I'll have to pass on that."

"But they're amazing seats!"

"I'm sure they are. But, you know. The *Yankees*."

"I know, I know," he says. "I wish it was for the Mets but they're the firm's tickets."

"Well," I say, "I guess you can't control the taste of the people you do work for. Speaking of which, you working on any interesting cases lately?"

"Oh God." He runs a hand through his already disheveled hair, making matters worse. "I'm working on a terrible case right now."

"Tell me about it. What's so terrible?"

"This young guy, maybe twenty, not his first offense, he's going down on a whole mess of charges and I can't think of any way to help him out."

"What'd he do?"

"He got pulled over in a random check. The arresting

officer's looking over his license and registration—nothing wrong there—when suddenly he spots some tools in the backseat and decides to take a closer look. Turns out to be burglary tools, so the cop keeps looking, finds a few items in the trunk that sure look like stolen goods along with some marijuana in the glove compartment."

"That's rough," I say.

"And how."

"You're telling me." I say this, not because it necessarily makes sense for me to be the one saying it in this context but because it's a guy thing to say, the kind of thing we guys say to each other to show support. I suspect it's like sorority sisters jumping up and down and squealing when they see each other— minus the cheerful aspects, of course.

"The terrible thing is," Steve goes on, "my client's such a good guy."

"Well, wait a second. If he committed armed robbery, maybe not such a good guy."

"But that's it. He wasn't armed. And anyway, it's burglary, not robbery."

I'm tempted to hit myself in the forehead for saying something so stupid. Of course I understand the difference between robbery and burglary.

Steve continues about his client. "He just does these... *things* sometimes but he doesn't even own a weapon. He doesn't believe in violence."

"OK, that is nice. And really, the marijuana charge? Why do we even charge people with that shit anymore?"

"I know, I know. But like I say, he's going down this time, hard. He's got those priors, and with the quantity of charges—"

"Wait a second," I say. "I read about this case."

"You did?"

"Or maybe I saw something on the TV. One of the two. You say he was pulled over on a random check?"

"Yes, but—"

"Was he speeding?"

"No, he was well below the limit, but—"

"Was he driving erratically? Was there anything at all wrong with his car—a tire low on air, a taillight out, anything at all other than just a random check to cause the cop to pull him over?"

"No to everything. He hadn't even smoked any of the pot in a long time, but—"

"Oh my God, the vehicle itself wasn't stolen, was it? Because if it was, I don't think we can get Mr. Nice-Guy Burglar off."

"No, it was his car. The license and registration all checked out. But—"

"But nothing! This is so easy!"

Steve Miller practically drops his coffee mug. "It *is*?"

"Yes! All you need to do is open up a can of constitutional whupp-ass on the D.A. and that arresting officer."

"*What*?"

"Constitutional whupp-ass! You say, 'My client's rights have been violated!' You say, 'My client committed no illegal acts that raised probable cause that he should have been pulled over in the first place!' You say, 'You are trampling on the rights guaranteed by the United States Constitution! This is a clear-cut case of illegal search and seizure. What's next? Police entering private homes randomly, without search warrants, in the hopes of finding evidence of crimes? What is this, the old Soviet Union? *Are we now living in a martial state?*'"

I'm out of breath and Steve's stunned.

"Really?" he says. "I say all that?"

"Well, hopefully you say it better, since you are the attorney. But basically? Yeah."

"I don't know what to say," he says.

"You mean my argument's that off-base?"

"No, it's that *on*-base. That's the thing—how could I have missed that?"

"Welllll…"

"Well, what?"

I don't know how to say the following because: 1) it's a hard thing to say to someone you barely know and 2) I don't want to lose this job, but…

"The drinking," I say.

Steve raises his eyebrows at me.

"I'm not saying you have to give it up entirely," I continue before I lose my nerve. "But, you know, maybe cut back a bit? And maybe not every night?"

I don't know what he's going to do. Hit me? Fire me? But then his eyes mist over.

"You're absolutely right, Johnny. No one else has had the guts to say that to me, but you're absolutely right."

Geez, I hope he doesn't hug me right now. He's probably got booze coming out of his pores from the night before.

But no, he doesn't try to hug me. Instead, he does the guy thing. He clears his throat loud, pushing the emotion away.

"So, about those Opening Day tickets. I know it's just the Yankees and not the Mets, but they really are amazing seats. They're those ones right behind home plate."

"You mean the ones that go for something like eight hundred dollars per seat per game?"

He nods.

"I've read about those things. Those really are some great seats."

"Well?"

"I don't know. I get kind of busy come April."

"But it's for Opening Day."

"Yeah, well, I'll think about it." What I'm really thinking is: Do I really want to go to a game with Steve Miller? I mean, sure I'd love to sit in those seats, even to see the Yankees, but what the hell would we talk about all night? It's not like we've got anything in common.

"Good enough," he says. "I've got your card. I'll give you a ring when it gets closer to Opening Day."

"So, what was that snort about?" I finally ask when Sam and I break for lunch a few hours later.

"It's just: Only you, Johnny."

"What the hell does that mean?"

"Do you think Steve Miller asks everyone who does work

on his house to go to the ballpark with him? You think he asks the maid to go to the opera? You're painting that guy's living room. You're doing blue-collar work for a white-collar guy and he's all, 'Ooh, Johnny, will you be my best friend?'"

"He didn't ask me to be his best friend," I scoff.

But she ignores my scoffing, instead going on with, "Will you go to Opening Day with me?' I swear, if the guy wasn't already married, he'd be asking you to be his Best Man."

"Ohhhh, go listen to Allison Iraheta."

Men at Din-din

A month after Billy and Alice's wedding, it's a fairly seasonable March evening and it finds me standing package in hand outside the door of their new house.

The call came from Billy three days earlier.

"Alice and me'd like you to be our first dinner guest," he said.

"Really? Both of you?"

"Well…"

"Wait a second. You sure Alice wants me there too or was this just your idea?"

"Well, when I suggested it, she didn't exactly say no way or threaten to divorce me, so…"

A note on why Billy and I talk the way we do, Alice and Sam too. Even though we live in Danbury, it has been pointed out that we sound like New Yorkers. This, I say, makes perfect sense. Danbury is a small city, a melting pot of many cultures with a multitude of sounds and smells, but for those of us who've spent our lives here it's a different story. While Danbury is technically in the state of Connecticut, it's home to the last several highway exits on I-84 before you hit New York State. On top of that, we're only an eighty-minute train ride from New York City. Hey, if you came from a place whose nickname was Hat City, said nickname having been rendered meaningless when John F. Kennedy refused to wear a hat to his inauguration, thereby decimating the hat industry in general and the industry that was then the city's pride and joy in particular, you'd be reaching for straws too. Let the rest of the state talk like they're part of New England. In Danbury we've got our own agenda.

Knock, knock.

My hands are sweaty as I knock. I don't know why I'm so nervous. This is just dinner—me, my oldest guy friend and his new bride. I tell myself being nervous is stupid but I'm relieved and maybe just a little disappointed when Billy answers the door alone.

"You made it!" he says. He says this like it should have been hard or something.

"Well, you know," I say, "it's not like I had to drive to a whole other town or something. What's this, like seven minutes from my house?"

"Come in," he says.

As I step past him into the house I think that my friend looks nervous too for some reason. I also notice that he suddenly looks older. We're exactly the same age, but his hairline's starting to recede a little bit, he's got a slightly well-fed overlap of his belt that I don't remember ever seeing before, an honest-to-God striped polo shirt with not a single stain on it, and I swear there's a crease in his chinos. He looks, for want of a better word, married.

"Hey, I like what you've done to the place," I say following him into the living room.

This is not a strictly accurate thing to say since, as far as I can tell, they haven't done anything with the place, unless you call stacking pictures to maybe be hanged later against the walls and scattering a few pieces of lawn furniture around the center 'doing something.' But it is what you say when you're invited into a new home. I mean, what's the alternative? 'I *don't* like what you've done with the place'?

"This is just temporary." He waves his hand. "Between planning the wedding, the wedding itself, the honeymoon and having to sell both our places and buy this one, we haven't really had time to make firm decisions on the interior design."

"You have had a busy year," I acknowledge.

"Plus, Alice wants everything to be just perfect. She says there's no point in rushing to buy things just to fill space. She says if we do that, we might only end up regretting our hasty purchases. And then where'll be? We'll either have to live among stuff we hate or sell it all and buy new all over again. Alice says it's best to wait until we find the exact items we fall in love with."

No doubt. It sounds like Alice says a lot. Geez, I don't remember her being so chatty growing up.

"Well, when you're ready to paint the place," I say, surveying the Navajo White walls, an unimaginative color I hate when it comes to walls, "hit me up. Speaking of Alice, where...?"

"Oh, they're in the kitchen."

"Wait a second. 'They're'—"

And then I notice it for the first time. The sound of feminine chatter and laughter. Whenever I hear that sound of women chattering and laughing, paranoid as it may seem, it sounds to me like they're planning something. A coup maybe.

I lower my voice, hiss at Billy. "There's another woman in there. You and Alice aren't trying to fix me up on a blind date, are you?" I would like a woman of my own but blind dates can be so humiliating.

"What?" Billy takes a step back, like he's afraid I'm about to grab him by the polo collar and punch him in the nose or something. "God no. Alice would never be a part of trying to fix you up with someone. I've suggested it before, like maybe with one of her available friends, but she says absolutely not. She says you're unfixable. In fact, she didn't really want to have you over tonight at all but—"

"But I asked her to," a feminine voice says.

I turn around and standing there is Three Sheets.

Three Sheets looks much better without the purple maid of honor dress, the updo hair and the bleary eyes.

But I don't notice that right away. I'm too busy looking at Alice.

Alice looks better than I've ever seen her. With her chestnut hair pulled into a high ponytail and no makeup, she looks even better than she did on her wedding day. Marriage agrees with her.

"Oh!" I say. "I almost forgot!" I hand over the package I've been carrying, a brown paper bag.

Alice gingerly opens the folded-over top—I don't know what she's expecting, snakes in a can?—and extracts my present. She holds it up for all to see.

"That's great!" Billy says with genuine enthusiasm.

"Wow," she says, "a six-pack of Sierra Nevada Pale Ale. You shouldn't have."

"Hey," I say, feeling pleased with myself that I remembered Aunt Alfresca's advice when I was little to never go anywhere empty-handed, "I figured it'd be rude, you having me to dinner and all, if I then went and drank all your beer on you."

"Well, you definitely outdid yourself."

Three Sheets takes a step forward. "I wanted to thank you."

"For…?" I'm not so sure I want to know.

Maybe Alice doesn't either, because she breaks it up with, "Here, let me go put this on ice and get us something to eat." She casts a meaningful look at her cousin. "You going to help me?"

"Oh. Right!" Three Sheets says.

That's another thing about women. At any given social occasion, they can't travel from one room to another solo. It's like they never heard of divide and conquer. To them it's all safety in numbers like maybe there's a masher waiting between the stove and the chopping block or something.

"Let me get us a couple of beers," Billy suggests, leaving me alone with the lawn furniture. See? If Billy were a girl, he'd need me to go with him. And if I were a girl, I'd probably feel the need to go after him whether asked or not. But I'm a guy. I can handle being alone for a few minutes with the lawn furniture. I'm not scared of any mashers, not scared of any shadows—

"Ack! What the hell was that thing?" I say, jumping out of my skin, having felt something rub hard against my calf and then seen a black furry blur run down a hallway toward what I presume are the bedrooms.

Billy pokes his head into the living room. "Did it look like it could be the size of a cat?"

I think about it. "I guess so. I mean, it wasn't the size of a horse and it wasn't the size of a spider."

"Then it was the cat." He disappears, comes back in with

our beers.

"Why in the world would you get a cat?" I study the label on the bottle of beer he hands me. "Sierra Nevada Pale Ale." I tip the bottle toward him admiringly. "Nice beer."

"Thanks," he says, takes a slug of his beer. "Alice's idea. The cat, I mean. She says it's good practice for us. We both want to have kids, but neither of us have any experience, neither of us has younger siblings or ever did any babysitting. Alice says it'll be good for us to see if we can love something other than each other without fighting all the time about how best to take care of it."

"Geez, Billy, that's a big commitment. A cat." I'm thinking: the crease in his chinos, the practical discussion about furniture buying, the cat—Billy has changed so much in the past month since he got married, I'm half amazed that he's still drinking regular beer and not some high-brow brand; or even worse, mixed drinks with strange names.

"Here we are!" Three Sheets says brightly as she follows Alice back into the living room like Alice is the lead in a two-car train and Three Sheets is the caboose.

Alice is carrying a square white dish upon which are arranged four appetizers that look to be about one-inch by one-inch square. It's all very geometrical. And small.

"Sit," Billy says as Alice sets the plate down on the redwood table that's got a hole for an umbrella but no umbrella, indicating I should take what is clearly the best piece of lawn furniture in the house, the chaise.

I straddle the end, reach for one of the appetizers—I see now it's a square of toast with a dab of some kind of pasty stuff on it with a sliver of something else on top of the paste—and pop it into my mouth.

"It's good," I say to Alice.

Before she can thank me for the compliment, which I'm sure she would have, Three Sheets starts to talk, making me all nervous again.

"I wanted to thank you in person for what you did at the hotel," she says.

"It was nothing," I say, not really sure where she's going with this.

Nervous, I pop another appetizer in my mouth.

"Really good," I say to Alice.

"To me it was everything," Three Sheets says. "I've been in that situation before—drunk, really drunk, and then… *stuff* happens."

"Yeah, well, we all—" I cut myself off from saying anything stupid by shoving a third appetizer into my mouth. I make the OK sign at Alice with my thumb and forefinger as I swallow.

"And then after stuff happens," Three Sheets goes on, "what usually happens is the next day I get so nervous worrying that maybe I was too drunk to use birth control correctly and worrying I might be pregnant, the nervousness makes me skip my period and then I get really sure I'm pregnant and I freak out and then—"

"And then she calls me," Alice says, "having called me at each stage in a panic, and I talk her through every step of taking a pregnancy test and everything turns out fine."

"Thank you for saving me from all that panic," Three Sheets says.

This is too much. Is this what it's like for Billy now all the time? All this talk of women stuff and periods?

"Um, you're welcome?" I say.

"Seriously," Alice says, "thank you from both of us. If you'd taken advantage of Dawn like I originally thought you had, I would have been getting panicked calls all through my honeymoon. When I didn't get any calls, I knew I was wrong about you."

"Wait." I point my finger at Three Sheets. "Your name is Dawn?"

I realize my mistake as soon as the words leave my mouth. Why oh why must I always commit the insanity of doing the same dumb shit—the same dumb shit that falls under the heading of *just being myself*—over and over again.

Alice goes from civil to fishwife in one second flat. "Oh my God, Johnny, you are so gross! You went to a hotel room with my cousin with the original intention of sleeping with her and you didn't even know her name?"

I could point out to Alice at this juncture that Three Sheets—I mean, *Dawn*—was the one who invited me to that hotel room when she didn't even know *my* name. But I don't do that because I can tell Alice maybe doesn't have the most respect in the world for her cousin already and if Alice thinks I'm a skunk for not knowing Dawn's name, what will she think of Dawn for not knowing mine?

"Yeah," I say, popping the fourth appetizer into my mouth, "I'm a real creep that way." I indicate the empty plate. "Hey, you got any more of these? They're great."

"No, I don't," Alice says through gritted teeth.

"You don't?" I feel my eyebrows go up. I was kidding when I asked if there were any more because of course I assumed there were. Who serves just four little square thingies to four people and calls it an appetizer?

"No," Alice says. "They're called *amuse bouche*. They're special miniature hors d'oeuvres meant to whet the appetite. There aren't meant to be a lot. Just one each."

Oh.

Oh.

"*Amuse bouche*," I whisper to Billy once the girls are back in the kitchen. "How was I supposed to know?"

"I know, I know." Billy waves his beer at me. "You're telling me? It's like a minefield sometimes. Women. They're always coming up with something new all the time—cats, periods, little tiny foods no one's ever heard of before except maybe in France. It really keeps you on your toes."

"Wow," I say, "I guess you've had to make a lot of adjustments."

Billy tilts his beer at me. "That I have, my friend."

I think of the way Billy talks about Alice, like her every word is golden law, and how she looks at him. Even when she looks at him like, "You idiot," it's obvious she's thinking 'No matter how big an idiot you are, I just love you so much.'

"And you've loved every second of it," I say.

"That I have," Billy says.

Alice and Dawn return with plates and I notice, thankfully, that the plates each have more than four one-inch-square items on them.

"Oh, is it din-din time already?" I say.

Alice's eyebrows shoot up. "Din-din? Did you really just say din-din?"

I feel the blush in my cheeks. To avoid Alice's scoffing gaze I look at Dawn. "It's something Big John used to say every night. Big John's my dad. See, my mom died having me so my dad felt he had to be both mom and dad so whenever he served dinner at night, even if it was burritos, he'd always say, 'Din-din's ready.' I think he though it made him sound like June Cleaver."

"Can I get you another beer?" Billy says.

"Din-din." Alice snorts.

"Aw." Dawn ignores her cousin as she covers my hand with hers and gives it a little squeeze. "Din-din. That's so sweet!"

"Well, that went well," Billy says.

Dinner has passed uneventfully, meaning I haven't said anything further to piss Alice off. On the contrary, Alice actually looked pleased when I thanked her for remembering my pescatarian diet by not serving anything with meat. Now Alice and Dawn have gone into the kitchen to fetch dessert and coffee while Billy and I enjoy another beer and a little Mets talk. After Billy complains, yet again, about the annoyance of what was once Shea Stadium now being called Citi Field, a sentiment I concur with wholeheartedly, a silence falls over us, into which I hear drop:

"Lucky finally knows!" That was Alice.

"Are you kidding me?" Dawn says.

"Yes! After all this time. For months I kept wondering: When is this idiot going to realize that his fiancé is sleeping with his half brother, the Greek prince?"

Alice knows someone who has a Greek prince for a half brother?

"So how did Lucky find out?" Dawn asks.

"He caught them together!"

"No!"

"Yes! He went over to talk to Nikolas about something and the door was open a crack. There's Elizabeth in her black bra and panties, straddling Nik."

"No!"

"Yes!"

"So what did Lucky do?"

"Oh, this is the best part. He quietly walks away before they see him. Then he goes back home and completely trashes the place. And when Liz stops by later? Lucky says he doesn't know who did it, that he just found it that way, that maybe Luke did it while on one of his benders."

"He did not blame it on his father!"

"He did!"

"What a dirtbag!"

"I know!"

"So what do you think Lucky's going to do now?"

"Revenge? Something else? I don't know. All I know is, whatever he does, he'll probably have tears in his eyes while he's doing it. Lucky's always got tears in his eyes. He's such a wimp."

I can't believe what I'm hearing. Someone they know just caught his fiancée in the arms of his half brother, the Greek prince, and they're laughing at the poor guy? These women are vipers! I look at Billy, to see if he's similarly disturbed by all this, but he mostly just still looks bummed about the stadium we grew up with as Shea now being called Citi Field.

As Alice and Dawn return to the room, I can't contain myself. "What is *wrong* with you people?"

"What?" Alice says, like she doesn't know what I'm talking about.

"Don't act all innocent," I say. "I heard you." I wave my finger back and forth between Alice and Dawn. "I heard both of you. You were laughing at your poor friend Lucky—"

"Our *friend?*" Alice says.

"You think they were talking about real people?" Billy says.

"Well, I…What? You know about all this?"

"We were talking about a TV show," Dawn says.

"Yeah," Billy says, "a soap opera. It's called *General Hospital.*"

"Oh," I say, feeling incredibly stupid. Then, to escape that feeling, I say, "Soap operas are stupid."

"Excuse me?" Alice has her hands on her hips now.

"I only said—"

"Soap operas serve an important sociological function."

"I only meant—"

"They provide millions of people with escape from their own mundane and depressing lives."

"OK, but—"

"They cheer people up because viewers realize that however bad they've got it, the perfect-looking and well-dressed people on soaps always have it worse. They give viewers something to bond over with each other in an often confusing and lonely world. They provide a nondestructive form of—"

"Geez, Alice, all right already. You don't need to write a thesis on it."

"Oh, no?" She gives the dangerous head nod here. "Well, maybe I do. You obviously think that soaps are an inferior form of entertainment, no doubt because it's a genre primarily enjoyed by women. Men always feel the need to devalue anything women admire or enjoy. Well, tell me, how is your vaunted sports some kind of superior entertainment? You talk all the time about earned-run averages and quarterback ratings and how badly the Nets suck – who does any of that matter to?"

I look at Billy, shrug my shoulders. "Us?"

"Do you think," Alice says, "a hundred years from now, anyone's going to give a shit that Mark McGwire hit a lot of homeruns while doing steroids?"

She's got a point there.

"God, you piss me off."

And, back to the kitchen goes Alice.

"You should never have knocked soap operas, man." Billy

shakes his head.

"You ever watch one of those things?" I say.

"Sure," Billy says. "Well, now I do. *General Hospital.* You should try it sometime." He tilts his beer bottle at me, winks. "It's a good show."

"No shit."

"And Alice is right. Lucky's a douche."

I know Billy said earlier that they didn't invite Dawn and me on the same night to fix us up, that Alice says I'm unfixupable, but as the evening winds down I'm getting this nagging feeling. I get this idea into my head. Billy and Alice are a happily married couple, Dawn's right here, she looks much better than she did at the wedding, particularly since she's not half as drunk, she's Alice's cousin, if we start dating and wind up—who knows?— getting married, I could spend the rest of my life having evenings like this, just the four of us hanging together. Well, maybe without all the bad and awkward moments of tonight. But other than that? Yup, it could be just the four of us. Billy and Alice. Me and my wife. Men and wives. I'm thinking that, but I'm also thinking: Poor Dawn. Still alone at her age. Someone should throw her a mercy date.

Which is why I lean over and say in a low voice so as not to be overheard by Billy and Alice, "Hey. You wanna go out sometime?"

"You mean like on a *date*?" Dawn says this so loud, the neighbors must've heard her. Certainly Alice did.

"Well, I…"

"Aw, I'm sorry, Johnny." Dawn covers my hand with hers like she did earlier. Come to think of it, that little move of hers coupled with her "That's so cute" about my din-din story coupled with the fact that it was her idea to have Alice have us over at the same time in the first place—all of that's what gave me the impression that maybe my invitation would be welcome.

"I already have a boyfriend," Dawn goes on. "Actually we're sort of engaged to be engaged, which is another reason I'm grateful for you not taking advantage of me at the wedding. Imagine how awkward that would have been, me having my usual pregnancy scare only this time also not knowing if the baby's my almost fiance's or yours? It'd be like something on *General Hospital*."

Ouch. I just got rejected by someone I never really wanted to go out with in the first place, at least not for anything to do with her personally.

Then I look over at Alice and for once she doesn't look annoyed with me. On the contrary, she looks like she feels sorry for me.

Pissed. Sorry. Pissed. Sorry. In a world where Alice is mostly just mad at me, I'll take looking like a pathetic loser if it means she stops being mad for a few minutes.

Dawn's gone and I'm getting ready to head off.

"Can I use your...?" I gesture with my hand down the hallway.

"Sure thing," Billy says, so I go to hit the head before hitting the road.

Then, as Billy and I are saying our final goodbyes, standing at the door trading a few last comments about the Mets, Alice heads down the hallway. I hear a lock click, followed thirty seconds later by...

"*Fucking Johnny!*"

"Oh, shit," Billy says. "You leave the lid up on the toilet?"

I nod.

"She's so skinny, her ass gets wet when that happens. You better get out of here while you still can."

Men at Play

In my mind, I'm thinking in my best bass voice imitation: I'm in the *front row!*

Steve Miller called me up the week before.

"You're not going to believe this," he said.

I was on a job at the time, standing on a ladder, cell phone in hand.

"What?" I said. "Your wife wants to paint the dining room a different color for the fourth time?"

"Good one." He laughed. "You know you're a very funny guy?"

"So I've been told."

"Katie's happy enough with the dining room, at least for now. She loves the aqua."

People always do.

"No," Steve went on. "That case I told you about? The burglar with a heart of gold?"

"Yeah?"

"I won! I followed your advice to the letter, and I won!"

"Hey, that's fantastic."

"Well, the opposing attorney didn't think so. You should have seen her face!"

"I'll bet."

"Anyway, the reason I'm calling is: About that Opening Day game…"

I hadn't really wanted to go to a game with Steve Miller nor did I want to sacrifice a half day's work, and I even resisted for a long time, but then I asked myself: Aren't I my own boss, and isn't one of the perks of that the ability to say screw work for the day and just go play? Plus, when in my life am I ever going to get to sit in a seat that costs more than my last long-weekend vacation?

So here I am, and I keep trying to pump myself up by telling myself in that bass voice: I'm in the *front row!*

Which is inevitably followed by a smaller interior voice saying: Too bad it's for the fucking Yankees, the World Champs—how annoying is that?

That's right. Here I am at the home opener—Steve had kept calling it Opening Day but the Yanks were on the road for the season opener so this is just the home opener—at Yankee Stadium, which is another annoying thing. The Mets have to play at Citi Field now but of course the fucking Yankees get to keep the name of their stadium, even after the new stadium opened, even after the corporatization of America. The Yankees always get everything. I hate to be such a girl about things but it's so unfair.

Yes, I'm sitting here in an eight-hundred-dollar seat at fucking Yankee Stadium on Thursday, April 16, I'm surrounded by a halo of lawyers, and they're all wearing suits.

Steve had a ticket sent to my home, so I drove in myself and arrived after Steve and his other two guests, which turned out to be two out-of-town lawyers.

"Monte," the one said, holding out a hand with perfectly manicured fingernails, "Carlo."

"Um, Danbury," I responded, figuring it was some sort of weird lawyer greeting as I shook his hand, "Connecticut."

"No, Jersey," he said. "I'm from Jersey. Monte Carlo's my name."

"That's pretty funny," I said.

"Is it?" he said wonderingly.

Then Steve laughed. "Huh. It is. I never thought about it that way."

The other lawyer's name turned out to be John John III. I don't know why people do that to their kids. Giving someone the same first name as their last is bad enough to do once but then to go on to do it for the next two generations? And this guy'll probably do the same thing to his kid, but this time I was careful not to say anything that might make it sound like I was laughing at someone's name since Monte Carlo was still looking kind of sensitive.

"We call him JJ Trey," Steve leaned into me for the whisper.

Whatever.

So now I'm sitting here in the front row, surrounded by my halo of lawyers, they've all got their suits on since they came straight from work, ties loosened now, expensive jackets draped across their laps. And what am I wearing?

My usual going-to-the-game uniform: relatively clean T-shirt, jeans, work boots. I left the Mets cap at home. Who says I'm not sensitive to the people around me?

Yes, I'm sitting here, blowing off work on a gorgeous spring day, right in the front row, right behind home plate where I've never sat in my life, Steve at my side, Monte Carlo and JJ Trey behind us, and I could care less. Because it is, in the end, only the fucking Yankees.

"What do you want to eat?" Steve asks. "Whatever you want—eat, drink—it's on the house, comes with the tickets."

"I'm thinking sushi," JJ Trey says from behind us, "with an ice-cold Stoli."

"Something Italian," Monte Carlo says. "Maybe calamari or a nice risotto? And a Rob Roy."

Geez, where am I, the ballpark or a restaurant in Manhattan?

"Johnny?" Steve says. "What would you like? Really, anything you want. A porterhouse steak? Shrimp Caesar salad? Maybe a nice bottle of champagne to go with it? Some Veuve Cliquot?"

"I don't know," I say. "I was thinking more like a couple of hot dogs with mustard and a Bud."

Steve is crestfallen. "I'm not sure if you can get that here."

Fucking Yankees. Fucking Yankee Stadium.

It's the third inning, the score is Who cares? to Who cares? and I decide to take a little walk, see if I can scare up some hot dogs and real beer.

And what do you know? It takes me a while, I have to take

the escalator up to the cheap seats and walk halfway around the stadium, but eventually I find what I'm looking for.

As I head back to my seat, coming up behind Steve and Monte Carlo and JJ Trey, for the first time I notice the people sitting to our right, two of whom are women. Both women are wearing business suits, the one right next to our box looking kind of sloppy in hers, while the one a little further down looks crisp and not at all like any woman I've ever seen at Shea; I mean Citi Field. She hasn't even removed the jacket of her suit, despite that it's turning into a very warm day. Her hair is a pretty auburn color, thick and up in some kind of twist. She happens to turn briefly as I approach and I notice that her skin is like china—I hope she doesn't burn in this sun—and that her eyes as they meet mine are an incredible shade of blue-green. I also notice that she looks bored out of her skull.

I'm thinking about how pretty and bored she looks, thinking about how eventually every seat in every stadium in the land will one day be filled strictly with bored people who are only there because their companies have season tickets but who have no real love of the game, when my attention is pulled away by the sound of my own name. Problem is, I realize almost immediately, no one's talking *to* me; they're talking *about* me.

"Really?" JJ Trey pops a sushi roll into his mouth, follows it down with a delicate sip of his ice-cold Stoli. "You invited your *house painter* to the game?"

"What's next," Monte Carlo says, swirling the swizzle stick in his Rob Roy, "you going to ask your garbage man to the opera?"

I don't know what I expect when I hear this—that Steve will laugh with them, sell me down the river? That he'll say inviting me was just some big joke?

But he doesn't do any of this.

"Come on, guys," he says, "Johnny's amazing. He's really funny."

"Right." Monte Carlo snorts. "Like him laughing at my name. The guy's a real laugh riot."

"I'm serious," Steve says. "Not only that, he's really

smart too."

Now it's JJ Trey's turn to snort.

"I'm telling you," Steve says, "the guy's like some kind of legal savant." He casts his eyes to the right, to the two women sitting next to our box, and lowers his voice. "He's the one who gave me the idea of how to get my last client off. My client was facing some serious time, the prosecutor had a solid case and—"

Enough of this. It's nice of Steve to defend me this way, but he shouldn't have to sell me to these two guys.

I "ahem" loudly, as I pass Monte Carlo and JJ Trey's seats, resume my seat beside Steve, hot dogs and beer in hand.

"Hey, Johnny." Monte Carlo taps me on the shoulder. "Steve here says—"

But he doesn't get a chance to finish, because just then my cell phone rings. I'm going to ignore it—I'm at a ballgame, after all, even if it is the Yankees—but then I notice people all around us yakking on their cells, and I figure what the hell.

But my hands are full of hot dogs and beer. I look around me for a place to put them as the cell keeps ringing, notice the two women in the box beside ours staring at me.

"You want one?" I say, indicating the hot dogs. The one in the rumpled suit shakes her head like I might be a pervert or something, but Blue-Green Eyes smiles politely as she says, "No, thank you." There's something about her voice that's instantly familiar, but I can't place it and anyway the phone's still ringing. I have the longest ring in the world before it'll switch to voicemail; the long ring is because sometimes when I'm working an exterior and I'm up high on the ladder, I prefer to get down to terra firma before picking up. As I set the hot dogs and beer on the ground, however, I do think about how politely Blue-Green Eyes responded to me. I always think it says a lot about a person, how they treat strangers and people who are dressed inferiorly to them in a social setting.

"Could be work," I say apologetically to Steve as I flip open the phone.

"Hello?" I say, listen as the caller identifies himself.

Steve nudges me. "Is it work?"

I shush him, speak into the phone, making my voice go all excited. "Are you kidding me? I finally made the team?"

"What team?" Steve says, and I can feel Monte Carlo and JJ Trey lean forward, interested.

"The Mets," I say, covering the mouthpiece with my hand as I listen to the voice in my ear.

I respond to the voice, "This is fantastic! When do you want me to show up for practice? This may surprise you to hear it, but playing shortstop for the Mets has been my lifelong dream!"

The voice in my ear and I go on for a time, before I finally end the call with, "Looking forward to seeing you next week!"

I snap my phone closed, pleased with myself, retrieve my beer and hot dogs. "You sure you don't want one?" I say to the women next to me, who are both eyeing me now like, "Who is this guy?"

When they shake their heads, I shrug, take a bite of the first dog.

All around me there's silence. Well, except for the roar of the crowd. Finally Monte Carlo says from behind, in awe, "You're going to be playing shortstop for the Mets?"

The laugh comes out of me so abruptly, I practically choke on my dog. "Um, no," I say.

What is this guy, high?

"You mean that phone call?" I say, and Steve nods. "Oh, that was just a ticket seller. I don't know how they got my number, but every season they call up with the same routine, 'We've got some exciting opportunities for you this year at Shea.' Well, now they say Citi Field, which really pisses me off."

"I know, right?" Steve says.

"Of course by 'exciting opportunities,' they mean they have season tickets they want me to buy. Like that's going to ever happen. I can't be blowing off work every day. So I just play with them, pretend I don't understand what they're talking about, act like I think they're offering me a contract to play. They keep trying to sell me and I keep acting excited about my new career with the Mets. It goes on like that until I tire the guy out." I shrug. "The guy today didn't last too long."

"That's pretty funny," Monte Carlo concedes. "When I get phone solicitors, they just annoy me."

"Hey," I say, "you should see me at home when someone calls the wrong number."

Next to me, I see Blue-Green Eyes smile as she watches the Yankees play. I figure it can't be the Yankees making her smile. It must be my charm.

JJ Trey taps me on the shoulder. "Steve says you're some kind of legal savant. Make a case for me."

What is this guy, high? "About…?"

"Anything. Just make something up. This game's lousy. I'm bored."

"OK," I say, thinking, thinking. I don't usually get put on the spot like this with abstract cases. It's more like I only think about it when I'm reading the paper or when Sam's watching one of her crime shows on MSNBC. But if this guy wants to challenge me, I'll play.

"Hmm… OK, my *favorite* loophole showed up in a Kansas law a year or two ago."

"You see what I mean about this guy?" Steve says proudly, loudly. "What kind of *nonlawyer* has a favorite loophole? I don't even have a favorite loophole!" When he says this, I see Blue-Green Eyes shoot me a sharp look, but I'm so excited to be talking about my favorite loophole that I don't stop and wonder what it might mean, instead plunging enthusiastically on.

"Like I say, this happened a year or two ago. In an effort to discourage abortions, the state of Kansas created a safe harbor for parents who abandoned their children at any hospital in the state. That may also have included fire departments and places like that—I'm a little hazy about some of the finer details. The interesting part is that the state neglected to clarify when the drop-offs were allowed relative to the age of the child. As a result, crafty parents with difficult teenagers began abandoning their kids at Kansas hospitals. Now, of course it's generally illegal to abandon a child but because the law was so poorly worded, several teens were abandoned, including some from out of state, until the law was redrafted."

"I remember reading something about that," Monte Carlo says. "What a mess."

"Exactly," I say. "Naturally, some instances resulted in criminal charges. Residents of Kansas couldn't be prosecuted for abandoning their teenagers until the loophole was closed. But say if for some insane reason someone decided to live in Florida and that same person tried to abandon their child in Kansas? The parent would have relied on the Kansas law, obviously, but Florida would have rightly relied on its law prohibiting such abandonment."

"'If for some insane reason someone decided to live in Florida'?" JJ Trey echoes. "What do you have against Florida?"

I shrug. "General principle."

"I love this guy!" Monte Carlo says. "We could use someone like him at the firm in Jersey." He punches me fraternally on the shoulder. "Hey, why don't you go back to school and get your law degree? You'd be terrific at it."

"Because I'm in paint," I say. "It never lets you down."

"Didn't I tell you?" Steve says like a proud father. "Johnny's great!" And now he's not modulating his voice at all as he crows, "Like I said, he's the guy who gave me the idea of how to get my burglary client off!"

And now Blue-Green Eyes is giving me the hairy eyeball something fierce, but I'm not bothered by it so much anymore because I'm generally used to women giving me the hairy eyeball, plus I'm finally in my element. I'm at the ballpark, even if it's the Yankees, and I'm surrounded by guys who think I'm wonderful, even if I don't dress like they do or if I make my vastly smaller fortune at something they consider to be an inferior job.

"Paint, it never let's you down," JJ Trey echoes. "Geez, I'd love to work at a job I could say that about."

Yes, I'm finally in my element—it's amazing how hard the guys laugh when JJ Trey complains about the vintage car he paid one hundred thousand dollars for that his mechanic can't fix and I tell him exactly how to fix it because I owned one once only mine was a thirty-year-old rust bucket I paid fifty dollars for, keeping it on the road with rubber bands and duct tape—and now I'm finally into the game too, actually watching the field, actually noting the Yankees are up, actually noting A-Rod at the plate as he tips one back and...

Omigod. The ball is coming my way, sort of; I've caught balls in the cheap seats before, but I've never been so close to a ball when it meets the bat, ricocheting off in my general direction, so of course I do what any red-blooded male would do. Even if it is a Yankee baseball, I leap from my seat, arm fully extended, hand out to make the catch as I stumble past Rumpled Suit and trip right into the lap of Blue-Green Eyes, knocking whatever fruity drink she's holding all over the both of us.

"Excuse me," she says, and I'm thinking there's that politeness again, only this time there's no accompanying polite smile. "What do you think you're doing?"

"Trying to catch the foul tip?" I wince out my ask-answer.

"You can't do that in these seats," she says matter-of-factly.

At first I'm thinking she means that that's not *done* in these seats, that the people who occupy these way-too-expensive eight-hundred-dollar seats are way too high brow to do something so mundane, so lower class as to try to shag a foul tip. And I'm about to let rip on her with a piece of my mind about such elitist bullshit when I see her hand come over my shoulder to point straight ahead of the two of us.

"See that thing?" she says, and now I see exactly what she's pointing at. "It's called a protective barrier."

And of course I see it, of course there's a protective barrier there, to protect people who are lucky enough to sit behind home plate from getting concussions from being so close to all those foul balls.

"They put that there for a reason," she says.

Christ, I feel like an idiot. But up close like this? Those eyes are bluer, greener, and so damn intelligent. I'm a sucker for an intelligent woman.

"Geez, I hate the Yankees," I say.

She surprises me by answering, surprise in her voice, "Me too. I can't stand them."

And I'm thinking how cool this is—we both hate the

Yankees! But I'm also thinking: Then why is she here? And then I'm answering myself: Oh, right. Undoubtedly she hates all sports and is only here, like almost everyone else, because they get free corporate tickets, which gives them an excuse to take the afternoon off work.

Still, we have something in common—we both hate the Yankees! It's been a long time since I had anything in common with a woman, unless we're talking about Sam. And then I think about how she smiled at me earlier and before I can second-guess myself I blurt out with:

"You wanna go out with me sometime?"

"No."

"Are you married?" I ask, in a way hoping she is; at least that would explain the instantaneous no, although I don't recall seeing any rings on her fingers.

"No, but I'm not crazy either," she says. "And I don't go out with guys who are responsible for helping criminals run free. Now if you wouldn't mind…" She gives me a meaningful look and I feel myself blush as it strikes me with full-force that I'm still sitting in her lap.

I make my way back to my seat, wondering what she meant about the part about not going out with guys who are responsible for helping criminals run free.

As I sit there, my shirt now sticky from her spilled drink, Steve leans across me and acknowledges Blue-Green Eyes with a nod of the head. "Helen," he says.

"Steve," she acknowledges in return, her single word as grudging as grudging could be.

Something about those one-word acknowledgments—it reminds me of a cartoon I used to see when I was a kid. This wolf and this sheepdog. They'd walk to a field together at dawn, lunch pails in hand, acknowledge each other with a one-word greeting—something along the lines of, "Joe"; "Scott"—and punch a time clock. Then the wolf would spend the day trying to steal the sheep while the sheepdog would spend the day outsmarting the wolf. At the end of the day, at dusk, after a day of fighting, they'd punch out and acknowledge, "Joe"; "Scott" like what had just happened had happened but also somehow as though it had not.

That's what Steve and Helen remind me of: the sheepdog and the wolf.

"You know her?" I say to Steve, impressed that my too-often-drunk customer knows such a woman.

"Of course," he says. "That's Helen. Helen Troy."

And everything in the world, or at least a lot that's happened today, makes perfect sense when he adds:

"She's the District Attorney."

Men at Play II

I answer the phone. "Hello?"

"I'm calling about the 2006 Toyota. Is it done yet?"

"Oh, right, the Toyota. Yeah, it should be ready for pickup in the morning. We had to put a new engine in."

"*A new engine?*" the voice on the other end goes apoplectic on me. "But I only brought it in for an oil change!"

I hang up to the sound of Sam laughing, which is good. Sam hasn't laughed in a while.

"That never gets old," she says, "no matter how many times I hear it."

Steve Miller looks confused. "You just told someone you put a new engine in their car?"

"Right," I say, "but he says he only brought it in for an oil change."

"But you don't even do car repairs." He looks more puzzled still. "Do you?"

"No, but Snappy Oil Change and Auto Repairs does and their phone number is only one digit different than mine. I get wrong numbers all the time. What can I say?" I shrug. "It gets boring answering wrong numbers every day. Every now and then I need to spice things up."

"So you tell some poor schmuck that only brought his car in for an oil change that you replaced his whole engine?"

I shrug again. "He'll figure it out in the morning when he goes to Snappy and his car's all fine, still with the same engine and with no big bill."

"That's cruel."

"Or hysterical. All depends on your perspective."

Steve starts to laugh. "That is pretty funny."

"Exactly," Sam says. "That's what I was saying."

"Whose turn is it to deal?" Big John says.

It's five o'clock on Friday afternoon, officially rendering our Weekly Friday Night Poker Night our Weekly Friday Afternoon Poker Night, which is why I'm still fielding calls for Snappy. We used to start our games at a more civilized hour, like seven or eight, but since both Billy and Drew are married now, and neither of their wives like them to be out too late...

Yup. Our games begin at five now. Christ, it's even still light out. I mean like, *really* light.

Well, it is when they arrive, but we don't see the light where we play, which is in my basement. It's not so easy for Big John to get down the stairs, what with the MS and all, but on good days he'll use his cane, and on bad ones me and one of the other guys will carry him. He says it's worth it. He loves watching Sam play, loves that she's my friend.

"In the old days when I was growing up," he likes to say, "we never heard of such a thing. But you kids these days? You've got everything. Computers. Cell phones. Lesbian best friends. You got it made."

If I'm lucky, he doesn't say it within Sam's hearing. She gets very sensitive about being regarded as just another technological advance.

We've been meeting like this in my basement every Friday night for years—Billy, Drew, Big John, Sam, me—only tonight we added Steve Miller to the mix. Well, I added him. I don't know how it happened. Honest to God! One minute, I was thanking him for giving me that free ticket to see a team I'm wholly uninterested in play a game I was wholly uninterested in, during which I managed to completely humiliate myself in front of a woman I found to be intriguing, and the next minute he's casually asking me what I have planned for Friday night, I casually tell him about the poker game, he sincerely states how he'd give his right nut to have a guys' night out of poker just once, and before I know what's happening I find myself saying, "Hey, why don't you come by?"

And now he's here! In my basement! Am I ever going to be

able to get rid of this guy?

Sam arrived a little before the others, like she always does, in order to help me set things up. She helped me put the snacks out—my favorite snack, the one I like to call Chips In A Bowl; it's a very delicate operation, transferring the chips from the bag—and make sure the fridge in the basement was stocked with beer. She also helped me cover the pool table with the large sheet of plywood we always use for our Friday games, setting the chairs up around one end because whenever we try to use the whole table, it gets kind of hard to deal the cards all the way across. It was while we were moving the wood together that she told me about Renee.

"Yup, she finally moved out."

"I kind of figured when I saw the moving van and all. Your idea?"

"Hers. She says I don't know how to be in a relationship."

"You OK?"

"Yes and no. Yes, because I think I've known all along that Renee wasn't The One. But no, because I'm tired of things never working out. What do women want?"

She was asking the wrong guy.

"I really like the way you've got this place set up," Steve says, taking in all my framed sports posters, the chandelier over the table with each light a hula girl, the painting of the dogs playing poker. He was particularly tickled when we told him we were playing over a pool table. "I should do something like this at my place."

"You think your wife would like that?" I ask, dealing the cards. It's kind of tough picturing Katie Miller, who has her Royal Doulton displayed in a ten-thousand-dollar breakfront, having a true appreciation for the dogs-playing-poker picture.

"That is always the question, isn't it?" He sighs. "Probably not."

I study my cards. Not a bad hand I've dealt myself. Three queens and I swear one of them's winking at me. If only that queen were a real woman. That wink'd never happen in real life.

Sam, seated to my left, tosses one card down. Shit. She

thinks she only needs one card?

"Give me—" she starts to say, but she never gets to finish because just then someone's cell goes off.

"Christ," Big John says. "I thought we made a rule about this."

Billy, Drew, Steve—they all color slightly as hands go into pockets, searching for phones.

"Sorry," Steve says, locating his phone, realizing it's not him. "I didn't know there was a rule."

"Could be Alice," Billy says.

"You are so pussy-whipped," Sam mocks him.

"Oh yeah?" Billy says. "Well, you wish you were."

I shake my head at my best friends. Always with the petty jealousy.

"Nope," Billy says, "it's not mine."

"It's Stacy," Drew says. "I gotta get this."

Geez, I wish a wife were calling me.

As Drew fumbles his phone open, he drops his cards on the table and now everyone can see his hand.

"Christ," Big John says, throwing his own hand down. "Why do we even bother playing?"

"Hello?" Drew says, shushing us. We can only hear his side of the conversation clearly, but whenever Stacy speaks on her end, we hear a "Waawaawaawaa" sound, kind of like the teachers' and parents' voices in those old Charlie Brown cartoons.

Drew: "No, it's not nearly done yet. I just got here. Well, a half hour ago."

Drew: "No, I won't drink too much."

Drew: "Yes, I'll remember to eat something. I'll eat something right now."

He crams a few chips in his mouth.

Drew (slightly garbled): "A quart of milk, a pound of angel-hair pasta and a leek. Leeks—are they the really skinny green onions or that big huge thing?"

Drew (less garbled): "Right."

Drew (whispering now, like maybe we won't hear him— we're right there): "I love you too, babe."

Drew: "Right, not too late, gotta go, I'm holding up the game, no, yes, I love you too, yes, leeks, no, bye, love you."

When Drew snaps his cell shut, he looks exhausted, like he's just run a marathon.

"Man," Billy says sympathetically, "you barely got out of there alive. I know what it's like."

"Tell me about it," Drew says with a heavy sigh. "Women. What is it they want?"

He looks around the table one by one, like he's expecting an answer somewhere.

Billy shakes his head, Steve shakes his head, I shake my head, Drew shakes his own head.

"Don't look at me," Sam says. "I still haven't figured women out."

"I'll tell you what women want," Big John says authoritatively. He pulls a cigar out of his pocket, chomps one end. He never lights the thing. He just likes to chomp.

"*You?*" I laugh. I don't mean the laugh to come out quite so mocking. But really. When was his last date—over thirty-three years ago? The only woman I've seen him with since Mom died is Aunt Alfresca. And I mean, she's Aunt Alfresca. It's not like she's a real woman. What could Big John possibly know about real women and what they want?

"I'm going to choose to ignore that mocking laugh," Big John says, still chomping. "Sure, I could choose to be offended and then further choose to withhold valuable information from you. But that wouldn't be very big of me now, would it?"

"Yes, but what could you—" I start to say, but Billy cuts me off.

"Stop mocking, Johnny," he says.

"Seriously," Drew says. "We've got wives. We need this information."

"But he hasn't been married in over thirty-three years!" I object.

"So?" Billy points out. "It's not like she divorced him."

Big John jabs his cigar in Billy's direction. "You make an excellent observation. Francesca died long before she had the opportunity to start hating me, so I think it's safe to say I know a few things about women."

Four heads swivel in my direction—Billy, Drew, Steve, Sam—as though expecting me to raise a further objection. Instead, I relax back against my chair, fold my arms across my chest, wave one hand expansively in Big John's direction.

"Be my guest," I say. "Educate us."

"Your basic woman," chomp, "is a completely different animal than your basic man." Big John gestures with his hand abruptly, palm down, like he's telling a dealer in Vegas that he wants no more cards. "*Completely*." Then he looks at Sam, adds, "Well, except for Sam."

I snort.

"No, it's true," Billy says. He gathers up the deck of cards. "Take what we're doing right now. When women want to talk about something with each other, they simply say that's what they want to do and then they go for coffee or a glass of wine and just talk. But when we men want to talk, we have to pretend we're really doing something else instead. Like we're doing now." He starts to deal. "It's like we can't engage in direct human interaction. It's like we always have to be *doing* something, engaged in some other activity, in order to give us an excuse to interact. It's kind of like we're still caught in some early stage of development, like kids engaging in parallel play."

Sam stares at Billy. "Where'd you get all that from?"

Billy shrugs. "Alice," he says, like it should be obvious.

"Exactly," Big John says, picking up his cards, arranging them in his hand. "In the entire history of the human species, what man has ever said to another man, 'Let's get together and *talk*'? Never gonna happen. Just like I was saying: *Completely* different animals. Women may like to think they want everything to be equal—and I'm sure equal pay must be a good thing—but mostly they're just fooling themselves, men too. They want men to be *men*, *different*, but then they also want men to be sensitive too. Like in bed."

"Oh," I say, not even caring that I'm holding two aces, "you are *not* about to tell us about your sex life with my mother."

I know it makes me sound childish, like I'm still ten years old, but I don't care. Who, no matter how old they are, wants to hear anything that will make them picture their parents in bed doing stuff together?

"They like you to be hard but soft," Big John says.

"Dad!"

"Hey! I wasn't even talking about sex anymore. We'll get to that another time. Now where was I?"

"Hard but soft," Steve provides, not even pretending to look at the cards he's holding. So much for parallel play.

"Right, hard but soft. By which I mean, they want you to be a *man*. They want you to be decisive, firm. And they want you to treat them like equals. But they also want you, at least sometimes, to treat them like women. Like that whole door-opening thing? Oh, they want it."

"Absolutely," Drew says.

"No, they don't," Steve says.

"It depends on their mood," Billy says.

"How should I know?" Sam says.

"No, they really don't," Steve says.

Big John ignores him. "Oh, and here's another tip. When it comes to Valentine's Day, their birthdays, or any of a million dates they say are important but really aren't to you? You are *dead* if you forget."

"Word," Drew says, like Big John's just spoken the wisdom of Solomon or something.

"Oh! Oh! I almost forgot about—" Big John starts, but he doesn't get a chance to finish because I cut him off.

"This is ridiculous," I say.

He looks hurt. "Which part?"

"All of it. Hard and soft at the same time, dates to remember, the whole door-opening thing—which, may I point out, none of you can seem to agree on. You don't really know anything, do you?"

"Honestly?" Big John says.

I nod.

"No." He shakes his head. "I have no idea. No one does."

Then he brightens. "But I know one thing."

This ought to be good.

"You have to figure out on your own what a particular woman wants," Big John says with certitude, "'cause they're sure as fuck never going to tell you."

Finally. Something we all can agree on.

"I know something too," Sam says.

Et tu, Sam? Really? Sam, who's had more failed relationships with women than I have, chiefly because I've had almost zero relationships *to* fail at, is going to educate us all on what women really want?

"If the women in question are adults," she says, "they don't want a man called Johnny."

"Oh, gee. Thanks."

"They don't want one named Billy either," she says. "Grown women don't want men with little boy names."

"She's right," Big John says. "That whole E-sound thing."

"The E-sound thing?" I echo.

"The E-sound thing! The E-sound thing!" he says impatiently. "Like names that end in 'y' or 'i-e.' Back when I was on the market, in the late sixties and early seventies, chicks loved the E-sound thing. If your name was Vinny or Bobby or Robby or Billy or Jimmy—"

"I get the idea, Dad," I cut him off before he can name every guy's name he can think of that ends with an E sound. Christ. The E-sound thing. He says it like it's a documented syndrome or something.

"Some guys," Big John goes on, "would even purposely E their own names just to get chicks, like if they'd been Sam for the first fifteen years of theirs lives, all of a sudden—bam!— their names are Sammy."

"I'd pound anyone who tried to call me Sammy," Sam says.

I can't believe I'm taking part in this conversation.

"Some guys would even take it too far," Big John goes on, "transforming names that should never have the E sound at the end, like this one guy I knew who kept trying to get us all to call him Briany. Briany!" He snorts. "Can you believe it?"

I can honestly say, I cannot.

Billy looks concerned. "Do you think I should change my name to Bill?"

"No," I say.

"No? Why not?"

"Because Alice already married you even though you have the whole E-sound thing going on." I can't believe I just said that. "Obviously, it doesn't matter to her."

"*Or*," Billy says, considering, "maybe it's *always* bothered her but she's never come out and said anything, making this like one of those things your dad was talking about before—you know, the things men are supposed to figure out on their own because the women are never going to say anything?"

Big John ignores Billy's concerns, continuing with his own nostalgia trip. "Even I went by Johnny back then. Your mother loved it when we first met. She said it made me sound like a rock star." His wistful look dissipates as he heaves a heavy sigh. "But those were different times. That was then, and this is now. Now, no adult woman wants a guy named Johnny."

"But you're the one who named me Johnny!"

"I know, right?" He sighs again. "Christ, what the hell was I thinking?"

And what was *I* thinking having this crew of screwballs over for a night of poker? Oh, right. We do this every week. Still, next week, I'm doing something different. I don't care what it is, it's going to be different.

Who knew the source of all my problems with women, all these years since I became an adult, was my name?

As people are moving to depart a few hours later, after we've finally managed to get in some solid rounds of poker, with minimal interruption from people's wives phoning cells, Steve hands me a slip of paper.

"What's this?" I ask, reading the scrawled handwriting on it. "Allenty?" Underneath whatever the hell Allenty is there's written a phone number.

"Sorry." Steve looks embarrassed. "I've got a lawyer's handwriting. That's supposed to say Helen Troy."

"Who's Helen Troy?" Sam asks.

God, I've got nosy friends.

"Just some woman I sort of met when Steve and me went to the game yesterday," I say.

"You met some woman at the game yesterday," Billy says, or maybe I should start calling him *Bill* now, "and this is the first we're hearing about it?"

Really nosy.

"I didn't *meet* her," I say, exasperated. "We were never even formally introduced. I just sort of, you know, fell in her lap and knocked her drink all over her when I was trying to catch a tipped ball."

"You *like* her," Big John says, getting excited.

"I don't even know her!"

"But you want to, right?" Drew says.

"No. Yes. Maybe. I don't know."

"Hey," Steve says, tapping the card. "It's no big deal. You're single, she's single, and she needs some painting done on her house. So I told her I knew a guy who did good work and that I'd have him give her a call. I even told her it'd be my treat—you know, to make up for me opening up a can of constitutional whupp-ass and kicking her ass in court over that case you helped me with."

"Who are you?" I laugh nervously. "The fairy fucking godmother?"

"Just call her," Steve says. "What have you got to lose?"

Interlude II:
Goes to Motive

Hey, even I wonder about me sometimes, why I do the things I do, wonder about the choices I make. So I can't very well blame you if you're doing it too right around now, can I?

Like I can't blame you if you've been wondering all along just what I've seen in Alice for the last quarter century, why I've carried a torch for that woman. After all, it's not like I've ever been unaware that, at least where I'm concerned, Alice is the prickliest pear ever.

What am I saying, prickly pear? Alice can be a real bitch.

Oh, you thought I didn't notice? Believe me, I noticed.

And now here comes this Helen Troy person. While maybe not quite as prickly as Alice upon first meeting, it's not exactly like she was all warm and fuzzy toward me at that Yankees game either. Well, I did sit in her lap and spill her drink on her. What were her words when I asked her if she'd like to go out sometime? Oh yeah, right. She said, and I quote, "I'm not crazy." Not exactly words of encouragement, I'll grant you that. Why, then, have I not been able to stop thinking about her since? Why, then, when Steve gave me her number and told me to call her about that paint job did my heart beat just a little bit faster?

Who knows why we love whom we love?

Not that this is love, yet. I mean, I only met the woman once. But I do have this whole quarter-of-a-century thing with Alice to account for. Plus, it's not just a matter of why we love whom we love but also why we're even attracted to these people in the first place.

Most people blame just about everything on their mothers.

But I don't have that luxury. Me, I blame it all on Aunt Alfresca. Sure, Big John tried to be both father and mother to me, what with all his din-din talk, but Aunt Alfresca was really the *in loco* maternal figure. And what kind of example did she set me?

It was always tough love with Aunt Alfresca, but somehow, I knew it was love nonetheless. All that harshness, all that talk about me killing her sister. Over the years I've come to realize that maybe Aunt Alfresca thought that if she was too soft on me, *I'd* be soft. Maybe she thought if she showed pity, I'd pity myself.

The thing is, I never pity myself. I may get briefly angry with the world or frustrated, but I never pity myself. Even when things go spectacularly wrong, like with women, I just figure that's the way things are and move on.

Me with women: it's like me with the Mets and the Jets, how you have to learn to like defeat or you'll go crazy. Looks like, under Aunt Alfresca's tutelage, I've learned to love defeat, which is why I accepted it and even expected it all those years with Alice.

Of course maybe I liked Alice all those years and like Helen now because I prefer a challenge. On the other hand, my whole love life has been one big challenge, so that can't be it.

I think I'll stick with the Aunt Alfresca theory.

All of the above: this falls under the heading of Nurture.

There's just one problem. This time, with Helen Troy, if I ever do get a real shot?

I want to beat Nature and Nurture.

I want to win.

Paint Job

Call?

   Don't call?

   Call?

   Don't call?

   Ca—

   "I can't believe you're being such a girl about this," Sam says.

   "Girl?" I say. "What are you talking about?"

   "You're acting like a girl. Call; don't call. Call; don't call. *Call her*. It's not like it's a date or something. It's just a paint job."

   "Right. Just a paint job."

   I pick up the phone, start to punch in the number from the slip of paper, stop.

   "Are you just going to stand there?" I say.

   "What's the big deal?"

   "I just feel funny talking on the phone with you standing there like that. It's like when a guy's trying to take a pee and some guy comes in and starts using the urinal right next to him. It feels awkward."

   "You're being ridiculous about this."

   I just keep staring at her, waiting.

   "Fine," Sam huffs, heading for the door. "Let me know how it goes. I'm sure the conversation will be scintillating." She imitates a masculine voice, "'I'm calling about the paint job?'" Then she does a hyper-feminine one, "'Oh, yes, I need some painting done.'" She's still carrying out her imaginary conversation as the door closes behind her.

   Fucking Sam.

   Now she's made me lose my nerve.

   I put the phone down, go to the sink, have a glass of water, wipe my sweaty palms on my jeans.

Phone Call, Take Two.

This time I make it through all of the numbers.

"Hello?" I hear the voice I've been replaying in my mind ever since the Yankees game.

"Hello," I say, "this is Jo—"

And then I stop. I was about to say "Johnny Smith." I've said my own name, how many times in my life? Thousands? Millions? It's not exactly a hard name to say, Johnny Smith, but today it sticks like a flytrap. I guess it's because of what Sam said and then Big John reinforced at the poker game about the whole E-sound thing and how grown women aren't interested in men who still have boys' names.

"Ja?" the voice on the phone says. "Ja who?"

"Not Ja." I clear my throat, force the unfamiliar name out, "It's John Smith." Then, in case she doesn't know who I am or why I'm calling, I add tentatively, "The painter?"

"Oh!" she says. "Steve said you'd be calling. But I thought he said your name was Johnny."

"That Steve." I laugh awkwardly. "He's such a kidder." More awkward laughter on my part. I make my voice go serious, even more masculine than usual, so there'll be no mistaking I'm a man and not some overgrown boy. "No, it's John. Really, it's John. So, about that paint job…"

The following Saturday sees Sam and me going through our usual workday routine.

"But you hate working Saturdays," Sam said when I told her about the job.

"I know," I said.

"You like to stay home on Saturdays and watch the game on TV," Sam said.

"I know," I said. "But Helen says she has to work during the week. Helen says she'd like to be there the first time I come. Helen says it's not that she doesn't trust workers in general or me per se—"

"Geez, would you stop with the 'Helen says' and the 'per se'? You're starting to sound like Barry."

"Billy."

"Whatever."

"So." I shuffled my feet. "You going to come with me?"

"On a Saturday? Hell, no. I wanna watch the game on TV."

"Oh, come on, Sam. It's just one Saturday, just one game. So we don't see it? We can still listen to it on The Wave."

"Christ, Johnny, you're like a little kid too nervous to be with the girl he likes so he has to enlist some kind of chaperone. I keep telling you: it's just a paint job. It's not a date."

I shuffled my feet some more, put on a hangdog expression. When none of that worked, I offered to pay her double time.

"Fine," she said.

"Oh, and when we're there? My name's John now, not Johnny."

"John," she said. "Christ, now I've heard everything. You're even worse than a girl."

We make the usual stops: the paint store—on the phone, Helen said she wanted us to do the dining room in maroon, a color I highly approve of—and Leo's.

Leo's is hopping. I count six customers, although one of those is Mrs. Leo, who sits at a corner table reading a fashion magazine while fingering a thick strand of pearls. I always think of her as Mrs. Leo because I've never known Leo's last name and never heard him use her first name; Leo always refers to her as The Little Lady. She doesn't work in the coffee shop, but she comes in a lot and when she does, Leo always stops whatever he's doing and crooks his elbow, escorts her to a table.

"Hey, Leo," I say while he's putting together my order, "how long have you and The Little Lady been together?"

"Oh." He thinks about it a bit. "Seventy-six years since we first met. Seventy-three since I talked her into marrying me."

Wow. Some people don't live as long as these two've been married.

"Did you always know she was the one?" I ask.

Leo laughs. "If I ever thought it was anyone else, I've forgotten." He grows serious. "Why this sudden interest in my marriage? You've never asked these sorts of questions before."

"I don't know." I shrug. "I guess I've been thinking a lot lately about love. How people get it. How they make it last."

"Making it last? That's easy."

I'm thinking all the divorced people in the world would disagree but I keep that thought to myself.

"How's that?" I say.

"You learn what makes the other person happy and then you just keep doing it."

Wow. He makes it sound so easy, and yet somehow it sounds so hard, all at the same time.

I realize I better get going, don't want to be late, but when I'm halfway to the door I think of one last thing to ask Leo. I could ask Sam, who's waiting in the truck, but I know she'd only laugh at me.

"Hey, Leo." I feel my face color. "Does my hair look OK today?"

Leo smiles. "Never better."

"Come in!" Helen calls when we ring the bell.

I think the house a person chooses says a lot about a person. It can say, "This is my castle." It can say, "I am a slob." Helen Troy's house says, "I make a decent living but I don't have a lot of free time to worry about decorating."

Helen's place, from what I can see of it as we stand in the entryway, is barely furnished. Oh, it's not as bad as Billy and Alice's place, with their lawn furniture. It's more like the pieces are all generic and the walls are mostly bare.

But who cares about her lack of distinctive furnishings because...

I thought I'd remembered exactly what she looked like but the memory's nowhere near as vivid as the reality when she walks into the room. It's like—whoosh!—there should be some kind of advertisement warning about this: "Helen Troy, now available on Blu-Ray."

Gee, she's pretty. Unlike at the Yankees game, she doesn't have a business suit on. She's got on basic jeans that on anyone else would look just that, basic, but on her they look amazing. Her thin sweater is a cornflower blue and she's got a multicolored scarf hanging casually around her neck. Funny, I've seen that puzzling fashion accessory on various women for the last year or so—scarves tied in all sorts of different ways, of which Mika on *Morning Joe* is a strong proponent—and I've always thought it looked pretty ridiculous. A scarf provides warmth when needed; it's not a fashion statement. Me, I only wear a scarf if my neck is cold. But on her it doesn't look ridiculous at all. On her it looks—

"Do you think you might introduce us," Sam cuts into my thoughts before hitting hard with, "*John?*"

Geez, I hope Helen doesn't notice the way Sam said that, in that sarcastic tone, like I'm using an assumed name or something.

But if Helen does notice, she doesn't say anything. The introductions go as well as introductions can go, Helen leads us to the room she wants painted maroon—or Spiced Pinot Noir, as we like to say in the trade. I show her the color tile, feeling completely thrown by her physical proximity—I think the side of her breast may have touched the side of my arm, plus she smells so good—as I verify this is exactly what she had in mind and then she excuses herself to do some work in her office, saying to let her know if we need anything.

I don't know what I was expecting. But man, that was over too quick.

Half the day goes by before I see Helen again.

I'm listening to The Wave pre-game show when I feel a tap on my shoulder. I take my earbuds out and turn, expecting to see Sam but instead find Helen.

"What are you listening to?" she asks.

"The W—" I stop myself from finishing saying Wave,

remember how she hates the Yankees, how she undoubtedly hates all sports. I cannot let her know I'm listening to the Mets pre-game show; for once I realize ahead of time that the biggest mistake I could make in my life would be to *just be myself* here. Thinking fast, thinking as fast as I can of what a sophisticated woman like her might like, I finish with, "Opera."

"The wopera?" Her pretty brow furrows. "What's the wopera?"

I think to crack a joke, say it's the Italian opera, which would be a perfectly politically correct thing for me to say since I'm half Italian, but if I made that joke, she might think I'm prejudiced if I didn't go ahead and explain about it being OK because I'm half Italian, and if I did explain it would take too long and spoil the joke. Damn, talking to a woman like Helen is complicated. So instead I just say:

"The opera. Just the plain opera. I meant to say the opera but I got a tickle in my throat."

Good one, Johnny. I mean John. Saying you have a tickle makes you sound so manly mature.

She cocks her head and I realize she's listening to the squawk of The Wave that's still coming out of my earbuds.

"That's funny," she says. "It sounds like they're just talking, not singing."

"Yeah," I say, hurrying to turn the sound off, "it's this crazy opera station. The announcers like to talk, like, forever, before they get down to the really good stuff—you know, the opera."

"Right."

I'm not sure if that 'right' is some form of agreement or if it's like, 'This nonsense you're spouting makes you sound like a high-strung maniac so I'm just going to say *right*, a nice neutral word, and hope you shut up and go away without shooting anybody.'

But I'm thinking it must be a somewhere-in-between 'right,' because when I don't say anything immediately in response, she says, "Can I get you and Sam some lunch? I was about to make something for myself."

"Oh no, that's OK," I say in a hurry, not wanting her

to bother on our account, "we already had lunch. We bring our own."

Instantly, I feel like a little kid, like the boy who's still brown-bagging it while all the more mature kids buy their food in the cafeteria.

"Something to drink then?" she offers. "A cup of coffee?"

Even though I've had more than my share of coffee today, I'm practically flying on the stuff, I don't want to look like such a little kid that I brown-bag it *and* am not old enough to drink coffee.

"Sure," I say, "coffee's always good."

"Sam?" Helen calls across the room. "Coffee?" she offers when Sam looks over.

"Nah," Sam says, "I'm good."

"Come on," Helen says and it takes a full minute for me to realize she's inviting me to follow her into the kitchen.

I only hope she doesn't hear it when Sam whispers, "Only you...*John*."

"How do you like it?" Helen asks.

She's got one hip pressed against the counter in her kitchen. It's a big kitchen, one of those massive kitchens that you see these days with everything in it, but for some reason I get the impression she doesn't do a lot of cooking there. And that hip. I like that hip that's pressed against the counter just fine.

"Hmm?" I say dumbly.

"Your coffee—how do you like it?"

"Oh, sorry." Why do I always feel like such an idiot around this woman? Maybe that's because I am one. "Black's fine."

She pours me a cup. It's one of those jumbo ones that look like you could fit the whole pot in it. Then she pours one for herself.

I take a sip. "Good coffee," I say. Brilliant, *John*.

"You sure I can't make you something to eat?"

"No." I take another quick sip of my coffee as if to prove my point. "I'm good with this."

She just stands there.

"Well, don't let me stop you," I say. "You were about to make your own lunch, right?"

I think I'd like to watch her make her lunch. At the Yankees game, all I really got to see her do was sit in her seat. But now I'm at her house, I've got Helen Troy in Blu-Ray, and if she makes her lunch, it'll be like seeing a character come to life—it'll be like Action Helen Troy!

But she doesn't make her lunch. Instead, she takes a sip of her own coffee, swallows and says, just as I'm taking another sip from mine, "So, you're the guy that gave Steve the loophole for how to get his favorite burglar off."

I nearly spit out the coffee in my mouth.

"What?" I say. "No. What are you talking about? God, no."

"But Steve said—"

"Oh. Steve said." I wave my hand dismissively. "We all know about Steve."

"What do we all know about Steve?"

I raise my jumbo cup of coffee towards my mouth, make a drinking gesture but don't actually drink any.

"Steve likes coffee?" she asks.

"No. Well, yes. Probably. But what I meant was"—and here I lower my voice to a whisper—"he drinks a lot of alcohol."

I can't believe the person I'm turning into. First I tell Steve that Sam's a cokehead. Now I tell Helen that Steve's an alcoholic. Is there no one I won't sell down the river for my own personal amusement or gain?

"What does that have to do with anything?" she says.

"It's just that he gets confused about things sometimes. I mean, he's a good attorney and everything, don't get me wrong." Geez, I've got to be careful about what I say. It was Steve who got me this job, Steve who's paying for me to do it. "He just gets a little muddled on the details sometimes."

"What does he get muddled on, for instance?"

"Why don't you tell me what he said, for instance, and then maybe I can help you?"

"He said you have this thing, that you love finding the

loopholes in difficult cases, so I naturally figured—"

"Oh. That." Another dismissive wave of my hand, combined with an awkward laugh. "See, there's your muddle right there."

"Where?"

"Steve and I were talking about ice fishing and I was saying how I like the part where you make the hole in the ice to sink your line into."

"How did Steve get loopholes out of ice holes?"

I shrug like, You got me. Then I make that heavy-drinker gesture again with my jumbo cup.

"So let me get this straight," she says. "It's not loopholes you have a thing for, it's ice holes?"

"Oh, yes," I say, "from when I was little and my dad used to take me ice fishing. Ever since he got MS and can't get around as well anymore, I like to remember the times when we used to be together on the ice, sitting around the ice holes."

Well, at least the part about him having MS is true.

"That's sweet," she says.

Hey, I'm on a roll here.

"Not only do I like ice holes," I say, "but I like sinkholes."

"Sinkholes?"

"I mean, I'd hate to get my truck stuck in one, but they're so interesting, the way they just appear all of a sudden. And peepholes, I like those too."

"Peepholes?"

"It is always good to see who's on the other side of the door so you know whether you want to let them in or not. Oh, and blowholes—you know, whales. They should be saved."

"So," she says slowly, reviewing my case item by item, "you like ice holes, sinkholes, peepholes and blowholes?"

I nod.

"But not loopholes?"

I nod again.

Hole this, hole that—even when I'm determined not to *just be myself*, I'm such an asshole. I just can't help it.

"That's somehow charming," she says. "Also seriously odd."

Well, one out of two.

"Oh, and one other thing I like," I say.

She waits for it.

"Opera," I say, waving one of my earbuds at her in the hopes that she'll forget all this business about holes and remember what a cultured guy I am. "I really like opera. Do you like opera?"

She looks startled at this. "I guess. Doesn't everybody?"

Then before I can think of anything further that's either brilliant or idiotic to say, she excuses herself telling me she has to get back to work.

It's a while before I realize that she never even made her lunch.

"Hey, Boss," Sam says at around three in the afternoon. "Isn't it quitting time yet? Come on. It's Saturday."

"I hate it when you call me Boss," I say, and it's true. It makes me feel like a slave driver instead of someone who pays her a fairly generous wage for driving me crazy. "Let's just finish this up today. That way we don't have to come back."

"But I thought you like her."

"Maybe. I don't know. But even if I did, she'd never want to—"

"Of course she would!"

"Ya think?"

"Absolutely! The way she asked you to come get your coffee in the kitchen, I could tell she didn't want me to come too. And then the way you two talked in there for so long. I could hear what you both were saying. I could tell she liked you."

"Seriously? But she said I was seriously odd."

"But she also said you were charming. Really, I can tell about these things, at least when it comes to other people. She totally likes you. You should ask her out."

Suddenly I'm nervous. "But you said this wasn't a date, that it's just a paint job."

"It's not a date, *yet*—"

And Sam proceeds to go on and on about how she can tell about these things, convinces me that Helen has practically said yes to me already. She does such a good job of persuading, that by the time we really are finished painting the dining room, I send her on ahead to start loading up the truck while I remain behind, saying goodbye to Helen.

"So listen," I say, "I was thinking…Since I like opera and you like opera, maybe sometime we could—"

"No," she says.

No??? Already with the *no*? But I didn't even get the chance to fully ask yet!

Paint, Paint, Paint

No???

I'm so stunned by the instantaneousness of her negative reply I just walk to the truck. It's not until I'm inside, the door safely shut, that it occurs to me that I may not have even had the manners to say goodbye. I just walked away.

"So?" Sam says eagerly. "How'd it go?"

"She shot me down."

"*What?*"

"Before I could even fully finish asking her, she shot me down."

Now it's Sam's turn to be stunned. "How could I possibly be so wrong about something?"

"I know, right?" The only reason I say this is because it's the thing you say in these situations. But inside? I'm thinking, *What the hell was I thinking of listening to Sam?* She's even worse than I am with the opposite sex, which for her happens to be the same sex so you'd think she'd at least know something!

And yet, a strange thing happens. As we're pulling up the drive to the condo, with Sam still puzzling about how she could be so wrong and me still puzzling about why I ever listen to Sam in the first place, my cell phone rings.

Well, that's not the strange part, my cell phone ringing, because it does have a tendency to do that from time to time. No, the strange part is, that when I look at the displayed number, underneath it says *H Troy*.

I start to answer the phone but then Sam starts to scream, "Don't answer it until the vehicle is fully stopped!"

"Why do you always have to be such a spaz?" I say. "Look. It's stopped. I just stopped."

Geez. Sam may be my best friend, but she's so bizarre sometimes. Like she's got this cell-phone fetish. She read that cops are cracking down on people talking on them while driving, which I must admit is a wise thing, so she worries I'll get arrested, but she carries things too far.

Still, I don't have time to dwell on Sam's weird little idiosyncrasies right now because...

"Answer your damn phone!" Sam screams at me. "It drives me crazy how you always let it ring and ring before answering."

"Hello?" I answer the phone.

The only problem is, as I'm answering it, half my mind's obsessing: How did she get my number? I called her about the paint job after Steve gave me her number and told me to call. But I never gave her my number, which means she would have had to call information to get it, but there's more than one John Smith in Danbury, Connecticut, she may not even know I'm in Danbury, Connecticut, and anyway, this is my cell. It's like the Nixon era all over again: When did Helen Troy get my cell phone number, and how did she get it?

See? This is the problem with starting to like a woman. Your mind starts pretzeling itself around all kinds of minor details, wondering what this or that little thing means, wasting valuable brain space on stuff a person shouldn't spend so much time on. Make that any.

"John?" I hear Helen's voice. "I called Steve and got your cell phone number. I hope that's OK."

Phew. At least now I've got that burning question answered.

"Sure," I say, forcing a casual tone into my voice, "that's fine."

Inside, I'm not casual at all, a forced attitude that's tough to maintain anyway with Sam staring at me like I'm a specimen on a slide. Inside, I'm an inferno of curiosity: Why's she calling? Did she change her mind? Has she decided to go out with me after all? Or did I just leave a paintbrush at her house?

"Listen, I was wondering..." she says. As she leaves that awkward pause, I'm reminded of something. I *know* that awkward pause. It's exactly how I sounded when I was trying to ask her to the opera.

"Yes?" I prompt.

"The thing is…I was thinking…"

"Yes?" I prompt, more eagerly still. I can't believe this. Sam was right all along. She is *so* going to ask me out.

And then she asks me what she wants to ask, to which I respond with a simple, "Yeah, sure, we could do that," before clicking shut the phone.

"That was Helen, wasn't it?" Sam says, getting excited. "I was right, wasn't I? She just called to ask you out?"

"Not exactly," I say.

"How do you not-exactly ask someone out?"

"She wants me to come back next Saturday, paint another room for her."

Sam's totally dejected. "That's not only not-exactly asking you out. That's not asking you out at all." She starts to brighten. "But maybe—"

But she doesn't get to finish because there's a sound of rapping knuckles on the driver's-side window.

I look out and see a statie standing there. And not just any statie. It's the guy who lives across the quad from me. He's always zooming into the lot in his state trooper's car, going way too fast. I worry he's going to hit some little kid some day. Then there's the way he walks, all barrel-chested, like every time you see him he's just come from the gym. Not to mention the way he talks to people. One time I heard him tell some guy who was just walking by his unit with his daughter, "Keep your kid out of my flowers." Who says that about a three-year-old? The kid wasn't even hurting his stupid flowers. I hate that guy, and I don't even know his name. Come to think of it, I don't know anyone's name up here, except for Sam's. The way I am with the condo is kind of like how I am about getting supplies for my business. Even though I've been at both for years, I never really invest myself, like I could be moving on or doing something different any day now.

I roll down my window. "Can I help you, Officer?" I can't

believe I have to call a neighbor 'Officer.'

"I saw you with your cell phone," he says, all official. "Did you initiate that call before or after you came to a complete stop?"

"I didn't initiate anything," I say. "She called me."

He sighs wearily like I'm an idiot. "Did you answer your phone before or after you came to a complete stop?"

"After."

"I hope you're telling the truth," he says eyeing me suspiciously.

I'm wondering: What can he do? If he suspected me of drunk driving, he could do a Breathalyzer. But he's got nothing on me. How can he prove the relationship between when I stopped my car and answered the phone unless he saw me the whole time? And anyway, I think indignantly, I'm telling the truth – the car was stopped!

"It was stopped," I say coolly, "completely."

"OK, I'll let you go this time, but watch it. You do know it's against the law in the state of Connecticut to be talking on a hand-held device while operating a motor vehicle, don't you?"

"We had read something about that," Sam provides cheerily.

"Don't give me a reason to arrest you," he warns.

I hold my hands up. "I wouldn't think of it."

He struts away.

"What a creep," I say.

"And that walk," Sam says. Then she punches me on the shoulder. "Hey, you've got another chance with Helen!"

When I get to Helen's house the following Saturday I see there have been some changes since the last time I was here. She's fully decorated the living room that we painted and it looks more homey now, lived in.

This time, we're supposed to work on the dining room, painting it the burnt gold color she requested when she called me again in the middle of the week.

"Burnt gold is a very classy selection for a dining room," I told her at the time. Immediately, I felt like a dork for saying it. Who talks like that? Oh, right. A painter. To make matters worse, I told her that in the trade we refer to burnt gold as Egyptian Sunset.

When Sam and me got there, I noticed for the first time that the dining room looked as decoratively barren as the living room previously had, but I shrugged, figuring it didn't mean anything, and simply got down to work.

Now I've got my earbuds in again, painting away while listening to The Wave. I'm wishing Sexy Caller would call in again—it would be so excellent if she became a regular—when I feel a tap on my shoulder. There's Helen, looking good again, another pair of jeans, another thin spring sweater, another scarf.

"Listening to anything good?" she asks.

"Oh, you know, the opera again."

"Which opera?"

"Hmm?" I stall, totally thrown by this.

"I said, which opera?"

"Oh, you know, Beethoven."

"I thought Beethoven wrote symphonies."

"Oh, yeah, it's a symphony. You know the opera station. They like to mix it up every now and then. They're wild and crazy like that."

"Can I get you and Sam some coffee?"

Once again, Sam declines. And once again, I find myself alone in the kitchen with Helen. Only this time, there's no talk about loopholes, so I acquit myself pretty decently and the conversation goes relatively smoothly.

I compliment her on what she's done with the living room and she starts talking about how difficult it was to make decisions about individual pieces. As she's talking, I start wondering what it is I like about her so much. Sure, she's really pretty. But a lot of women are pretty. She's smart, but I know there are even smarter women, like Supreme Court justices. She's funny, but Sam's funnier and Sam's easier to be with too, although I am starting to relax around Helen. So what is it? And then it hits me. There's no formula for why we like who we like. It's just something that happens. It just *is*.

"So what do think?" she asks.

"Hmm?" I obviously missed something here.

"About the choices I made for the living room? You don't think it's off in any way?"

"Off?" I think about it, the sofa and chairs with their big fluffy pillows and floral patterns. It's a little feminine for my tastes but..."No, I don't think there's anything off about it. You know, it's, like, pretty. It reminds me of a woman."

"Good." She smiles, looks relieved. "That's very good."

Another Saturday, another room in Helen's house.

This time, she wants her bathroom done.

"Geez, Johnny, you must really like this woman," Sam said when I told her Helen called again. "You're giving up all your Saturdays for her. It's like the Mets never existed."

"I still listen to the games on The Wave," I said, feeling huffy about it. "So, you coming Saturday or not?"

"Not. One of us has to watch some of the games live and I'm pretty sure you can do a bathroom by yourself. Besides, if you're on your own, maybe you'll get up the nerve to try asking her out again."

Helen wants the bathroom to be in a soft moss color—OK, it's called Young Forest—and this time I don't make the mistake of saying something dorky like that it's a very classy selection for a bathroom.

I just think it to myself.

Upon arrival, I note that just like the week before with the living room suddenly being fully decorated, now it's the dining room that's been transformed. There's a sleek table with a flower arrangement on it and a breakfront with delicate china.

"It's funny," I say in the kitchen a few hours later, after she's tapped me on the shoulder, I've told more lies about the opera, and she's asked me if I want any coffee, "the way you asked me to come back this week to do your bathroom."

"What's so funny about that?" she asks, suddenly looking awkward and flustered. "I just need my bathroom painted."

"Yeah, I get that. But this is the third week in a row."

"So? What are you getting at?"

"It's just that most people usually just have one room that needs to be done, like Steve having me do his dining room, although in his case his wife has me do it over and over again." I think about how Helen keeps asking me to do more rooms and how the whole place looked so barren when I first saw it and how now, as I do each room, she's filling those rooms with stuff. "Hey," I say, a light bulb finally going on in my brain, "did you just buy this place recently?"

That's got to be it. She only just moved in, hasn't had time to do anything with the place, and now she's starting to.

"No," she says, "I've been here five years come September."

Oh, well, there goes that theory.

But if she's been here for five years, and she hasn't bothered doing anything about her environment in all that time, why the sudden urge now to change everything?

Somehow it reminds me of when a bird starts putting together a nest—nesting, I think it's called.

I finish the coffee, finish the bathroom, but contrary to Sam's expectations, I do not try asking Helen out again.

I tell myself if she calls me back to do one more room, I'll ask her then.

The following Saturday, as I'm painting Helen's bedroom Tranquility Sea, as I'm rehearsing in my head the persuasive lines I'm going to use later when I ask her out, it hits me:

Why else would a woman suddenly change her whole place after five years?

There can be only one answer.

She's doing this all for some man. Somehow, this nesting involves a man.

This is borne out by the fact that she doesn't ask me if I want any coffee; that she does ask me to step out of her bedroom so she can change, emerging a short while later in a plain T-shirt and shorts instead of her usual jeans; that she does race to the door when the doorbell rings, her ponytail bouncing behind her like a schoolgirl; the way that she shouts over her shoulder, "I won't be back until later—can you lock up?"

When I hear the door click shut, I hurry to the window to see who rang the bell for Helen, who's tearing her away from our Saturday coffee together. I peek through the curtains, not even knowing what I'm expecting, secretly hoping it's just a girlfriend and they're going shopping, and who do I see holding the door to a red Porsche with Jersey plates…

Monte Carlo? Helen's doing all this to impress Monte Carlo?

"I'm not letting you go back to that hellhole," Sam informs me.

"It's not a hellhole," I say. "It's a respectable cape."

"I don't care what the accurate architectural description is. I'm not going to let you go back there and be used by that"— she pauses, strains to think of a despicable enough word, finally settling on—"*D.A.*"

"It's a paying job, Sam."

"We have other paying customers. Lots of them. We don't need her."

True, we don't need her. But one of us still likes her.

"It's not fair," Sam says when I don't respond. "You do all the work and now some *shyster* from New Jersey's going to get the girl?"

"We don't know he's a shyster."

"His name's Monte Carlo and he's from New Jersey. What else do we need to know?"

"I don't know why you're getting so upset about this anyway. We did the living room and the dining room, I did the bathroom and finished the bedroom. Steve paid us for the one room and she paid us for the rest. The kitchen's all tile. There's nothing left to paint. We're done."

Only it turns out we're not exactly done.

Monday morning I'm at another job, my cell rings and

it's Helen.

"Helen!" I say, surprised.

"I have one more thing that needs painting," she says.

Sam's shaking her head at me: no.

"But I thought we did every room," I say, wondering what I missed. Maybe a closet?

"Can you come again this Saturday?" Helen asks.

"This Saturday?" I echo.

Now Sam's practically hopping up and down. She grabs my free arm in one of her hands, grabs my paintbrush out of the bucket and scrawls across my forearm in screaming magenta, *No more Saturdays!* It's like my arm's a mirror in a horror flick. I feel like I've been violated here.

"I can't really do that," I tell Helen.

"Then what about the following Saturday?"

"That neither. See, the first Saturday was a favor to Steve that just got out of hand. But we don't normally work Saturdays. You know, even us house painters deserve a real weekend."

I don't know where that last proletariat outrage came from but I see Sam pumping her fist in the air: Yes! Blue-collar workers of the world, unite!

"So you see," I go on, "it looks like I can't hel—"

"What about tomorrow instead?" Helen says. "I could take the day off. Could you come then?"

"I can't believe you're going back to that hellhole," Sam says the next morning.

She came by while I was still eating breakfast, asked if she could borrow a bowl of cereal, finished all my milk.

I ignore her, read the side of the cereal box instead. It looks like if I save five box tops and send them in with this form, I can get a decoder ring.

I put my dish and glass in the sink, run some water in them.

"I'm ready to roll," I say. "You coming?"

"This early?"

I shrug. "I figure I'll get an early start, get it over with."

"Did Helga ask if you'd come earlier?"

I feel my cheeks color. I also notice that while Sam had previously honored Helen by calling her by her real name, she's revoked that privilege now that she's decided she doesn't like her anymore.

"Oh, you are so whipped, Johnny."

"So, you coming?"

"We should start saving these." She rips the box top off. "No," she says. "You want to go back to that hellhole, you go alone."

I pull up to Helen's and it's only eight-thirty in the morning. I haven't gotten to a job this early in, like, ever.

"So what am I working on today?" I ask Helen without preamble once she's ushered me in. We're standing at the edge of the hallway leading from the living room to her bedroom and there's a door about halfway down I've never noticed before. I gesture at the door with the can of paint I'm holding, Arizona Ecru, which is basically the color she asked me to get even though she didn't exactly call it that. "The basement?"

"No!" she says, moving quickly so her back's against the door.

"What have you got down there—Norman Bates's mother?"

"It's just a mess down there." She relaxes. "This hall," she says. "I want you to paint the hall."

"Oh. Right. Well, let me get to it then."

A few minutes later, I'm prepping the walls when I hear the sound of the TV click on in the kitchen. Next thing I know, I'm hearing Joe Scarborough and Mika Brzezinski going at it with some guest on *Morning Joe*. I can't help myself. Like a moth to a flame, just like if I were at home I find myself drawn to the TV.

"You watch this show?" Helen says when she sees me in the doorway.

"Of course," I say, but instead of looking at her for once, my eyes are all over the TV.

Joe and Mika have That Guy on. You know That Guy. I

hate That Guy.

Before I even think about the fact that Helen's sitting right there, I go off on the TV like I'm at home and it's Sam sitting there instead.

"Can you believe That Guy?" I start. Later I won't be able to recall exactly what I said, only that it involved politics, the Constitution, and the inadvisability of wearing yellow plaid on television.

"You're really smart," Helen says when I'm finished.

"Yeah, well." I feel like an idiot.

"No, I mean it. Funny too."

Now I feel like a funny idiot.

"There's something I've been wondering, John."

"Yeah?"

"You *are* smart. You listen to opera. You have sophisticated political views."

This could be taken as being condescending and yet I don't hear that in her voice.

"Well," she adds, "except for the part about the yellow plaid."

"I know," I say ruefully. "The ad hominem attack has always been my weak suit."

"Um, exactly." She laughs, then turns serious. "That's what I don't get. You could probably be almost anything you want to be. Why a house painter?"

This is not the first time I've been asked this in life. Really, with the exception of Big John and possibly Aunt Alfresca, just about everyone I've ever known has asked me this question at one point or another.

I sigh, preparatory to launching into the litany.

"Sure, I'm smart. I even graduated Magna Cum Laude. I could have worked on Wall Street like my friend Billy, not that that's anything to brag about these days. I could have been a doctor if I was more interested in science. And no offense? I definitely could have been a lawyer."

"No offense taken. But I still don't get it."

"Well, see, that's one of the problems with America. Just because a person can be a certain thing, everyone thinks they should do it, like it's a requirement. Like you have to make the most money or work at the most professiony profession you can get a job at."

"Professiony profession?"

"A slightly poor choice of words. My point is: What's wrong with making a decent, even if it's not fantastic, living at something you love?"

"And you love paint?"

I realize Big John's always been right about one thing even as I say the words, "It never lets you down."

Helen doesn't say anything to this and I hear Willie Geist asking the eternal *Morning Joe* question: *What, if anything, have we learned today?*

"That's my cue," I say, hooking a finger toward the doorway. "Time to get back to work."

Helen's voice stops me. "John?"

I turn around. "Yeah?"

"I was wondering...would you like to get together and do something sometime?"

I'm not processing this. "Like what? You want to help me paint the hall?"

"No, I was thinking of something outside the house. You know, at night. Or in the afternoon, if you prefer."

Is she asking me out?

No, she can't be.

"We could go to—" She stops herself. "What do you like to do in your free time?" She brightens. "The opera! That's what you like, right?"

Sam, You Made the Pants Too Long

"Helga asked you out?" Sam is incredulous.

When I arrived home from Helen's I found Sam on my couch, watching a replay of the 1986 World Series, the year the Mets won.

"Can you believe Darryl Strawberry was on *Celebrity Apprentice*?" she said. "How the mighty have fallen. And that former governor of Illinois was on too. You know, the one whose wife ate a tarantula on that other show?"

You really can't make this stuff up.

But I didn't have time to dwell on the fickle nature of fortune just then, or on how reality is often stranger than fiction—I mean, a disgraced governor whose wife ate a tarantula and a world champion baseball player who had more ups and downs than a yo-yo, both on Donald Trump's *Celebrity Apprentice* together; the mind reels—because I had to tell her about Helen right away. I was bursting with it. I had to tell someone. Which is how we got to...

"Helga asked you out?"

"I don't know if I'd go so far as to say she asked me out, per se."

"There you go with the per se again. What's per se about it? She either asked you or she didn't."

"Well, see, that's the confusing part. She asked if I'd like to get together and do something sometime. You know, something other than me painting her house. But it's not like we set a specific date and time or anything. So when you get right down to it, it's kind of like with two guys who don't know each other so well when they run into each other someplace and one of them says, 'Hey, we should get together and have a beer sometime' and the other says, 'Yeah, let's do that,' and then it's a crapshoot whether they actually do it or not because nothing's been formally set in stone."

"I hate that," Sam says.

"I know, right? Because you don't want to be the one to call first, because what if the other person was just being polite and didn't really mean it? You don't want to force getting together on someone who really doesn't want to get together with you. But then, what if the other person calls first and you're not really sure they're sincere—maybe they're just being polite? Maybe they don't really want to get together after all? Or maybe *you* don't want to get together and you're just—"

"But you do want to get together with her, right?"

"Well, yeah."

"So put on your big boy pants and call her."

"Call her?" The idea sounds so…intimidating.

"That's what I just said, isn't it?" Sam shakes her head in disgust. "Only wait until tomorrow so you don't appear too eager."

"Right. I don't want to appear too eager. I'll wait until tomorrow."

This is good. I've got a plan, or at least a plan is forming, and I don't have to do anything about it until tomorrow. This is really good.

"As far as it being a date or not goes," Sam says, "maybe you can figure that one out when you're actually on it."

Sam's right. Why am I getting myself so worked up? This may not even be a date. Maybe Helen just wants to hang out. Or maybe she's just, you know, slumming.

There's a depressing thought.

"So," Sam says, "where are you going to take her on this date that may or may not really be a date?"

"Oh, Christ." I groan, remembering that part. "The opera."

Sam makes a face like she's smelling dead fish. "*The opera*?"

"I know, right? But now she thinks I'm some kind of like,

I don't know, *opera aficionado*, so I have to go through with it. I guess people like her like the opera. There's just one problem."

"What's that?"

"I don't know a fucking thing about the opera!"

I think about that, add:

"Or dating D.A.'s."

I think about that, add:

"If this really even is a date."

Google is my friend.

Come to think of it, Google is everyone's friend these days. Well, except for people who worry that it's the beginning of the end of civilization as we know it. But for the rest of us?

Sam's standing behind my shoulder as I sit before the computer. She's swigging from one of my beers that she took from my fridge.

Not that I'm keeping track of these things.

"Google 'Connecticut' plus 'opera'," Sam advises.

"I know how to google," I say, feeling miffed.

But it turns out, Google is not my friend.

"Wow," Sam says. "The Connecticut Opera went out of business in 2009?"

"I know, right? Says here it was in existence for sixty-seven years. I didn't even know it was there, and now, when I finally have a use for it, it's gone?"

"What are the odds? If you'd met Helga last year, you wouldn't be in this mess now. The Connecticut Opera would still be there. You'd think the economic downturn would have been more considerate about your love life. You'd think it could have waited just a few more years before destabilizing the arts."

"You're telling me. Great. Now what do I do? She's expecting the opera."

"So? Take her to one in New York. It's more romantic anyway. If it turns out to be a date after all, you'll be much better situated for it, geographically speaking."

But 'New York City' plus 'opera' proves to be just

as disappointing.

It's May now, and it looks like the opera season ended in April.

"Opera has a season?" I'm stunned. "What does opera think it is—baseball?"

"It's totally crazy," Sam says. "Who knew?"

"Great. There's no Connecticut Opera anymore. I'm not even in the right season. Now what?"

"Keep googling. There's got to be something. Someone somewhere has got to be performing an opera, even if it's in someplace you've never heard of."

Which is exactly what I finally find. In some dim corner of Connecticut, in a tiny town I never even knew existed, they're doing *Tosca* the following weekend.

"I've heard of *Tosca*," I say. "I think it's one of the big ones."

"Really? You know what it's about?"

"No, but I can always google later—so I look, you know, informed."

"You really don't know anything about opera, do you?"

"Do you? Anyway, what's there to know? I know that people sing really loud for a few hours, and in the end, someone usually dies."

"Perfect," Sam says. "Call her to see if she's free, then order the tickets."

"You make it sound so easy."

"It's not?"

"Well, no. Like, what am I going to talk to her about all night? What am I going to wear?"

"What are you going to *wear*? You sound like a girl!"

"Be that as it may…"

"You wear a tux."

"I do?"

"Sure. Didn't you see the pictures on the site for that fancy New York opera house?"

"Yeah, but that's New York. I don't think people who go to see no-name opera companies in no-name towns in Connecticut wear tuxes."

"Trust me, you need a tux. You want to impress the girl, right?"

I sigh. "I suppose." Then I brighten. "Hey, at least I do have a lot of experience wearing tuxes—you know, from my eight times being Best Man and all."

"You are *not* going to wear some white and purple monstrosity like the one you wore to Bailey's wedding."

"Billy. And the tux wasn't my fault. *I* didn't pick that color scheme out."

"Still." Sam steps out of the room.

"So," I call after her, "I ask her if she can go, if she says yes I order the tickets, then I rent the tux. But there's still that one problem."

"Hmm…?" I hear Sam rooting around in my kitchen cabinets, looking for snacks to go with her beer.

"What do I talk to her about all night?"

"How should I know what you talk to her about?" Sam pokes her head around the corner. "I suck at that sort of thing."

Great. Looks like I'm on my own with that one.

I call Helen the next day, she says yes to going to the opera on Saturday night, so after work I find myself at *Maury the Magnificent! Your Place for Tuxedos and All Your Formal Wear!*

All those times I've been Best Man, the grooms have gotten the tuxes for the wedding party from one of those chain stores. I thought about doing that, but then I thought: Isn't Helen special? Shouldn't I get a really special tux for this occasion, like maybe even buy one so it doesn't have that other-people-probably-had-sex-while-wearing-this-thing feel to it? When I looked in the book, however, the only non-chain tux shop I could find was this one.

And now I'm here and I'm thinking, *This place is so small.* Dusty too. I'm also thinking, *What was I thinking? This is Danbury! How many people in Danbury need to buy a tux—enough to justify a whole privately owned shop?*

I'm thinking about leaving, maybe going to the usual place

where people like Billy rent them, when a guy comes out of the back room. He's about as old as Leo from the coffee shop, but hunched over, with a horseshoe of white hair around his pink scalp, steel glasses perched all the way at the tip of his comma-shaped nose, red suspenders holding up his gray slacks, and a measuring tape draped around his neck like a stethoscope.

Too late to back out now.

"You Maury?" I ask.

He spreads his arms. "In the flesh. What can I do for you?"

"I need a tux," I say.

He studies me in my work clothes: jeans, T-shirt, Mets cap.

"Well, of course you do," he says in a flat voice, like it's an observation anyone passing me on the street might make: *See that guy over there? He needs a tux!*

"Rent or buy?"

"Buy."

"Good choice. Good choice."

He moves to stand behind me, starts measuring my shoulders.

"Every man should own a tux," he says.

"I know, right? Plus, it'd be great for your business."

"True." He bends to measure my inseam. "Special occasion?"

"First date."

"Oh," Maury says knowingly, "I know all about those."

"Well, it may not be a date exactly. That part's still up in the air."

"There's a woman involved?"

"Yes."

"And you're renting a tux?"

"Obviously."

"Where you taking her?"

"The opera."

"Sure sounds like a date to me. But it's the off-season."

"Yeah, I heard that, but I found one anyway."

"Very nice. Very nice. Which opera?"

"*Tosca.*"

"Good choice. Good choice."

But then I'm wondering: Is it? When I invited Helen, I forgot to tell her which opera. What if she's already seen *Tosca* before? Will she be bored?

Since Maury seems to know all about opera, I confess my concerns to him.

"Operas aren't like movies," he says. "There aren't a few hundred new ones made every year. People who go to the opera tend to see the same ones over and over again. It's not like there's much difference between one opera and another anyway. People sing. People die. So long as she likes opera, you should be fine."

He walks over to a display of tuxes. "What were you thinking?" He holds out sleeves of two different tuxes for my consideration. "The Cary Grant or the George Clooney?"

"There's a difference?"

"Most definitely. With the Cary Grant, you get the shawl collar. Very classy."

"I guess I'll take that one."

"Here." He hands me the tux. "Go try it on and then I'll check the length."

I wonder why he measured me if he's only going to hand me something off the rack and then check the cuffs later, but I figure it's his shop. He must know what he's doing.

I'm almost to the dressing room when I hear a phone ring.

"Better get that," Maury says. "It's that time of day."

"Wife?"

"Girlfriend."

As I'm pulling the dressing room curtain shut I hear, "Hello?...Sylvia!"

I don't want to be eavesdropping, so I force myself not to hear. When I come out a few minutes later, Maury's off the phone.

"Let's take a look at that fit," he says. "Hmm...just as I suspected. Everything else is fine, but I think we need to take the cuffs up a half inch, maybe just a quarter, so they break perfectly across the tops of your shoes. Here, let me chalk them."

As he's down on the floor near my ankles, chalking, he begins singing softly.

"Trousers dragging, slowly dragging through the street/Yes! I'm walking, but I'm walking without feet!"

"What's that song?" I ask.

Maury looks up at me, stunned by the gaps in my education. "It's 'Sam, You Made the Pants Too Long', 1932. You don't know 'Sam, You Made the Pants Too Long'? It's a classic, every tailor's favorite song. And believe you me, you do *not* want to be on a first date walking without feet."

"I see your point."

Geez, Maury seems to know a little bit about everything. He's a regular polymath.

Maybe he knows how to talk to women too.

"So, um," I say awkwardly, "that was your girlfriend on the phone?"

"One of them," he says.

Maury's got more than one girlfriend? He's a regular stud— the guy really is magnificent!

"Maybe you can help me then," I say. "How do you talk to women?"

"What do you mean, how? You open your mouth. Words come out. If you're lucky, they make sense."

"Yeah, I get that part. But you've got more than one girlfriend. What do you talk to women about that makes them want to go out with you more than once?"

"Oh, that's easy."

"It is?"

"Sure! You don't talk. You listen."

"But how is it a conversation if you don't say anything?"

"Well, of course you say *something*. You ask them questions, show an interest. Find out what interests them and then just let them talk and talk." He laughs knowingly. "Believe me, they'll do it."

"What kind of questions?"

"Gee, kid, do I have to go on the date for you?"

Ouch.

"Just ask questions. 'What's your favorite color?' 'Do you really think the Cold War is over?' 'Do you like your pizza plain or with pepperoni?'"

"Just ask questions," I echo, as if making a mental note.

"Really, it doesn't matter what you ask them, so long as it comes across that you're soliciting their opinion. Women love to have their opinions solicited. Makes them feel like what they've got to say actually matters."

"Make her feel like what she's got to say actually matters," I echo.

"Oh, but be sure to pay attention when she's talking. There can be hell to pay if you don't. Some women like to trip you up that way. Like you think they've answered your question? You know, maybe you've asked what her favorite color is? And she says blue right away, but then she goes on and on and on with details about it. Before you know it, your mind is drifting to other things, she changes her answer to yellow, you totally miss that part, her birthday comes, you give her a blue sweater, think you did great remembering her favorite color. Turns out, the part you didn't hear was when she amended it to say blue *used* to be her favorite color, until her father was struck and killed by a drunken driver driving a blue car. Before you know it, the relationship's over. Swear to God." Maury holds up a hand. "Happened to me once."

"Wow, that must have been rough."

"Nah, it wasn't too bad actually. She used to wear yellow all the time and I could never quite figure it out until the end there. It was like dating a yield sign. I never was crazy about yellow."

"OK, I think I'm getting this. I not only ask questions but I also listen carefully to all the answers, no matter how long or digressive."

"Right. Oh, and if you get the woman into bed? Offer to paint her toenails afterward. They really go for that. Tends to seal the deal on a second date."

Wow, this guy's a regular font. And I have had practice painting toenails with Sam.

"So that's how you get through a first date," I observe. "Ask questions, make her feel like her opinion actually matters, listen to the answers."

"No, that's how you get through dating, period."

I've got a burning question that I've been wondering about for years. Billy and Drew probably have the answer now, and Big John had it once, but I've always worried if I asked any of them, they'd laugh at me. But Maury? Once I pick up my tux later in the week, I'll probably never see the guy again.

"How," I ask, "do you get women to make the leap? You know, from being girlfriends to being wives."

"Now *that* I couldn't tell you."

"No?"

"No. Never been married. I can get them all to date me, but none of them have ever wanted to get married. So. What do you think—the classic white silk scarf or the one with the fringe? You can't wear a tux without a scarf."

"Do these have names, like the tuxes?"

"Of course. The plain white silk's the Henry Fonda. The fringe is the Robert Downey Jr."

"I guess I'll take the Fonda."

"Good choice. Good choice. Now for some shoes…"

You feel a winter breeze up and down the knees
The belt is where the tie belongs…

A Night at the Opera

Knock, knock.

Who's there?

Me, the guy in the Cary Grant shawl-collared tux with the white silk Henry Fonda scarf and my palms are sweating. Geez. When was the last time I went on a date? Hell if I can remember. If this really is a date.

Helen opens the door and damn she looks pretty. She's wearing one of those snug-fitting cardigans that have come into fashion. This one's a vivid red with some swirling black sequins and sparkly shit. The way the top buttons are open to reveal the hint of a low-cut black tank top, the way the button that strains across the breast area screams *There are breasts under here!*—man, this is *not* your grandma's cardigan. I've never taken an interest in women's fashion before but now I see it definitely has its merits.

"Wow," she says by way of greeting, "you're wearing a tux."

"Yeah, well, the opera." I shrug.

And that's when my gaze travels downward and I see, not the black skirt or black slacks I'm expecting to see beneath the lovely breast cardigan, but rather, faded jeans and a tattered pair of sneakers.

Sneakers? Really? She's wearing *sneakers?*

Doesn't this woman know how to dress for the opera?

I been driving all night, my hands wet on the wheel...

It really does feel like I've been driving all night, the place the opera's at being clear across the state. And my hands are definitely wet on the wheel—still a bundle of nerves.

It doesn't help that the wheel is an unfamiliar wheel. Sam's fault. Sam said, "No way can you pick up Helga for a first date in your work truck." Sam said, "What—she's going to be wearing a fancy gown or something and you're going to have her driving around in a vehicle that advertises your painting business on the side? Really classy." Sam said, "You need something that looks cool, something that will impress the chick." Then Sam made me go to a car rental place where she managed to find me a yellow Porsche for the night.

I feel like I'm driving a banana.

This is nothing like the cool red Porsche that Monte Carlo had.

And now the radio on the rental is stuck so it only gets one station where all they seem to play is old '80s rock, the kind of stuff you'd be excited to hear if you were in a smoke-filled bar getting ready to shoot some pool.

I apologize for the lack of opera or classical music to get us in the mood for the big show, but Helen is being a good sport about it.

"That's OK," she says, drumming the dashboard and playing a pretty decent air guitar. "I love this kind of music. 'Red-eyed Love' is a classic."

What is it with women that they can never get the title of that song right? Sam always makes the same mistake and I always correct her by pointing out, "What the hell does red-eyed love even mean? Like that's something to aspire to?" To which she always replies in her typical childish fashion, "Oh, yeah? Like 'Radar Love' makes so much more sense?"

But I don't correct Helen like I would if she were, say, Sam. Helen may not know how to dress for the opera. Helen may not know the right title of a song. But who cares?

She's here.

With me.

The fact that the radio is stuck on one station turns out to be a good thing because for the two-hour drive Helen seems happy to just listen to the music, which saves me from having to make conversation. Maury said I should ask her questions about herself, but I don't know what to ask, and now at least I can feel like my date's having a good time without me even having to do anything.

But when we arrive at 2 Grand Junction, the address for the opera, I'm confused.

It's not just that we're in some podunk Connecticut town I never even heard of before this week, but we're on a lonely stretch of rough road and the hand-painted wooden sign at 2 Grand Junction reads Verdee Farm.

"This can't be right," I say, peering down a long dirt driveway. Are those bales of hay in the distance? The GPS says this is where we're supposed to be but it makes no sense.

"What's wrong?" Helen stops singing along with Fleetwood Mac's "Sweet Little Lies" long enough to ask me.

"This place." I squint. "Is that an actual farmhouse back there? Are those cows?"

"Um, John," she says. "When you found this place on the Internet, didn't you look around the website at all?"

"No, not really. I saw that they were offering a performance of *Tosca* and how to order tickets."

"Oh. Well, when you invited me, I took the time to google and I read all about this place. It's a real farm."

"No sh—" I correct myself. "No shenanigans?" I can't believe I just said shenanigans. "Really? I figured the Verdee part was after that guy who writes a lot of opera. And the farm part—I don't know, I guess I just figured it was some kind of affected opera thing. Like maybe they were trying to downplay the elegance, thereby somehow making it more elegant."

"That guy who writes a lot of opera spells his name V-E-R-D-I."

Who knew?

Apparently Helen did.

I nose the Porsche into the drive and I'm nearly at the farmhouse when a gray-haired man in overalls ambles over toward the car, standing right in front until I pull to a stop. I see him eye the front plate, which is a New York plate, and then peer at me in my tux. I could swear I see his mouth utter the words "City slicker." I roll down the window.

"We're here for the, um, opera?" I say.

He walks to my side of the car.

"Well, of course you are, but you need to park over there." He points far to the right. "Performance is in the barn. Do you have your tickets?"

I reach into my pocket, pull out the e-tickets to show him.

"Good for you," he says. "Riffraff're always trying to sneak in to see the show for free. You go on now. I'm Vern, by the way." He tips his hat at Helen. "The missus, Dee, is in the barn. She'll take your tickets."

I drive over to where Vern pointed and park the yellow Porsche between two pickup trucks. Quickly I stride over to the passenger side and hand Helen out of the car. Then I offer her my arm. When she tucks her hand in the crook, it feels good. As we walk toward the barn we see other people—or should I say folks?—strolling in the same direction. They all have on jeans with flannel shirts or T-shirts, work boots or sneakers on their feet. As we near the barn I see a sign that says, *Tosca—2Nite!*

I lean down a bit and whisper, "Am I the only one who feels like I wandered into an old *I Love Lucy* episode? Do you think if I refuse to marry the farmer's daughter I'll get thrown in the hoosegow?"

"Don't worry." Helen pats my arm. "If you do, I'll get you out."

Dee turns out to be a short woman, her jeans belted high over a firm mound of belly, her red checked cowgirl shirt tucked in, a bandana around her neck. She's got Dolly Parton hair.

"Nice to see a man who knows how to dress for the opera," Dee says, assessing me approvingly.

"Is this, um, a real opera?" I ask handing her the tickets.

"Oh yes," she says. "We have operas here all through the months that the big operas are closed. No one can make a living as just a farmer anymore. Gotta find new ways to innovate. Popcorn?"

Behind her is a machine, steadily popping away. I hadn't been planning on eating popcorn at the opera. I look down at Helen, raise my eyebrows and she nods.

"Sure," I say.

"What size?" Dee says. "We've got The Little Buckaroo, The Medium Calf and The Large Red Hen and The Jumbo Squealer, which is an extra-good value—it comes in a souvenir bucket." She holds up a massive cardboard bucket that has *Tosca!* printed on it. Dee's a good salesperson.

I reach for my wallet. "I'll take the, um, Jumbo Squealer," I say, because I don't want to appear stingy plus I can't bring myself to utter the words 'Little Buckaroo.'

"Good choice," Dee says, filling the bucket to overflowing and taking my money. She hands me two programs, which are really just folded sheets of colored paper. "Vern'll show you to your seats."

Vern has a flashlight, just like a real usher. As he leads us through the barn I notice the rafters are decorated with little white Christmas lights. When we get to a wooden ladder, Vern gestures with his flashlight. "You ordered the deluxe tickets. You're in the balcony."

It takes a moment to realize he means for us to climb the wooden ladder. Helen figures it out first actually and I realize the ladder's no hardship as I follow behind her, watching her backside sway in a fetching manner, although it's not all that easy negotiating the wooden steps while holding The Jumbo Squealer in one arm. When we get to the top, I discover that "balcony" here means "hay loft." Helen gets comfortable right away, sitting down and crossing her legs in what used to be called Indian style before it became wrong to say that. It's a little more awkward for me to get into that position what with my high-polish see-yourself-in-the-shine black patent leather Douglas Fairbanks Jr. shoes; yep, Maury talked me into the shoes. It was either the Douglas Fairbanks Jr. pair or the Jay-Z pair with the sequins.

"This is kind of, um, *nice*, isn't it?" I say to Helen, offering her the popcorn.

"It is," she says, taking a large handful. That makes me happy. I always think it's strange eating with women who will hardly eat anything in front of you, like they think if you don't actually *see* them consume anything you won't *see* the effects on their bodies of what they do consume when you're not around. Me, I like to eat and see people eat.

"But I can't believe," Helen continues, "that you didn't investigate that website more carefully. You weren't expecting any of this, were you?"

"I can assure you," I say, picking a piece of straw out of a Douglas Fairbanks Jr., "I did not."

"It's OK." She smiles. "It's nice here and Dee's right. The tux looks good on you."

Then she bends her head to study the program and I do the same.

"Do you see any names you recognize here?" I ask. Then, to show off, I add, "Like Luciano Pavarotti?"

I've been doing some homework on opera.

"Pavarotti's dead," she says without looking up.

Clearly, I haven't been doing *enough* homework.

I note that there's nine main characters in the opera, one female and eight males. The female, Floria Tosca, a celebrated singer, is to be played by Sally Pickett. The eight male characters? They're all to be played by Brick Pickett. Somehow Brick's got to be a tenor, a baritone, and a bass, and, when he's A Shepherd-Boy, an alto. I don't know much about singing, except for what I do in the shower, but even I can tell: that can't be easy.

"Wow," I say. "Low-budget production." Inside I'm wondering if Sally and Brick are also going to play the soldiers, police agents, altar boys, noblemen and women, townsfolk and artisans. If so, they'll bring new meaning to the word 'virtuoso.'

"Pickett is the last name of Vern and Dee," Helen informs me. "Sally and Brick are their children. Really, didn't you read anything on that website?"

No, but clearly someone else read *everything* on that website.

"You knew it was going to be like this?" I ask.

"Well, no," she says. "I don't think that even having read

about this place I could have envisioned anything quite like this."

Then it hits me. She knew, or at least had some inkling, of how bizarre this was going to be. And yet, still she came.

"Shh," she says as the Christmas lights dim and Vern shines his flashlight on a clearing at the center of the barn. "Show's about to start."

"Have you seen this one before?" I whisper to Helen.

"If I have," Helen says, eyes glued to the stage, "I never saw it like this."

Should I hold her hand? Should I not hold her hand? Does she want me to? Will she get upset if I do? Will she get upset if I don't?

What are you, Smith, I say to myself in disgust, *twelve?*

I don't hold her hand.

"Wow," Helen says when the Christmas lights are turned on, much strangeness and several arias later, "that was different."

"I know, right?" I agree. "It was particularly strange when Brick was playing Sally's lover, them being brother and sister and all, but at least they didn't kiss."

"I know, right?" she says right back at me. "Still, it's amazing what good singers they were, especially Brick."

"No sh—" I stop myself again, and find myself still unable to come up with anything better than, "No shenanigans. He and Sally really sang their little hearts out."

They did. In fact, they were actually shockingly good. Which somehow made everything that much weirder.

As we reach the bottom of the ladder, Vern makes his way over to us, accompanied by Brick. I'm surprised the kid doesn't look exhausted. Playing all those parts, even though he wore the same costume for each one—jeans, work shirt, boots—must've been a real workout.

"My son says you were a real inspiration to him tonight," Vern says to me.

"It was awesome," Brick says. "Seeing you up there in that tux, I felt like I was singing in a real opera house."

"Can you come back again next month?" Vern says. "The kids're doing *Aida*. I can get you a discount on your tickets."

Geez, maybe Sam's right about me. Even I'm beginning to think it's a little bizarre, the effect I have on other men. If only I could have that same effect on women. Or at least one woman.

I'm thinking the last thing in the world I want to do is come back here next month in my tux and watch Sally and Brick play lovers again. Well, maybe not the last thing I want. That would be getting a horrible disease. Or having the Yankees win the World Series again. But I don't want to hurt anyone's feelings, so instead I say, "Maybe. I'll have to see how my schedule looks."

"Good man," Vern says.

The moon is lying on its back as we exit the barn.

"You want to get something to eat before the long drive back?" I ask Helen.

She thinks about it for a moment, shrugs. "Sure. I could eat."

We get in the car and drive.

I don't know what I was expecting. No, I *do* know what I was expecting. I figured that after the opera, we'd go to a nice, quiet, romantic little place—soft candlelight, maybe I'd even order wine instead of beer, you know, the kind of place where sophisticated people go for an after-show bite after they've seen a real opera. But I'm driving and I'm driving through all these little podunk towns and all I can find open is…

"Subway OK with you?" I wince out the question.

"It's perfect," Helen says. "I'm starved. That popcorn wasn't very good, was it?"

"No, it wasn't."

In fact, after our first handfuls we barely touched it. Dee Pickett might have had great hair, but her culinary skills sucked.

We enter the Subway and wait in line behind the group of teenagers ahead of us. As we wait, we study the menu.

I'm starved too. And what I'd most like to order, despite

being a pescatarian most of the time, is the foot-long Italian combo, maybe two. All that meat, all that cheese, maybe add extra onions…But then the counterperson is asking me what I want—I didn't even hear Helen order; I was too busy dreaming about my sandwich—when all of a sudden it occurs to me: If there's an opportunity to kiss her later, if this really is a date and there's even a chance in hell that my lips might touch Helen's within the next two hours, do I really want to smell and taste like an Italian combo with extra onions? I quickly look through the rest of the menu trying to find a food option that will fill me up without making me smell or taste like anything bad.

"I'll have…I'll have…"

And now the counterperson is drumming her fingers against the side of the cash register and another crowd of teenagers are behind us.

"I'll have…" I reach into the fridge that's on the customer side of the counter and grab the first thing my hand touches. "This Snapple. This Diet Pink Lemonade Snapple. Yeah, that's it."

The counterperson looks at me in disgust. If she were a guy, I'll bet she wouldn't be looking at me that way. If she were a guy, she'd probably think I was hysterical. But no.

"You spent all that time," she says, dripping contempt, "deciding to just have a Snapple?"

"*No*, I'm not *just* having a Snapple. I'm also having a—" and then inspiration strikes—"salad!" Salads don't smell as much as sandwiches do, right? Or at least they don't if you don't really put anything smelly in them.

"What do you want in your salad?" the counterperson says, bored, as she takes out a plastic container.

"Lettuce," I say decisively. Everyone knows lettuce doesn't smell. It's the ultimate safe kiss food.

"What else?" the counterperson asks.

What else? What else can I put in that's not offensive?

"Tomatoes," I finally decide. Everybody loves tomatoes, or at least tomato flavoring, on pizzas and pastas, stuff like that. Tomatoes are safe.

"What else?" the counterperson asks.

"Nothing," I say because I know onions and peppers are out and while I happen to like olives, I'm sensitive enough to know that not everyone does.

"Dressing?" the counterperson asks.

Is there a dressing in the entire world that doesn't have some kind of strong smell or taste to it?

"None," I say.

"Great," the counterperson says and rings up our order. "One Diet Pink Lemonade Snapple, one salad and one foot-long Italian combo."

"Wait," I say. "I didn't order—"

"That's mine," Helen says, eyes large as she reaches past me to grab her sandwich.

I pay for the food and find us a table.

"Is this OK?" I ask.

Helen looks around the room and sees what I see, that every table is pretty much the same here. It's a Subway.

"It's fine," she says.

We sit, and she starts to eat. And eat and eat and eat.

Me, I just enjoy watching her. Like I said, I'd rather be with a woman who eats than one who doesn't. If my choice is between a thin woman who doesn't eat and a less-than-thin woman who enjoys her food without guilt, there's not even a contest.

Between bites of her sandwich, Helen helps herself to generous gulps of my Snapple. She's so busy eating, and I'm so busy watching, there's no opportunity for talking.

And now I'm wondering, worrying really: Is the fact that she ordered the foot-long Italian combo—with what looks like extra onions, I might add—some kind of female signal that there will be absolutely *no* chance of kissing tonight? Or maybe, it's just that she's hungry and likes the Italian combo, and she'll be offended if I *don't* try to kiss her? But what if *that's* the wrong thing, she gets grossed out by me trying to kiss her—knowing she has onion breath—and gets mad that I couldn't figure that out on my own? Or maybe it would just embarrass her and—

"You're not eating?" she asks, cutting into my kiss quandary and gesturing at my untouched salad with the remainder of her sandwich.

I look at the unappetizing salad: lettuce, tomato, no dressing.

"I guess I'm not hungry after all," I say.

She pops the last bite into her mouth, balls up the wax paper the sandwich came in, gets up and tosses it in the trash.

"Before we hit the road..." she says, pointing at the restroom door.

As I watch her walk through the door, I think that if she had a girlfriend with her, she could take that girlfriend with her into the tiny bathroom and then the two of them could discuss how the evening's going. I imagine the conversation would go like this:

Girlfriend: Are you having a good time?

Helen: [message unclear]

Girlfriend: What do you think of this guy?

Helen: [message unclear]

Girlfriend: I mean, c'mon. The tux, that so-called 'opera', that salad...

Helen: [message unclear]

With all the unclear messages, I turn my attention to the TV that's suspended from a corner of the ceiling. There's one of those cops shows on and the minute the cops read some guy his rights, the poor guy starts confessing everything, just spilling his guts.

Without thinking about what I'm doing, just as if I were at home watching with Sam, out loud I say, "Exercise your rights, idiot. Wait for a lawyer. If you don't, the prosecutor will—"

"What's that?" Helen asks, coming up behind me.

"Oh," I say, turning to face her. "Nothing. I was just...Hey, did I ever compliment you on your outfit tonight?"

"No." She gives me a funny look. "If you had, I'm fairly certain I would remember."

"Well, you do. Look nice, I mean. I mean I like your outfit. That sweater, plus you were smart enough to check out the website so you knew to wear jeans and sneakers...So, ready to go?"

Girlfriend: The guy's a douche, Helen.

Helen: [message unclear]

We get back into the Porsche, I key the ignition, turn on the radio to its one station expecting to hear more Golden Earring or Fleetwood Mac and…

Nothing.

OK, Smith, it's show time, time to put into practice Maury's advice to ask questions because that's what women like: for you to show an interest in them. But where to start, where to start…

"What's your favorite color?" I ask out of the blue.

"Blue," she says right away, then quickly adds, "no, green. I got in the habit of saying blue because people always say blue, but really, it's green."

"Why did you get into the law?"

"Because I like it. I like seeing justice done, when it works out that way."

"What's your favorite musical group?"

"I don't have one."

"Do you watch *American Idol?*"

"No."

"What are your hobbies? What do you like to do when you're not working?"

"I like to—" She stops for a minute, making me wonder what she was going to say, before she says, "I like to read."

"If you could be any animal other than a human, what would you be?"

She laughs, but when I glance over at her, in the dark of the car I can't tell if it's an amused laugh or a God-you-are-an-idiot laugh or maybe somewhere in between.

"Who are you," she asks, still laughing, "the D.A.?"

That's when I realize that maybe I'm executing Maury's advice incorrectly. Maybe instead of throwing a bunch of random questions at her that she can just give short answers to, I should pick one topic to focus on.

"Sorry," I say, feeling embarrassed. "I guess I just figured that with the radio not working at all, it might be nice to take the time to get to know each other a bit better."

"That could be good," she allows.

"So." I try to think of something to talk about that will invite more than a yes/no answer, finally settling on...

"Why don't you tell me about your family."

"Oh gosh." She laughs. "Where to start! OK, first, I'm the youngest. I have five older brothers."

"Wow," I say, "that must be..." I'm about to say "excellent," because for me it would've been—it'd be practically like having your own sports team all under one roof! But then I realize for a girl that might not be so excellent, that it might feel lonely or as though life is all one-sided against you. "That must have been difficult for you at times," I say in what I hope is a solemn or sympathetic voice.

"Are you kidding me?" She laughs again. "It was excellent. No one outside of the family ever dared pick on me. It was like I had my own little squad of enforcers. Well, not so little. Plus, they always got into so much trouble, doing things first, that by the time I got around to doing things, my parents thought it was mild in comparison or at least old hat."

"Are your parents both still around?"

"Oh yes. They still live in the same house I grew up in."

As she proceeds to tell me about what her parents were like when she was growing up and what they're like now, about her five older brothers and some of the scrapes they used to get into, I'm thinking: This is good. It's like we're having a real conversation.

"Having all those guys in the house," I say, disguising the glimmer of hope I'm feeling, "there must have been a lot of interest in sports, huh?"

"You're not kidding." She laughs. "The TV was permanently tuned to ESPN. Like the radio in your car with that '80s music—there was no other station."

"So then you must, oh, I don't know, *like* sports? I mean, except for the Yankees of course."

All the humor goes out of her voice. "No," she says

abruptly, "not at all. I listened to enough of that growing up. Anyway, being the only girl in the family besides Mom, I was always encouraged to be, you know, girly." Before I can ask any further questions, she turns the tables. "What about you? Tell me about your family."

Oh, geez. I didn't know that having a real conversation meant that *I* was actually going to have to answer questions and talk about myself.

"Well," I begin, and before I know it, I'm telling her about my mother dying right after birth, about Big John raising me and then developing MS later on.

"Your dad sounds sweet," she says. She probably says that because I left out the part about Big John loving chili and its aftereffects. "But growing up without any women in the house, with no female influence, you must be a real man's man."

"Me?" I make a face like 'don't be ridiculous' until I realize it's the left side of my face that's smirking and that I'm facing the road. "I'm not a man's man. I'm a lady's man." No, that doesn't sound right. "I mean I did have a female influence. I had Aunt Alfresca—that would be my mother's sister—the most female female you ever want to meet." *Not.* Sure, Aunt Alfresca cooked, but guys in the Mafia and the fire department cook too, and Aunt Alfresca was always the least female female in the world. Honestly, the woman was a human howitzer.

But none of that matters now because I'm making up stories about what it was like growing up with Aunt Alfresca, learning how to make cookies and all that crap that never happened and Helen's actually *laughing* at my stories. And then she's telling me stories about growing up with five brothers and how she used to get them to play Tea Party with her, which doesn't sound like it could be either funny or interesting and yet when Helen tells it, somehow it's both. And then we start talking about the night we've just had and one of us, I don't even remember which now, coins the phrase Barn Opera, and before you know it we're both laughing and I'm not even self-conscious anymore as we drive and laugh into the night.

Best. Date. Ever.

. . .

But then I screw it all up when we arrive in front of her house and I walk her to the door. Oh, I handle the mechanics of it all OK. I get around to her side of the car in time to open the door for her, I manage to walk beside her up the path without tripping over my own two Douglas Fairbanks Jr. shiny shoes. But when we get to the door?

"So, I really had a good time," I say.

Not exactly witty repartee, but nothing offensive either.

"It was fun," she says, back to the door. "Do you want to…" She jerks her thumb over her shoulder.

"No, I'm good," I say hurriedly, and immediately realize how wrong that sounds. "I mean, I'd love to come in, but I still have another long drive ahead of me. I've already done a lot of driving tonight. You know, something like five hours of it."

God, I sound like a blathering idiot. Of course I'd love to go inside with her, but I'm too worried. I've made it this far without alienating this woman. I just want one night where I don't blow anything. And if I go inside, I might louse that up.

"So," she says, looking up at me expectantly.

This is the moment I've been waiting for, hoping for all night. This is why I didn't eat that Italian combo, even if she did. Because this is the moment when I get to kiss the girl.

But what do I do instead?

I put out my hand and say, "So, um, thanks."

She shakes my hand. "You're welcome."

Why didn't I kiss her? I think as I walk back to my rental car, as I hear the sound of her door quietly clicking shut behind me. Because if I kissed her, what if I loused *that* up? What if she didn't like the way I kissed and she never wanted to see me again? What if the kiss was the thing that actually blew it all, the thing that ruined this imperfectly perfect night?

So I didn't kiss the girl.

Idiot.

I might as well have eaten that Italian combo when I had the chance.

Self-Help

"You need to call her and invite her out again," Sam says.

It's Sunday morning, breakfast at my place. Where else would we be? Sometimes I even forget Sam's got her own place.

"Since when did you become an expert on women?" I ask.

"I'm not an expert. Far from it. But you take this woman on a date and at the end of the night you shake her hand? You make no specific plans to do anything in the future, you don't even vaguely say 'I'll call you,' which everyone knows is almost always a lie, and then you shake her hand? She's going to think you don't like her. You do like her, right?"

I mumble something into my cereal because I don't want Sam to know just how much I do like Helen. It's scary liking someone this much.

Sam wisely interprets my mumble to mean yes.

"Then call her. Ask her out again."

Sam's right. If I'd tried to kiss Helen and she'd turned her head to the side, I'd think she didn't like me. Me? I didn't even try. What's Helen supposed to think?

Without giving myself a moment to rethink myself, I go to the phone, punch in the number.

"Hello?" Helen answers right away.

"So listen," I say, ever the smooth operator, "I was wondering—you want to do something together today?"

"I can't. I already have plans."

"Oh, OK then, thanks."

As I hang up, I'm wondering: Who's she got plans with— Monte Carlo?

Sam shakes me out of my jealous reverie by punching me in the shoulder.

"Ouch!" I rub the spot. "What was that for?"

"Schmuck," she says. "What was that all about?"

"What? I called her like you said I should, asked her out, she said she had plans."

"And you let it go at that? Anyway, who calls on a Sunday and asks the girl out for the same day?"

"Like you know what people do?"

"I know enough not to do that. And if I did do *that*, I wouldn't be so stupid as to say, 'Oh, OK then, thanks.' Schmuck."

"Don't hit me again!"

"Call her back. Ask her out for a day other than today. Schmuck."

"All right already. Just don't hit me again!"

I pick up the phone again, punch in the number again.

"Hello?" Helen says.

"Listen, I understand you already have plans today. It was very inconsiderate of me to assume you wouldn't. So I was wondering: Would you like to do something together at some future date?"

"When did you have in mind?"

"I don't know. I was thinking"—I look over at Sam, who mouths the word *Saturday*. "Next Saturday," I say.

"What did you have in mind?"

But I got nothing in mind. When I came up with the opera last time, I shot my load.

"I don't know," I say. Then I ask-answer, "Something?"

"That could be good," Helen says.

"Great," I say. "I'll call you later on in the week with the details."

I hang up.

"So," Sam says, "you have another date."

"Sort of."

"Well, since that date's not today, what do you want to do with the day—watch the Mets game?"

"I don't think I can," I say. "I think I need professional help."

• • •

By professional help, I mean Alice.

While Sam turns on the pre-game show, I punch in Billy's number.

Alice picks up and when she realizes it's me says, "Hold on a sec, I'll get Billy."

"No!" I practically shout. "I mean no," I say in a more reasonable voice.

"Did you dial the wrong number?"

"No." I never could have imagined before this moment that I could say no to Alice so many times in a row. "Actually, it's you I was looking to talk to."

"So talk."

But I realize I can't do this with Sam in the next room. I don't want to get laughed at. Well, any more than Alice will probably laugh at me.

"Not on the phone," I say.

"So come here."

That idea doesn't appeal either. Billy's never seen me so smitten with a girl before. He might laugh at me even more than Sam would.

"Not there either," I say. "Could we meet for coffee?"

"You mean now?"

"No, I thought that maybe while you're at work tomorrow, I could go somewhere by myself and pretend you're there too."

"What?"

"Yes, now. Unless you're too busy?"

"Actually Billy's getting ready to watch the game with Drew. I could use a break from the Mets, even if it's with you. Sure. Where do you want to meet?"

"Leo's in half an hour?"

But I'm so antsy to get going on this, I wind up leaving right away and get to Leo's twenty minutes before Alice is due.

Leo's is open seven days a week. But since I only come in on weekdays on the way to work, I'm surprised to see Leo working on a Sunday. I don't know why. I guess I just figured at his age the guy must want to take some time off.

"How was the big date?" Leo asks as he gets my coffee.

Leo knows pretty much everything about me except for the more beneath-the-surface stuff like boxers or briefs.

It's boxers.

I give him the Cliffs Notes version. He laughs about the tux and the Barn Opera, comments that it was good advice Maury gave me about asking women questions.

"Maury's always spot on about getting women," he says, "although not so hot on keeping them."

"You know Maury?"

"Everyone knows Maury," he says.

I didn't know Maury before last week.

"Everyone knows me," he adds expansively.

"True that. Hey Leo, you and The Little Lady have been together forever, right?"

"Forever and a day, yup."

"Can you give me any more tips on how you keep it going?"

"Well, remembering dates is a big one."

"Dates?"

I seem to recall at the first poker game Steve Miller came to, Big John discussing the importance of remembering dates. But I'd dismissed it at the time, figuring: What does he know?

"Oh yeah," Leo says, "women are all about the dates. Forget a birthday or anniversary and you're screwed."

"Screwed, huh?"

"The thing is, it's hard for a guy to keep all that stuff straight. I mean, it's not like it's important to me when any particular thing happened. I'm only glad that it did happen and that she hasn't left me yet."

"So how do you keep it all straight? What do you do, use one of those little Hallmark calendars?"

"Huh. I never thought to do that—that's not a bad idea. But no, over time, you learn tricks. Take the whole wedding anniversary thing, for instance. I can never remember: Did we get married on November 10th, 11th or 12th?"

"I'd think you'd at least remember your own wedding anniversary, Leo."

"I know, right? But wait until you get married. You'll see.

A woman can come up with so many anniversaries for minor things you'd never think anyone in their right mind would care about. First Time Holding Hands. First Kiss. First Time You Went To An Outdoor Festival Together. A woman'll get you so confused trying to remember all the minor anniversaries, the major ones can get knocked right out of your head."

"First Time You Went To An Outdoor Festival Together? No shit?"

"You don't even know the half of it. Wait til you're in the thick of the thing. You'll see."

"So if your head's always getting filled with all that other crap, how do you handle the wedding anniversary thing?"

"Oh, right. Well, what I do, see, since I do know it might be one of three days in November, I go shopping early November and put the present in the trunk of my car. But then I just wait. Because if I pull it out too early? I'm screwed, just as bad as if I pull it out too late. Believe me, I know. One year, I gave her the present on November 1st just to be on the safe side? The Little Lady wouldn't talk to me til December. Which sucked. It was a really good present!"

"So you just leave it in the trunk now?"

"No, I don't just leave it in the trunk now." I can tell Leo's exasperated with me for not getting this. "Well, I do leave it in the trunk. But then I just bide my time. Wait and watch—that's the name of the game."

"Wait and watch?"

"Oh yeah." Leo nods, wipes at a spot on the counter with his rag. "As soon as The Little Lady starts to look sour in the mouth, I go out to the car and voila!"

"Wow, that sounds like a lot of work, trying to stay one step ahead with a woman."

"Oh it is." Leo nods again. "But the right woman is worth it."

"Any other tips?"

"Yes. Be a good kisser. I'm such a good kisser, The Little Lady'll never leave me."

"So long as you have a present in the trunk by

November 10th."

"That too."

I don't think I've ever not noticed what Alice looks like or what she has on, but today I don't. As I sit at a table at Leo's and watch her come through the door, all I'm thinking about is Helen and how I'm hoping Alice can give me more profitable advice in dealing with her than I've received elsewhere.

Alice takes a seat across from me and before I know it Leo's scurrying over to take her order. Now this is new. I've never seen Leo come out from behind his counter for anybody before. At Leo's, the protocol is that you place the order at the counter and, if you're eating in, you go back to the counter to pick up your order when he shouts your number.

Alice orders a Chai Latte and Leo doesn't even blink. Me, I'm wondering what he's actually going to serve her since Leo's doesn't have Chai Latte on the menu.

"That's all," Alice says when Leo doesn't leave right away.

Leo puts a hand on my shoulder as he speaks to Alice.

"This guy here," he says, adding, "Johnny," as if there might be doubt as to whom he's referring, "is one of the finest guys I know."

What's Leo doing?

"Any woman," Leo goes on, "would be lucky to get him. Johnny's the kind of guy who doesn't just talk, he listens. Plus, he never forgets a significant date, nev—"

"Leo!" I cut him off.

He stops testifying long enough to look down at me in puzzlement. "What? I was only trying—"

I put one hand on the side of my face so Alice can't see as I urgently mouth the words, *This isn't the woman.*

"Oh?" Leo says. "Oh!" Then he looks at Alice, says, "I'll call your number when your coffee's ready," and leaves.

"But I didn't order—" Alice starts to say, but Leo's already behind the counter, making whatever he's going to make her.

"That was odd," she says to me.

"Yeah, well, you know." I shrug. "Old people. Listen, about what I wanted to talk to you about. There's this woman, see, and I really like her. Like, *a lot* I like her. And—"

Before I can go any further, she holds up her hand like a traffic cop.

"What?" I say.

"Please don't go there," she says.

"What are you talking about?"

She spaces the words carefully, like I'm an idiot. Great. Now she's a traffic cop and I'm an idiot. "I...know...Johnny."

She knows? How can Alice know?

"What are you—" I start to say, but she won't let me finish.

"I can't believe you'd do this to your best friend," she says.

What's she—

"What are you—"

"I know you've always had a thing for me. But I'm married to Billy now, *your best friend.* Plus, even if I wasn't, it's not like you, or me, we, it's not like we'd ever be—"

"Omigod." Now it's my turn to cut her off. "I can't believe this. You actually think I called you here to—what? I don't know—confess my undying love to you?"

"You mean you didn't?"

"No." I laugh. "God no!"

Alice isn't laughing. First she's mad at me because she thinks I'm in love with her. And now she's mad because I'm laughing at the idea. You can't win with women.

"I mean," I say earnestly, trying to save the situation, "it's not like you're unworthy."

"Gee, thanks."

"And there was a time where I would have given—"

"Number one-ninety-seven—order up!" Leo barks, saving me from myself. You gotta wonder where Leo comes up with this stuff. Alice and I are the only customers here, so how does he come up with Alice being one-ninety-seven?

Alice comes back with the drink Leo gave her.

"What'd he give you?" I ask.

She takes a sip, shrugs. "I think it's orange juice. So, you were saying…"

Well, we don't need to get back to *exactly* what I was saying…

"There's this woman I really like," I start again, then hasten to add, "who's not you."

Alice is still looking curiously grumpy about that last part—women!—so I hasten some more.

"It's just that I really like her and I don't want to louse this up. I've gotten some good advice from"—I'm about to say Leo but then realize Alice will not be impressed—"*various parties*, but they're all men. I feel like I need a real woman's perspective on what women like, on what women like in a man. And yet the only women I have to go by are Sam and Aunt Alfresca, and frankly—"

"I get it," Alice cuts me off. "I've met both Sam and Aunt Alfresca and I know exactly what you mean."

"Thank you," I say with relief. Finally, she gets it.

"Sam still call me Alex?"

"Pretty much."

"No, she can't help you. As for Aunt Alfresca…"

"I know, right?"

"So, you want to get the girl…" Alice mulls this over while I wait for her verdict. "Well, first thing, you've got to do something about your wardrobe."

"What's wrong with my wardrobe?"

Alice eyes me from my sneakers to my jeans to my Mets T-shirt and Mets cap turned backwards.

"Everything," she decides. "You dress like a boy."

"A boy? I know a lot of guys who dress like this."

"Right. And they're all overgrown boys. You need to dress like a grownup. Real shirts with collars, and no polyester. Real pants, like khakis, not jeans; come the fall, a nice wool blend. Real shoes, like a loafer or Docksiders. A real belt from time to time wouldn't hurt."

I'm starting to get really offended at the ongoing theme emerging here. "My clothes aren't real?"

"No, not really. And that hat. You've got to lose the hat."

"What's wrong with the hat?"

"Did you know that Barings Bank, the oldest merchant bank in London, was brought down in 1995 by a guy in a backwards baseball cap?"

"I did not know that," I say, feeling admonished. I slide the cap off my head, hold it in my lap.

"It's true. The guy's name was Nick Leeson. Look it up if you don't believe me."

"I believe you."

"Nearly everything that's wrong with this world can be traced to some guy somewhere wearing a backwards baseball cap."

"You've made your point."

"Hey, you're the one who asked for my help." She starts to rise.

"And I want it, I want it. Please." I wave her back down. "Sit." She sits.

"OK, I need to change my whole wardrobe. I get it. I can do this thing."

"Boxers or briefs?"

"Excuse me?"

Alice enunciates like I'm a moron. "Do you wear boxers or briefs?"

This is getting personal, but…

"Boxers," I finally admit.

"Good," she says, approvingly for once. Then she adds, eyes narrowing, "There aren't cartoon characters on them or anything like that, are there?"

"No!" Sheesh.

"Good."

"But that can't be all," I say. "I change my wardrobe and get the girl?"

"No, of course that's not *all*. You've got to talk to a woman, ask her questions about herself."

"So I've been told."

"Good. At least someone else is giving you some decent advice. But you've also got to take an interest in *her* interests. Most women don't want to hear about the Mets' latest trade."

"Yeah, I finally figured that out on my own."

"A woman likes to feel as though you're not just pretending an interest for her sake either. A woman likes to feel that you've found a way to like the thing for the thing itself so that when you discuss the thing, your conversations are lively."

The thing, the thing, she keeps saying "the thing"—what thing?

"The thing? Like, what sort of 'the thing' am I supposed to be taking a genuine interest in?"

"*General Hospital.*"

"*General Hospital?*"

"Only call it GH, makes you sound more in-the-know."

"And you're saying I should actually watch that thing?"

She shrugs. "Billy does."

"And he's been able to—what was that thing you said?—find a way to like the thing for the thing itself?"

"Yes. In the beginning, he said he couldn't see the appeal. But then he started treating it like any other sport. You know, finding a way to bring stats into it, earned-run averages for different characters. He says Sonny's box scores for getting different women pregnant are off the charts." She rolls her eyes when she says this last part, and I figure she thinks Billy's a dope for doing the stat thing with GH, but then I notice there's actually a lot of love in that eye roll.

"And you think if I start watching *General Hospital*—I mean, GH—that this woman will actually like me more?"

"Couldn't hurt. Every woman I know watches GH. It's like our universal language."

Inside I'm thinking, *But Helen's not like every woman. Helen's different, special.* I've learned quickly in this conversation, however, not to give voice to such thoughts. If I do, Alice will take the implication to be that she's not special. And besides, Alice must know what she's talking about when it comes to women. Why, up until I met Helen, Alice was the female yardstick I measured all other women by.

"OK, I'll change my wardrobe and start watching GH. What else? I've got a date with her next Saturday, but I haven't figured out where to take her yet."

"Do I have to do everything for you?" Alice looks around the room, spots stacks of real-estate booklets and *The Penny-Saver* on a ledge by the front door.

She goes over and grabs something.

What? Now she's going to tell me I need to buy a new home to impress Helen?

But no. She comes back with *The Penny-Saver*.

"Here." She tosses it at me.

"What's this?"

"*The Penny-Saver.*"

"I know but—"

"Really, do I have to do everything?" She grabs it back from me, starts flipping through. "There's an activities and events section here. It's always filled with all kinds of things—plays, flower shows, festivals—the kinds of things women like to be taken to. Here, you go through it. I gotta go. I'm meeting Stacy at the mall to do some shopping." She hands it back to me.

"But I don't know what—"

"Fine." Now she's really exasperated as she grabs it back yet again. "Here, look. The circus is coming to town."

"The circus?"

"Yes, the circus. Women love the circus. Win her a prize."

They have prizes at the circus?

I arrive home shortly afterward, *Penny-Saver* in hand, to find Sam lying on my couch watching the tail end of the Mets game.

"Where'd you go?" she asks.

"I met Alice for coffee. I thought maybe she could give me some advice about Helen."

"How'd that work out for you?"

"Not so good really."

"No?"

"No. I don't think she knows all that much more than we do."

"Why? What'd she tell you?"

"She told me to watch *General Hospital* and then she gave

me a copy of *The Penny-Saver.*"

Sam snorts. "Fucking Alex."

"Hey." I get an idea. "I need to go to the mall to get some new clothes anyway. Wanna come with me and hit the bookstore on the way back? I think maybe I need more help than mere human beings can give me."

The Kiss

Who should we run into coming out of J.C. Penney, just as we're walking in?

Alice and Stacy.

"What'd you get?" I say, eyeing the big bags they're carrying.

"New sheets," Alice says.

"Some dinnerware," Stacy says.

"How's Drew?" I ask Stacy. "I haven't seen him around lately."

"Busy. Working."

"Tell him we'll expect him for poker Friday night."

"What are you two shopping for?" Alice asks me.

"New clothes," I say, feeling embarrassed. She's with Stacy. Does everyone need to know what I'm doing? "Like you told me to."

"Wrong J," Alice says. Then she takes me by the elbow, physically turning me in a different direction. "You need to get your clothes at J. Crew."

"But that's so much more expensive," Sam objects on my behalf.

"Do you want to impress the girl or don't you?" Alice asks me.

I shuffle my feet. "I guess."

Once we're in J. Crew, Sam surprises me by being helpful in picking out clothes and I surprise both of us by looking good in them.

"Ready to hit the bookstore?" I say as we exit the mall.

. . .

Once in the bookstore, while Sam looks over the bestsellers on the front table I make straight for the Information desk. As I wait for the clerk's attention, Sam wanders over.

"What're you doing?" she asks.

I ignore her.

When the clerk finally turns to me, I lean across the counter and whisper, "Where do I find the books on relationships? You know, male-female stuff?"

"Christ!" Sam laughs.

"Shh," I say.

"Stop whispering and shushing people," Sam says. "It's a bookstore, not a library."

The clerk, no doubt trained to help people rather than laughing in their faces, leads us to a section with a big sign over it: RELATIONSHIPS.

Huh. How could I have missed seeing that on my own?

"Are you looking for any title in particular?" she asks.

"Not really," I say. "I was kind of hoping for something just generally self-help-ish. You know, something basic, like a how-to guide for how to have a relationship without lousing everything up."

"How about this?" she suggests, reaching for a yellow-and-black book in the center of the shelf.

"*Relationships for Dummies*," I read the title. "That's a little bit insulting, but yeah, this could work."

"There's also this," the clerk says, handing me another yellow-and-black book, "just in case you need something to help get the relationship started."

"*Dating for Dummies*?" I read the title. "Oh yeah. I could definitely use this."

"Oh, and if you need help in another department?" The clerk, now assured that I'm actually going to buy something, is suddenly very helpful. She reaches for the lowest shelf, extracts another yellow-and-black book.

"*Sex for Dummies*?" I'm offended. "Hey, there's no need to get carried away here. I *think* I can figure that one out on my own."

The clerk scampers off and I head toward the counter to pay.

"You coming?" I turn back when I realize Sam's not by my side.

I turn just in time to see her snag two books off the shelves. Sam waves the books at me: *Dating for Dummies* and *Relationships for Dummies*.

"Hey," she says. "If you're going to get educated, I'm certainly not going to let myself be left behind."

Monday afternoon at three finds Sam and me sitting on the couch in front of my TV. Arrayed on the table in front of us is a six-pack of beer so we don't have to keep running to the fridge, plus various bowls of salty foods.

"OK, let's do this thing," I say clicking on the TV to ABC.

Two minutes later, after a few teaser scenes and as the opening theme song plays, Sam says, "I can't believe I'm watching this."

"So what? I'm paying you, right?"

It's true. I need to do my GH research but I can't bring myself to watch alone, so I told Sam we'd break off work in time to watch every day this week. I had to promise I'd keep her on the clock until four to get her to agree.

Halfway through, I'm still confused. It's a lot to digest, so many characters, plus everyone's got a lot of history. I'm having trouble keeping all the characters straight although some do stand out.

"That Carly's crazy, isn't she?" I say.

"She's hot," Sam says.

"Do you understand why the Cassadines and the Spencers hate each other so much?"

"Not really. But it can't help, Elizabeth Webber Spencer being pregnant and no one knowing if the baby is from Lucky Spencer or his half-brother Nikolas Cassadine, the Greek prince."

I vaguely remember Alice and Dawn saying something about this situation a few months back.

When the show's over, we break out our *Dummies* books and read, lying perpendicular on different sections of the sofa, feet meeting in the middle. We do this every day that week.

As the week rolls on, there are certain characters we never discuss by name because their names strike too close to home. There's a Johnny who's a gangster, a Sam who's a female private detective, a Helena—a name very close to Helen—who's a bitch, a Steve who's a head surgeon, an Alice who's a maid. As far as I can tell, there's no Billy or Drew, and there's definitely no Monte Carlo. But this is a soap. Characters get added and subtracted all the time and this could change at any minute.

By the time Friday's episode rolls around, I feel as though I'm on much better footing.

"You know, this isn't half bad?" Sam says when it breaks for a commercial.

"I know, right?" I say. "And Alice was totally right about Sonny. He's got—what?—five kids from three different women?"

"Four," Sam corrects. "Alexis's second child is the daughter of Sonny's brother, Ric."

"Right." I slap myself in the forehead. "Why can't I ever remember that?"

"Maybe because Ric's not on the show? Plus, don't forget, Sonny also had a baby with Jason's girlfriend, but that baby died. And Michael isn't really Sonny's son, he's Jason's dead brother's son, even though everyone acts like he is."

"So how many does that really make with how many different women?"

"I don't know anymore. I'm starting to confuse myself."

"Too true. It's as bad as baseball with all the trades, trying to keep everyone straight. But Alice is right about Sonny. If he even looks at a woman, the woman winds up pregnant. Doesn't anyone on this show use birth control? And what is it with that guy?"

"I don't know, but if I wasn't a lesbian, I'd do him."

"What is it, the hair? Should I slick back my hair like that?"

I hold my hair back to demonstrate and Sam studies me briefly.

"Um, no," she finally concludes. "On you, that doesn't work."

Gee, thanks, Sam.

In order to change the subject from Sam thinking my hair doesn't look as hot as Sonny's slicked back, I ask, "You think my bookie's got a line on GH like he does on regular sports?"

"How should I know? He's your bookie." She thinks about it for a minute. "If he does, what would you want to bet on?"

"Who Sonny's going to knock up next."

"Oh yeah? Who's your favorite for that?"

"Carly."

"*Carly*? But they've already been married like four times plus they've already got one kid together and she's still married to Jax."

"I know, right? Still, I think they're due again. It's at least three-to-two odds, maybe even money."

"You don't win money on even money."

"True. If my bookie does have a line, who'd you pick?"

"Elizabeth," she says without hesitation.

"*Elizabeth*? But she's knocked up right now. I'm pretty sure he can't knock her up while she's knocked up. I don't think knocking up works that way. Don't you know anything about sex? Maybe *you* should've gotten that *Sex for Dummies* book that salesclerk kept waving at me."

I'm feeling pretty good about myself. I rarely get one off on Sam like that.

But Sam just gives me an elaborate eye-roll. "I didn't mean he'd get her pregnant *right now*. I meant after she has the baby. Elizabeth's fertile as hell, she has or soon will have had three different kids from three different fathers, and she's running out of sperm donors. Sonny'd make the perfect father for her next kid. Plus, they've both got great dimples."

"But their storylines hardly intersect."

"That's the beauty of it. I could probably get fifty-to-one odds from your bookie on a Sonny/Elizabeth hookup. I'll make out like a bandit."

She says this like this whole scenario might actually come to fruition.

When the closing credits roll, Sam turns to me. "Shall we get our books out and study? I can't believe we have to wait until Monday to find out what Lisa the surgeon's got up her sleeve."

Sam's hooked.

"Just so you know," I say, "my offer was strictly for this week only. If we start blowing off work regularly to watch GH, I am not keeping you on the clock for it come Monday."

"OK, OK. So...the books?"

"I've already memorized the parts on 'Getting Your Outside Ready' and 'Having a Way Cool Time.' Actually, I had something else in mind for today's study session. It has to do with that thing you said about Sonny, how if you weren't a lesbian..."

"I am *not* kissing you, Johnny!" Sam says for the third time.

"We have time to kill. The poker game doesn't start for another two hours and my date with Helen is tomorrow. Come on, you have to!"

"I do not. What part of 'I am a lesbian' do you not understand?"

"But that's what makes it perfect. It's not like you'll get turned on or anything. I just need the practice, to make sure I've been doing it right, should the occasion arise that I get the chance to kiss Helen."

"Of course you're doing it right. You're how old? How long have you been kissing women?"

"But that's the thing. What if all these years I've been doing it wrong? What if the real reason I've never had a successful long-term relationship is that secretly I'm the world's worst kisser?"

"Don't you think you'd know that by now?"

"How would I know it? Would some girl ever actually say to me, 'Gee, I'd like to like you...*if only you weren't the world's worst kisser ever'?*"

"Well, no, but—"

"Are you that confident you're *not* a lousy kisser?"

"Ooh, harsh."

"I don't mean to be harsh. I'm just trying to say, maybe we

could both benefit from practicing together?"

Sam doesn't say anything.

"Come on, Sam. You're my best friend. If I were dying and I needed a kidney, you'd give me a kidney, wouldn't you?"

"Yes, but if I gave you a kidney I wouldn't have to kiss you."

"Sam…"

"Oh, all *right*. But draw the blinds first. I don't want anyone to see this."

I draw the blinds.

"OK," Sam says, "how do you want to do this thing?"

"I don't know." Now that I've got my way I'm suddenly unsure. "Should we do it sitting down? Standing?"

"How should I know? It's your date."

"Maybe it'll happen after I walk her to the door, so I guess we'd be standing."

"That's an improvement. You wouldn't just like to shake her hand again like you did last time?"

I ignore that.

"Or maybe," I say, "it'll happen earlier. There'll be a naturally occurring opening—"

"What is that, 'a naturally occurring opening'? It sounds like something they'd say on The Science Channel about the aftereffects of a meteor."

I ignore her and just start again. "There'll be a naturally occurring opening in the date where we're sitting down somewhere and I say something that's funny and she laughs, or I say something that's at least not totally asinine and she tolerates it, or maybe we're both laughing at something happening around us that doesn't even have anything to do with us and as we're laughing our bodies just naturally fall toward one another and—"

"You're way over-thinking this, Johnny. If this is the sort of crap that goes on in your mind during an actual date, no wonder you never get around to kissing the girl."

"Remind me again why you're my best friend?"

"Because I'm standing here with the blinds drawn and I'm going to let you practice kissing on me even though I'm a lesbian."

"Oh right. That."

"Why don't we do it on the couch?"

"Really? You think so? Because what if I learn how to do it in one position and we wind up doing it in an entirely different position? Maybe the opportunity won't come until the end of the date when I'm walking her to the door and—"

"The couch, Johnny, the couch. Let's do it on the couch before I change my fucking mind."

Geez.

We sit.

We sit side by side. My hands are on my knees, Sam's hands are on her knees, and we're facing the TV.

"We probably need to face each other to do this," she says finally.

"OK," I say, turning toward her. "Can you take your glasses off? Helen doesn't wear glasses and—"

"—and you're sure that if you practice on me while I'm wearing glasses, even if your practice makes perfect, when you go to kiss a girl without glasses you'll somehow go back to lousing things up. Have I got that right?"

"Pretty much." It's embarrassing how well she knows me.

"Fine." She removes her glasses and carefully places them on the coffee table. "Now I'm blind as a bat, which could work to your advantage."

"OK, now maybe we should try to create a natural conversational atmosphere so this feels like it will when it's actually happening. Pretend I just said something funny and you're laughing."

"*HA!*" Sam barks.

Like a character in a comic strip, I'm practically bowled over backwards by the volume of that laugh. "Not like that. That sounds like you're laughing *at* me."

"I can't help it. That's my laugh."

"OK, then just smile, like you *would* laugh, like what I just said is funny enough for a laugh, but you're more restrained than that, more sophisticated, so instead you just have this smile on your face—you know, kind of Mona Lisa-ish."

Sam smiles. Then through her smiling teeth, she says, "You mean like this?"

"Perfect, if a little spooky. OK, now I'm going to lean toward you and put my hand on your shoulder. But in a non-threatening way, of course."

"Of course. We wouldn't want Mona Lisa to feel threatened before you kiss her."

"Now you put a hand on me somewhere."

Sam pulls away from me. "I can't do this," she says abruptly.

"But you promised!" I can't believe how much like an eight-year-old I sound, even to my own ears.

"I did not promise. There were no guarantees given here. I signed no contracts."

"Fine, that's all true." I sigh. "But I need help here, Sam, real help. Who else can I ask to help me make sure I'm kissing right? Alice? Aunt Alfresca? Alice would yell at me again, like she did when she thought the reason I wanted to meet her for coffee was to confess my undying love for her. And Aunt Alfresca—ick. She's a relative. Plus, even if she wasn't a relative? Ick."

"I take your point."

"Thank you."

"Maybe if we get drunker I can do it."

"Aren't we buzzed enough? We drank beer all through GH."

"I need something harder for this." Sam thinks. "You still got that bottle Mr. Papadopolous tipped you with at that job last week?"

"You mean the ouzo?"

Sam nods.

"Sure. You know I never drink stuff like that. Neither do you."

"Well, we're drinking it now."

I get the ouzo, two shot glasses, put it all on the coffee table, pour. Simultaneously, we knock back the shots.

"Ugh!" Sam wipes her mouth with the back of her hand. "That tastes like licorice!"

"I'm pretty sure it's supposed to."

"I hate licorice." Sam nods at the shot glasses. "Again," she instructs. "Doubles this time."

On the count of three, we knock our doubles back together.

Sam wipes her mouth with the back of her hand, then wipes the back of her hand on the thigh of my jeans. Fucking Sam.

"OK, I think I'm ready," she says. "Let's do this thing."

Finally!

A few more minutes of logistical discussion and we're back where we left off earlier with my hand on her shoulder in a non-threatening way and me saying, "Now you put a hand on me somewhere."

"Where somewhere?"

"I don't know. My waist?"

"Threatening or non-threatening?"

"Non. OK, now hold the Mona Lisa-ish smile as our heads just naturally move toward one another and—"

My lips make contact with Sam's lips. Hers are soft and taste like potato chips and beer and licorice. I imagine mine do too. For the longest time, we just stay there with our puckered lips touching, not moving them around or anything. Then, figuring this is not the part of kissing I need practice on, I gently part my lips and wait for her to part hers too. She does, and before you know it, we've got noses crashing and teeth clashing and tongues smashing like mad. I'm not sure what this is but it feels like the kiss equivalent of when a cartoon character is thinking dark thoughts and the thought bubble contains something that looks like $*%(^)*&!

And then to make matters worse, smack in the middle of it, I think of what it would be like to have my lips touch Helen's, to have it be her hand on my waist, and my boner pops *sproing!*

Sam and I practically push each other away, wipe our mouths with the backs of our hands.

What the hell was that?

"Let's never do that again, OK?" Sam says.

"Deal," I say.

For a long moment, we just sit there, catching our breath.

"You know," I say at last, "you're a good friend?"

"I know."

• • •

All during the poker game, things are weird between Sam and me, each of us barely nursing our beers, barely saying a word to one another. When the game breaks—early, because all the married guys need to head on home to their wives—Sam stays as usual to help me clean up. At least that's the same as it's always been.

"Listen," I say as we head up the stairs from the basement, each holding several empties, "I wanted to apologize for earlier. I realize it was asking too much, to expect you to practice…*you know* with me."

"Don't sweat it," Sam says, shrugging me off in an attempt to make like it's no big deal. "It was no big deal."

"But it was," I say as we hit the kitchen, deposit the empties on the counter, "particularly for you. When's the last time you kissed a guy?"

Sam blinks at me. "Never."

"Never?" I blink back at her.

Sam shrugs. "I'm one of those lesbians who's known I was a lesbian all along. There was never a reason for me to kiss a guy like that before."

"Christ, Sam." I pull my hair back with the palm of my hand. In some vague corner of my mind, I wonder if *this* time I look as hot as Sonny on GH with my hair like that. I shrug off the thought, let my hair go. "Then it really is a big deal. If I'da known…"

"Forget it." Sam waves her hand at me. "It was just that, it wasn't like it was *just some guy*. It was you."

I feel good again, on firmer ground, because now I know exactly what to say. "I know, right?" I say, almost too eagerly. "It was me, and it was you."

"Exactly." Sam heaves a sigh of relief. "It's like we're such close friends."

"*Best* friends," I amend.

"BFFs for sure," Sam agrees. "But that's what makes it so weird. Do you know what I mean?"

"I know exactly what you mean. It's like when you have really close friends—like you, like Billy—it's not like you ever think of...*doing stuff* with them. But because you're so close, or maybe the reason you're so close, there's a different connection, a click you don't have with other people that's almost like its own separate category of attraction—"

"Except it's not, not like what you have with Helen."

"Or what you'll have with whoever you replace Renee with."

"I hope that's sooner rather than later."

"You and me both." I pause. "Anyway, when you tamper with that separate category of attraction that isn't really an attraction, like we did earlier..." I pause again, not sure how to properly finish my thought.

But that's OK, because Sam finishes it for me with, "...you disrupt the natural fabric of the universe."

"Exactly!" I look at my best friend. "So, we good now?"

"Not exactly. I'm still a bit weirded out by all of this."

"What can we do to correct that?" Before she can answer, it comes to me. "I know! We'll do something normal together. We'll get out of here, hit the bar."

"You mean right now?"

"Why not? I'm sober again, aren't you?"

Sam thinks about this. "Yeah. I could drink."

"Great. We'll go to Pockets." It's a local bar that has a pool table. "Besides, I'd like to take my new pants out for a spin."

"The khakis? But I thought you bought those for Helen."

"So?" I'm just so glad Sam and I are about to do something normal together, get us past this hump of weirdness between us. "If I dribble on myself, I can always wash them. It might even work out better. That way, when I wear them with Helen, they won't have that just-purchased-for-this-occasion look."

"You know you're starting to sound like a girl? You sure I wasn't kissing a girl earlier?"

Fucking Sam.

Yes! She's insulting me!

We are definitely on the track back to normal.

• • •

Pockets is hopping. Or it's limping along as much as Pockets ever does but at least it's not completely dead when Sam and me hit it around eleven P.M. In the bar area there are maybe a half dozen people, there's twice that out on the terrace, and the same around the pool table even though no one's got their names up on the chalkboard.

"I'll rack," I say, crouching to put four quarters in the slot. "Here," I say rising, pulling my wallet from the back of my crisp new khakis and handing a twenty to Sam. "Get me a Sierra and get whatever you want for yourself."

As I rack the balls, I'm thinking how good I'm feeling, being out. I'm with Sam, my pants look sharp, and we didn't have to wait forever to get on the table.

I'm feeling even better when Sam returns with our drinks and, as she nears, I notice two women seated on a couch under a neon beer sign eyeing me. They're maybe in their mid-twenties, tight jeans, tight tank tops, tight figures, Jersey Shore hair, strong Friday night makeup.

They're definitely giving me the eye.

I tell Sam as much after I break, sinking two stripers, and accept my beer from her. I don't even add anything about her pocketing all my change.

"See those two girls?" I say.

"Yeah, what about them?"

"I can't figure out which one wants me more."

Sam nearly spews her drink on me.

"It's the pants, Sam, the pants. They're definitely working. I don't know why I didn't shake up my wardrobe sooner. All these years, I could've been getting laid like clockwork! Instead of, you know, intermittently."

"You want to get laid by those girls? But I thought you liked Helga."

"I don't, I do," I answer her questions in the correct order. "But it is flattering to feel, you know, desirable."

"And you think those two women desire you?"

"Yes."

"And you think it's because of the pants?"

Duh! "What else could it be?"

"They're lesbians, Johnny."

"Excuse me?"

"They're lesbians, I'm guessing just two lesbian friends who like to hang together but are not involved with one another. And it's not you they're finding hot." Sam gives a wave at the two women. "It's me."

And now things really are back to normal.

Oh, well. It was fun thinking women found me hot while it lasted.

Send in the Clowns

When I pick up Helen on Saturday, I'm wearing my new duds. I never could understand why women fuss so much over clothes but now I get it, even if those lesbians weren't really giving me the eye last night. With my belted khakis—washed and dried when I got home last night—collared shirt and pair of brown shoes that have those little rough suede laces, I feel like I'm dressed for success, like this could be the day my life changes. I don't even feel naked without my backward baseball cap.

It's a warm spring day and as I hand Helen up into the front of my work truck, I can't help but notice how the slight breeze causes the longish skirt of her sundress to hug the silhouette of her strong calf. Sam almost talked me into getting a rental car again, but 1) the banana yellow Porsche wasn't available when I called the rental place and I figured it'd be too strange if I kept showing up in a different car each time we go on a date, if we do indeed keep going out on dates, and 2) I figured in just this one thing I would be my true self—I paint for a living, no denying it, and if Helen can't accept me being a painter and everything that goes with that, like the work truck, maybe she's not the girl for me.

Helen doesn't flinch at the truck, nor does she ask me why I'm not driving a banana Porsche anymore, and I figure: so far, so good.

"It's a beautiful day for the circus," she says as I climb into the driver's seat.

After agreeing, I key the engine and as soon I do that, the radio which is always on springs to life and the truck is filled with the sound of The Wave.

I reach to quickly turn the dial before I'm outed as being a hardcore sports fan but Helen is holding the dial firm.

Recapping from the last hour, not all fans are in agreement about the latest trades by the Jets. In fact, as one of our favorite callers pointed out just yesterday…

There's a click as the host of The Wave cues the previously recorded clip and a new voice fills the truck.

What kind of garbage is this? the female voice says. I've heard this voice on The Wave only once before, the voice I immediately thought of as Sexy Caller. At the time it sounded naggingly familiar—like when you see some young actress nominated for an Oscar for a serious role and you can't place her big-toothed smile for the longest time until you remember, 'Oh yeah, right, she was in that really popular movie the critics hated'—but I couldn't place the voice then and I still can't place it. *First, Thomas Jones. And now, Kerry Rhodes. What the hell are the Jets doing? Does management not remember what it was like having a disappointing team? So they finally have one season that is not a disappointment and now they're going to get rid of some of the components in the equation that made them almost great in the hopes of getting someone better? Where is the loyalty in modern sports? Where is the sense of the people who helped you get where you are? Where is the—*

Helen shoots me a quick look and then spins the dial far away from The Wave. Well, of course she does. Except for Sam upon occasion, and Sexy Caller, women are never interested in listening to The Wave.

"What was that?" she says as music fills the truck.

"Oh, that?" Think fast, Johnny. Do you claim no knowledge of it at all? That might be safest. But it was right on that station and it came on just as soon as you keyed the engine. She's a D.A. Won't she find that suspicious? "I think it's called The Wave?" Come on, Johnny, you're not even fooling yourself here. Why would you have a station obviously preprogrammed on your radio and then pretend you don't know it? She'll know; she's got to.

"You have a station preprogrammed on your own truck and you're not even sure what that station is?"

See? I knew she'd be smart that way. Man, this dating stuff

is tough.

"Yes, it's definitely called The Wave," I say with greater certainty. "I don't really listen to it myself. You know, all that sports stuff. It's so boring."

"Then why was it on as soon as you turned on the engine?"

Oh, she is good.

And then inspiration strikes.

"Sam!" I practically shout, I'm so happy. It's the equivalent of screaming, "Yes!" when your team scores.

"Sam?" Helen's puzzled.

"You know, Sam, that woman that works with me?"

Helen nods.

"Well, see, Sam's this huge sports fanatic." True. "And Sam listens to The Wave, like, all the time." I roll my eyes. Of course I'm exaggerating. Sam doesn't mind The Wave occasionally but mostly she likes to just watch sports, not listen to people talk about it endlessly on the radio like I do.

"But Sam's not here," Helen says.

"And that is an excellent point," I admit. She's wearing me down. I'm still smiling but if this goes on much longer, no doubt I'll confess everything, including about breaking Mrs. Knox's window that time I was six and we were playing tackle basketball.

"But see," I go on, "when Sam works for me, she insists I have The Wave on the radio all the time—you know, as part of her bonus package. That Sam, she's such a nut. She says it's better than full medical."

"But Sam's not here," Helen says again.

She's not going to let this go.

"Yes, I do know that," I say.

"So why are you listening to Sam's station when she's not even here?"

All right with the thumbscrews already!

"Because," I say simply, "it was on when I got in the truck and I guess I just never changed the channel because I didn't even notice it. My mind was on something else. I was too busy thinking and I guess I never even noticed The Wave as anything other than background noise."

Which is true. I was too busy being both nervous and looking forward to my date with Helen that for once I didn't even pay any attention to what they were saying on The Wave. Although now that I did pay attention briefly when we first got in the truck, I'm thinking I agree with Sexy Caller. Where is the loyalty? It sucks, the Jets letting Jones and Rhodes go.

"What were you so busy thinking about," Helen asks, "that you didn't even notice a sports radio station playing all the way from your house to mine?"

"I was looking forward to seeing you and going to the circus with you," I admit, helpless under the onslaught of her prosecutorial prowess. "I was thinking of you."

I can honestly say that in the entire history of my life I have never said anything that charmed a member of the opposite sex like this.

But as I glance over now to see how Helen's taking what I said I see that she is just that:

Charmed.

It's a circus *and* a carnival!

For the rest of the drive here, we simply listened to music from the radio, which was perfect. After charming Helen, I didn't want to run the risk of *un*charming her. But now we're here and the fact that this is a circus *and* a carnival is perfect too. I don't know what I expected when I saw the circus listed in *The Penny-Saver*—maybe a few mangy elephants and an acrobat or two?—but I never expected that right next to the circus there'd be a whole carnival set up, with rides and games and everything.

I love rides.

I love games.

One thing I do not love is…

"Eek! A clown!"

Yes, I'm ashamed to admit, that was me going *eek*.

Helen looks at me. "Did you just say 'Eek!'?"

"I'm afraid so," I admit. "I can't help it. Clowns just freak me out."

"You're telling me," she says, smiles. "Ever since I was little, I wondered, why do they have clowns at circuses? Is the goal to make everyone want to run away?"

"I know, right?" I'm psyched. This woman is…there are no words for it. She just seems to get the things that I get. "I don't know what I was thinking inviting you here. I guess I forgot the clowns part of circuses."

"It's OK," she says. "When you invited me, for some reason I forgot all about the clowns too. Maybe we should just go to the carnival part instead?"

"Good idea."

As we're walking to the booth to buy tickets, a clown passes us on the right.

"Eek!" I say, laughing at myself.

"Eek!" Helen laughs right along with me.

The line is long and I realize I need to find something to talk about, something Helen will be interested in, so…

"I can't believe that Sonny," I say with a shake of the head.

"Sonny?"

"Is he the most twisted person in the world or what? He shoots Dominic when Dominic's not even armed, then when he finds out that Dominic is in fact his own son and that his real name is Dante, he blames everyone else under the sun for it." I do my Sonny imitation. "'Olivia, if you'd told me we made a baby together years ago, this never would have happened.' 'Patrick, if you told me the truth as soon as you learned it, I never would have shot him.' What is up with that? Like if Dante hadn't turned out to be his son, somehow it would have been perfectly acceptable for Sonny to shoot an unarmed cop? The man's got an ego the size of Port Charles. I mean, come on, if—"

"Um, John, what are you talking about? I don't remember hearing about any of this in the news. Is this some kind of court case?"

I'm stunned. "I'm talking about GH. You know, *General Hospital*? I thought all women were up on *General Hospital*."

I don't understand this. Have I been wasting my time watching this soap? Not that I think *General Hospital*'s a waste, not now that I'm into it. But maybe I should have been watching *The Young & the Restless* instead?

"Oh, *General Hospital*?" she says. "I don't know what made me think you were talking about a real case. Of course you're talking about *General Hospital*. I don't know how I could have gotten Sonny and Dominic and Dante confused with anything else."

"That would be hard to do," I say. "Then you do? Watch, I mean."

She waves a dismissive hand. "Of course. Well, I'm not usually home from work in the afternoon, so I just, you know, TiVo it for later."

"That's what I do too," I say, even though it's a lie; I don't want her to think I'm a lazy bum who shirks work to watch a soap. "I, you know, do that thing—I TiVo it."

Truth time. I know I'm a guy and all but I'm not great with modern technology. Cars I get. Computery type things? Not so much.

"So," she says, "you've been watching that for a long time, have you, *General Hospital*?"

I wave my own dismissive hand. "Forever. I've been watching since Sonny first got a girl pregnant by just looking at her funny."

And finally it's our turn.

"Two, please," I tell the ticket taker.

We're trying to decide which ride to go on first—decisions, decisions!—when we pass a game booth. It's a basketball toss. The barker's yelling at me, "Every player a winner! Don't be a chump. Win the little lady a prize!"

I wouldn't normally allow myself to be egged on by some guy inferring I could be a chump, but the barker really gets me with that "little lady" stuff. I remember how Leo always refers to his wife as The Little Lady and I decide this is something to aspire to: a little lady of my own.

"What do you think?" I shrug, raise my eyebrows at Helen. "Should I give it a go?"

She raises her eyebrows back, shrugs.

I pay my money for three throws, sink two of them.

"Not bad," says the barker. "You have your choice of these prizes." He waves his arm, displaying the lowest level of prizes adorning both sides of his booth. Let's see…We have a choice of a key chain decorated with a single feather or a key chain decorated with a single puffball. Hmm…That's a tough choice. Decisions, decisions.

"*Or*," the barker says, "you *could* try your luck again. Sink two out of three again and you get to choose from the next level."

The next level includes stuffed bears so small, if you made a circle with your thumb and forefinger the little bear could live inside.

I'm going to ask for the puffball key chain, just as soon as I can figure out how to say "puffball key chain" out loud without sounding like a complete moron, when Helen speaks up.

"Can I have a turn?"

"Absolutely." I hand the barker a couple dollars more.

Helen shoots and scores. Three times.

By going three for three she bypasses the mini-bear level completely, leapfrogging straight to the mini-medium stuffed fish.

"You're good," I say.

"Beginner's luck," she says.

"You want the fish, or you want to shoot again for an upgrade?" the barker offers. "You're on a roll."

"You go," Helen says to me.

So I pay and go, sinking all three this time. What can I say? Her sinking all three brings out the competitor in me.

Then she goes again, sinking two this time.

And we go on like that, alternating turns and alternating who gets two and who gets three until we're all the way up to trying for one of the giant bears on the very top row. I mean, these bears are so giant, a person's arms would barely fit around them; so giant, there's only one on either side. To go for the top row, it should be my turn since she went last, but she looks like she's having so much fun, so I say, "You take it."

And she does, sinking all three in rapid succession this time.

"Wanna go again?" the barker offers. "You sink two out of three and you can keep the giant bear *and* take one of those puffball key chains. The puffball's stuffed…"

What does he think I am, a patsy?

"No, thanks," I say. "I think we're pretty good on stuffed things for the time being."

"Come on," the barker says. "I'll bet the little lady would love one of those puffball key chains. I'll bet any other guy wouldn't stop now. What are you, a cheapskate?"

"I'm fine with just the bear," Helen informs the barker tersely.

The barker hands Helen one of the giant bears. It's purple and fairly hideous. It's maybe even creepier looking than a clown. Plus, I'm doing the math and I just realized that bear cost me about ninety bucks.

"Cheap chump," the barker mutters after me as we walk away.

But none of that matters because Helen's smiling, not a pained or barely tolerant smile like I sometimes get from women, but a genuine honest-to-God I-am-having-fun smile and I realize that I've never in my life done something so simple with a female as take her to a carnival and win her the big prize and how good this all feels.

Well, I didn't really win her the big prize, not completely. She won over fifty percent of that prize herself.

"Hey," I say, "where'd you learn to shoot a basketball like that?"

She shrugs. "I told you I have five big brothers."

"Oh, right," I say, remembering, "the brothers. So, what— they taught you all about sports?"

"Some. Or at least how to shoot a basketball. So that when they played there could be even teams. You know, three against three."

"That must have been cool," I say coolly. Inside I'm thinking, *This is great!*

"Not really," she says.

"No?"

"No. I only played because they made me. I don't really like basketball or any sports."

"Oh. Right. Me neither."

Despite that neither of us likes basketball specifically or sports in general, we spend a good part of the afternoon playing games at the carnival. We throw ping-pong balls into little glass fishbowls, toss softballs through the bull's-eye on a big board, shoot water pistols at a target. We're not really trying to upgrade prizes anymore—after the giant purple bear, what would be the point? Instead we're just sampling all the games, having fun. It's cool. It's kind of like doing sports-like stuff without doing actual sports.

"Are you getting hungry?" I ask, hoping the answer is yes. I'm starving.

"I could eat."

"What'll it be?" I say, glancing around at the various food booths.

"Maybe a hot dog and fries?" she says.

"Sure thing," I say.

We walk over to the hot dog/hamburger booth and as she places her order, I scan the menu, seeing if there are any non-meat alternatives.

"Are you looking for a salad?" Helen asks.

"Excuse me?"

"Maybe a tomato-and-lettuce salad with no dressing like you had at Subway?"

"Oh, that." I can't believe she remembers that particularly awkward moment in my life when I've been trying so hard to forget. "I actually do eat other things. It's just that—"

The guy behind the counter comes over with Helen's fries, asks me if I've decided what I want.

"Yeah, do you have anything with fish?"

"No," he says. "That's why we're the hot dog/hamburger stand." Thanks, buddy. But then he gestures with his spatula.

"That's where you want to go, the fish stand. They do fish sticks, fish filets, crab cakes, soft-shell crab sandwiches, fried clams, fried shrimp. They even do a corndog-type thing but with fish in the middle."

I pay for Helen's items, we find a table topped with a red-and-white checked oilcloth and I head over to the fish stand as she starts in on her fries. A few seconds later I'm back with assorted fish items, fries and an orange soda.

Helen's looking at me as I pop a fried clam strip into my mouth. "You like fish," she observes.

"Actually," I say, "I'm a pescatarian. I eat fish but not any kind of meat or chicken."

"I know what a pescatarian is. So why are you one?"

"It's a philosophical thing," I say. I always hate explaining this to other people. I don't want them to think I'm being all judgy about whatever they do. It's just a decision I made for myself. "I read this book once about how various animals, you know, become dinner. As soon as I read that, I just knew I'd never eat any of that stuff again."

"But I've seen you. At that baseball game, you were eating hot dogs."

"Oh, that. That's different. I have a special ballgame rule. Not that I go to many games—you know, only when someone asks me, because I don't really like sports. But at the ballpark it just seems like the thing to do, like a place with special rules. Also if I'm invited to someone's house and the main course is something I don't eat? I eat it anyway. No sense in hurting someone else's feelings over something that's already on the plate."

"So ballparks and houses of people who don't know any better is OK?"

"Pretty much."

"But other than that, no meat or chicken ever because you think it's wrong?"

"Not for other people. I'm not saying it's wrong for other people, just for me. You know, because of the book. I guess that all sounds really weird, huh?"

"No. Actually it sounds incredibly sweet."

And then Helen pushes the remainder of her hot dog away and reaches for one of my fried clam strips.

Did she just convert for me?

Every game played; food eaten.

"You want to go on a ride?" I suggest.

"Sure," Helen says.

We're standing right in front of the Ferris wheel, so...

Our carriage is halfway up the loop, going backwards, the giant purple bear between us, and Helen's peering over the side.

"I probably should have mentioned before this," Helen says, "but I'm not crazy about heights."

"How not crazy is not crazy? Is it like 'this is mildly uncomfortable,' like on a scale of 1 to 10, it'd be a 3?"

"More like a 7."

Christ, we've barely even gotten started.

"I'm not saying you necessarily should have said something earlier," I say, "but how come you didn't say something earlier? Like when we were still on the ground?"

"Because I didn't want to embarrass myself. It sounds so stupid. A grown woman scared of heights."

"Just close your eyes then and think of something pleasant like, I don't know, England."

"That's good, if a little strange. I think I'll do that."

Helen closes her eyes tight and keeps them closed as we go round and round.

"What's the number now?" I ask.

"Not bad," she says, sounding relieved. "It's back down to a 3, maybe even a 2."

"So it's only maybe about as bad as clowns."

"Clowns?"

"Yeah, earlier, when I said I was scared of clowns, you said you were too."

"Oh, that. I was lying."

"Lying?"

"I didn't want to make you feel bad, like you were alone in your fear. Actually clowns don't bother me at all."

"Just heights?"

"Just heights."

Which shouldn't be a problem, I'm thinking, now that she's got her eyes tight shut and her fear level is down to a 3, maybe a 2.

Only it becomes a problem when the Ferris wheel slows to a stop with our carriage swinging right up at the apex and Helen, sensing the stop and thinking the ride's over, opens up her eyes, sees where we are and…

"10! 10! I'm at 10!"

"Helen! Helen!" I shout over her shouts. "Look at me! Think nice thoughts!"

"I can't. England's not working anymore!"

"Then think of other nice things."

"Like what? There's nothing nice right now."

"Think of how much fun it was to win that bear earlier. Making all those baskets—you were excellent."

"That makes barely a dent," she says. "Maybe 9.5 now."

Why is the Ferris wheel taking so long to start moving again? Christ, I hope she doesn't jump just to get closer to the ground. What else can I tell her to think about that she'd think is nice? Cute puppies? But I don't even know if she likes cute puppies. Doesn't everyone like cute puppies, though? But what if she was bitten when she was little? Or what if she's a cat person? What if—

Then I remember something Leo told me.

"Significant dates!" I say in a louder voice than I intend.

"Significant dates?"

"Yes," I say in a calmer voice, even though I'm still feeling desperate to soothe her. "Significant dates." I start doing the math in my head. "It's the thirty-seven-day anniversary since I first met you at that Yankees game. It's the thirty-five-day anniversary since I first started painting rooms in your house." It's funny. I began reciting the dates to calm her down, but as I name each one, I realize these dates are all significant to me too.

"It's the one-week anniversary from when we went to the Barn Opera. It's the four-hour anniversary since I picked you up late this morning and it's the—"

"Forty-minute anniversary since I first stole one of your fried clam strips," she cuts in.

"Actually, I was thinking of something else, but that one works too."

"I can't believe you keep track of all that," she says softly. "What did you call them?"

"Significant dates." I'm beginning to feel like a moron. Maybe I'm the one who should jump out of this carriage.

"I can't believe you keep track of all that," she says again, "and that you think those dates are significant."

And then before I know what she's doing, she switches seats with the giant purple bear.

"Zero," she says, looking at me instead of over the edge at the big drop. "Right now my fear level is at zero."

And then we're falling toward each other until there's no space between our lips, and my arms are going around her with nothing awkward about it at all, and this is nothing at all like kissing Sam, *nothing*, nothing like kissing any other female I've ever kissed before. It's soft and urgent, it's comfortable and terrifying, it's natural and supernatural all at once. It's…

Wow.

Friendly Interlude

"This is getting serious."

That last comment? That was said by just about everybody.

We're all crammed into my place to celebrate Big John's fifty-fifth birthday. "We're all" equals me, Sam, Big John and Aunt Alfresca, Billy and Alice, and Drew and Stacy. Also present are Steve and Katie Miller. Katie looks like she doesn't know what she's doing there, at her painter's condo for a party for his father, but Big John wanted me to invite Steve. After Steve joined us for that first poker game, Big John decided Steve was "our kind of people," even if Steve is a lawyer and Big John worries he'll put pie-in-the-sky don't-be-a-painter-anymore ideas in my head. There are also a bunch of other people here—friends of the family etcetera—but they don't seem to matter so much.

At least the food is good. Aunt Alfresca doesn't do much well in the kitchen, but what she does well, she does really well, like her meatless lasagna. So the food, like I say, is good.

The conversation, on the other hand? Not so much.

I had briefly considered but then quickly rejected the idea of inviting Helen to the party for Big John. Meeting my friends one at a time? Even that seemed like a lot to ask of her, never mind the risk to me that one of them might say something to tip my fragile apple cart. But all of them at once? Forget about it.

"This is getting serious," Big John says.

"I believe someone may have mentioned that already," I say, refilling both of our red plastic cups from the keg in the kitchen.

"Yeah," Big John says, "but I mean *really* serious. You like this woman enough *not* to expose her to all of us?"

I never should have mentioned considering to invite Helen and then chickening out.

"Are you ashamed of us?" Aunt Alfresca says. "What are we, chopped liver?"

"No, I'm not ashamed. No, you're not chopped liver. You're—" I stop myself. Just what exactly is Aunt Alfresca? It's a puzzle.

"You know," Steve says, "you're not the only one who's getting serious."

"What do you mean?"

"Well, maybe *serious* isn't the right word. Maybe what I should have said is *happy*."

"Excuse me for asking," I say, "but just what the hell are you talking about?"

"Helen. Ever since you started painting her house and then taking her places, she's a lot easier to work across the aisle from."

I'm not sure I understand. "What, she's not working as hard to get convictions?"

"Are you kidding me? She still tries to kick my ass every time we meet in court. But at least now, she smiles sometimes when she does it."

This is news. I can't help but notice the changes that meeting Helen has caused in my life—the new wardrobe, trying to put my best foot forward, and all the other etcetera—but I never stopped to think before that I might be having some kind of affect on her too. I also never thought before that Steve, being the only person in my circle who knows both Helen and me, might know something, might be useful for insider information.

But I do now.

"What do you know about Helen?" I ask, trying to sound casual. I figure no one likes to feel used for insider information.

"Know about Helen?" Steve seems surprised at the question. "Nothing. We're just friendly adversaries. If you're looking for insider information, like what her favorite color is, I'm afraid I can't help you."

"Green," I say. "It was blue but then she changed it to green."

Before this moment, I tried to convince myself that other conversations were going on in the room, that people were not hanging on my every word. Well, allow me to disabuse myself of that notion.

"You not only know her favorite color," Drew says, "you also know the *history* of her favorite color?"

"Well, I don't know as that I'd put it quite like—"

"This is getting serious," Stacy says. Then she punches Drew in the shoulder. "Do you even know my favorite color?"

"Reddish-purple," Drew says proudly.

Stacy looks slightly mollified then her eyes narrow. "And before that? My favorite color before reddish-purple?"

Drew looks panicked. "Canary yellow?"

"*Sunshine* yellow." Stacy punches him again. "Schmuck. You don't know the *history*, not like Johnny does with Helen."

I feel kind of bad for Drew's shoulder, but it's nice having the spotlight taken off me, however briefly, that spotlight returning when Steve says:

"I'm sorry, I wish I could help you out. But you already know more about Helen than I could ever tell you, what with your knowing the history of her favorite color and all."

"Well, what about that other guy she's seeing too? That friend of yours, Monte Carlo?"

"Hold on here," Aunt Alfresca says. "That bitch is stepping out on you already?"

"She's not a bitch," I say, "and I don't think you can call it stepping out. I mean, I've only taken her out a few times. It's not like we're married or something."

"Are you *thinking* about marrying her?" Sam says. "This is more serious than I thought."

I ignore Sam.

"Seriously, Steve," I say, "what do you know about Helen and Monte Carlo?"

Suddenly Steve looks uncomfortable. A minute ago he was all happy to help, even if he couldn't, but now he's wary.

"I don't even know what you're talking about," he says. "What are you talking about?"

"One time when I was painting Helen's house, back before I took her out the first time. We're getting along just fine and all of a sudden she changes her clothes, next thing I know I look out the window and she's getting into a car with your pal Monte Carlo from Jersey. Then, the day after I took her to the opera, I called to see if she wanted to do anything that day and she said she was busy. I figured she must have had another date with him."

"What days were this?" Steve wants to know.

"What days? I don't know." I start doing the math. "Let's see…The time I was painting, today's the twenty-four-day anniversary from the day I painted that room. And the other? Today's the seventeen-day anniversary from when I took her to the Barn Opera, so the day after would have been sixteen days ago."

"Oh my God," Stacy says in a hushed voice, "Johnny's remembering significant dates." She looks at her husband. "Do you still remember all our significant dates?"

Drew takes his sore shoulder and quickly excuses himself to the bathroom.

"Actually," Steve says, "I meant days of the week. Do you remember what days of the week those things happened on?"

I don't even need to think about this one. "The first time was a Saturday and the second was a Sunday."

"Oh," Steve says, looking relieved but still wary. "Don't worry about it. It's nothing. I'm sure there's nothing romantic about it in the slightest."

"How can you be so sure? You said you don't really know Helen outside of work."

"True, but for one thing, if something were going on between Helen and Monte, he'd be bragging to me about it. And for another, I'm sure they were just doing lawyer stuff together."

"Lawyer stuff? On the weekend?"

"Yeah. You know how it is. We're all colleagues. And sometimes we need to get together and just talk over cases and, you know, lawyer stuff."

"But what kind of cases would they have to discuss? He practices in a different state plus they're on other sides of the law."

"Well, see, that's what makes it ideal. Them being from different states, they can just practice on each other—you know, do a little moot court."

Even Steve's wife Katie is looking at him like he's nuts with this one. "Really, Steven. You say they're doing a little moot court?"

Steve puts his hands out, palms up. "It's the truth. I swear."

"It sounds like things are going well for you," Alice says. "I'm glad. But you need to kick it up another notch so you don't lose momentum."

"How do I do that, kick it up another notch? I've already taken her to the Barn Opera and the circus/carnival."

"I agree, the Barn Opera does sound as though it would be tough to beat."

I can't tell if Alice is serious or if she's mocking me.

"So what do you suggest?" I ask.

"Invite her to dinner," Alice suggests. "Women love it when a guy invites them to dinner."

"You mean like a restaurant?"

"No, I mean here. Any guy can take a woman to a restaurant. But when you invite a woman to dinner and then actually prepare the meal for her, now *that's* something special. Just don't make spaghetti. Guys who think they can win a woman over with a plate of spaghetti are just dreaming."

"Invite her to dinner!" Sam says.

"Invite her to dinner!" Big John says.

Before I know it, everyone's saying it.

"What are you people," I say, "a Greek chorus made up of mice? I swear I feel like I'm in one of those movies where there's a whole bunch of brain-challenged mice always screaming stupid things."

"Hey, don't insult us," Billy says. "We're all just trying to help."

"And you need a *lot* of help," Alice says.

"OK, fine. Say I do invite her over for dinner. What do I prepare if I'm not going to be making spaghetti?"

"Oh, no no no no no." Alice wags a finger at me. "No way

are you ready to discuss the menu yet. First, you've got to prep this place."

What's she talking about? You prep a person for surgery. You prep for an exam. You prep a wall before painting it. But how do you prep a condo for a dinner date?

"What are you talking about?" I say.

"Well," Alice says, as though the answer's obvious, "you can't invite a woman to dinner at a place that looks like *this*."

"Absolutely not." Stacy shakes her head.

"Any woman in her right mind would run for the hills," Aunt Alfresca says.

I look around my humble abode.

"What's wrong with this place?" I ask.

I look at Sam for support, but she just shrugs, clueless. "I don't see anything wrong with it," she says.

"Try *everything*," Alice says.

"*Everything*?" I echo. "Isn't that a little extreme?"

"Not even close to being extreme," Alice says. "The paint job, the furniture, the lighting fixtures—everything's got to go."

"What's wrong with the paint job?" I feel particularly sensitive about this. I mean, paint: it's who I am. And now it's like she's telling me it's who I'm not, like telling a surgeon he just removed the wrong organ. Paint is one thing I know. Maybe Alice is right about everything else, but she's got to be wrong about this.

"It's not the *job*. It's the colors. You need colors that will say, 'I'm not just a guy who regards where I live like it's a large dorm room, a way station to some more important place in life that I may never get to. I'm a guy who knows how to make anywhere I live a home. I'm strong, sturdy, sensitive, fun and I know how to make a mean shrimp scampi.' Actually, I was going to say beef bourguignon—you know, the whole Julia Child craze; if you made her beef bourguignon, she'd be naked before dessert—but I know how you feel about meat."

I'm speechless. I mean, I always knew paint made a statement, of course I did, but I always thought it made one statement per color, not this smorgasbord that Alice is describing. How could

I have been so wrong about something so essential to my being?

"Seriously?" I say. "The right paint color can say all that?"

"Well, not on its own," Alice concedes. "That's an awful lot to expect from a single color. But when combined with the right furniture choices—tasteful pieces that don't say, 'This is here because I watch so much sports on TV'—and the right accessories…"

Alice proceeds to take me on a tour of my own home.

Of the main floor bathroom, she says, "You need a soap dispenser here. Every time I come over here and use the bathroom, I wonder, 'How am I supposed to wash my hands? This guy doesn't believe in soap.'"

In the kitchen, she says, "Paper towels are fine for spills but they're not meant to be used for everything. You need real napkins for when you eat and dishtowels. Some soap would be good in here too. Consider getting a scourer that doesn't look like you've had it for ten years. That thing is gross, Johnny."

She shows me how none of the rugs I have are any good ("Seriously? A football-shaped area carpet with 'Go, Jets!' on it? How old are you again?") and how all the things hung on the walls have to go ("Try to think beyond poster art. I know it will be hard for you, but just try.")

Her suggestions for my bedroom—"just in case"—are so extensive, I feel compelled to take notes.

And then we get to the basement.

"Really? I've got to do the basement too?"

"Everything," Alice says firmly. "What if she comes down here for some reason? It'll be awful for her after seeing what you're going to do with the rest of the place—everything being all normal and then discovering this. It'll be like in *Psycho* when they look in the basement and there's skeleton Mom in her housedress."

Alice looks around the room. "The sports memorabilia? Outta here. The dogs-playing-poker painting? Outta here. The chandelier with all the hula girls for lights?"

"Not the chandelier with all the hula girls for lights!" Steve interjects. "But I love that thing!"

Much as I love that thing too, even I can see that a woman might not appreciate its appeal.

"I get it," I say. "Outta here. I suppose next you're going to tell me that the pool table's gotta go too?"

Alice considers this one. "Nah, the pool table can stay. It's the right kind of manly. You know, Paul Newman, *Color of Money* and everything. But everything else?"

"I get it," I say again. "Outta here."

We all troop back upstairs. And as I'm trooping, I'm thinking of all the things I have to do before I can invite Helen over for dinner, before I can kick things up a notch. Who knew a guy had to do so much, *change* so much, just to get the girl?

"Thanks for all the help," I tell Alice once we're back in the living room.

"Don't thank me. I'm doing it for me, not you."

"How's that?"

"The way I figure it, the happier you are in your world, the less I have to see you in mine."

"Oh. Well, whatever the reason, thanks anyway."

"One other thing," Alice says.

"Hmm?"

"You need to get a cat."

"A cat?"

"Women love cats."

"Word," Billy says. "A cat is the way to any woman's heart."

"I am *not* getting a cat," I vow.

"And that Christmas tree," Alice says. "It's June. That thing's got to go or she'll think you're a freak."

"Really? The Christmas tree?"

"You said you were leaving it up until something good happens," Sam says.

"True."

"So maybe you meeting someone you like enough to have over for a dinner you're actually going to prepare is that good thing?"

"Aren't we ever going to have cake?" Big John says.

Extreme Makeover

"Throw pillows, Johnny? Really?" Sam says.

"I know, right? But they're on The List."

The List is a sheet Alice foisted on me, things she felt I needed to get to properly decorate my place so Helen will find me to be the perfect male, and Sam and me are in Home Goods.

"So what do you think?" I start holding up pillows for Sam's inspection. "The red? The green? The gold?"

"Definitely not the red. With the new green couch it'll look too much like Christmas or something, like you're obsessed with the holiday, like you're the kind of guy who leaves his Christmas tree up for months after the fact just waiting for something good to happen—like, you know, a freak."

"Thanks a lot."

"And not the green either. It's the wrong green. It'll clash with the couch."

"So the gold then?'

"Definitely."

"Velvet stripes, braided cord or plain silk with tassels?"

"I can't believe we're having this conversation."

"I know, right? Still, velvet stripes, brai—"

"All three. I don't know much about decorating, but I'm fairly certain that since people always talk about 'throw pillows' plural, not 'throw pillow' singular, if you don't get at least three you'll look like you don't really know what you're doing, plus chintzy."

"Thanks, that actually sounds like good advice."

I wrap my arms around all three pillows, which takes some doing.

"You know," Sam says, picking up one of the red ones,

"maybe I should pick up a couple of these. In case I get lucky this weekend."

"What's going on this weekend? Did I miss something?"

Well, did I? I have been pretty obsessed with the Helen situation lately. Wars could start and end, even crazier stuff could happen like, I don't know, Big John and Aunt Alfresca falling in love, and it would all totally zoom right over my head.

"No, you didn't miss anything," Sam says, "because I didn't say anything about it before. I was kind of worried you'd laugh at me."

"Oh, good. I get a chance to laugh at you for a change? I definitely want to hear this."

"I've decided to try speed-dating."

Sam waits.

"You're not laughing," Sam says.

"Maybe because I don't think it's funny. Worrisome, maybe, but not funny."

"Why worrisome?"

"I don't know. Isn't it a little shallow, interviewing a whole bunch of people in rapid succession in the hopes of finding a spark?"

"Nah, I'm thinking more like it's super-efficient. I'll be able to talk to forty women in two hours. Normally it'd take me forty separate trips to the bar to accomplish so much. I'm getting older. I've done slow dating and that hasn't worked out for me, so I figure why not try something with a little speed? And if I have nothing to show for it at the end of the night, I will have wasted only one night, not forty."

"When you put it like that, it sounds like an eminently sensible idea."

"You're still not laughing at me? Why are you not laughing at me about this?"

"Who am I to judge? I'm holding a bunch of throw pillows I neither want nor need and yet will buy anyway in the hopes of creating an impressive enough total package to wow one woman."

"Yeah, I've kind of been meaning to talk to you about that,"

Sam says as she gathers her own set of three throw pillows.

We head toward the registers at the front of the store.

"It's just this whole thing," Sam says, "all of it. Changing your name to John, getting a new wardrobe, reading books on relationships and dating, buying throw pillows—isn't it a bit much? It's like you're erasing the real you and replacing it with someone entirely different all to impress one person. What happens if it doesn't work out? Do you get rid of the throw pillows and put the hula girl chandelier back up? Or what if it does work out—do you go on being someone who's not really you for the rest of your life?"

Sam's making too much of this.

"You're making too much of this," I say. "It's just surface stuff. It doesn't change who I am at core. It's like slapping a fresh coat of paint on something. Don't get me wrong. You know how much I love paint. But paint doesn't alter the foundation of a structure. I'm still me under it all. And anyway, it's not like the old me was doing so well. And anyway, part two, you're buying the throw pillows too."

Score! Sam doesn't have a comeback for that last item. A momentarily comeback-less Sam—if I was smart I'd be worried about this state of affairs.

We get to the registers and wait in line holding our pillows. We wait and wait until eventually we're up next. As I'm putting my pillows on the checkout counter and the young guy behind the register starts scanning my items, Sam turns to me.

"Oh, and before you even bother asking? I know I kissed you and everything but I will *not* have sex with you just so you can test out if you're doing it right in case you get a chance with Helen."

In every person's life there's at least one moment where they're having a personal conversation and it's just fine because there's plenty of background noise to camouflage their words, but then the noise disappears just as the most awkward thing gets said.

I turn to the lady behind us in line who's looking at me like I'm some kind of freak then back to the young guy behind the register who's looking at me like I'm some kind of god, and I realize this is my moment.

"Gee, thanks, Sam. Do you think maybe you could have saved that little pronouncement for when we were alone?"

Sam shrugs. "I had to get it out of the way."

"Throw pillows?" the young guy behind the register asks me earnestly. "I used to think they were just girly. But do you think maybe I should get a few? Maybe I could get more random chicks to make out with me that way, you know, even if they won't have sex with me as a test-run for someone else?"

"Go for it," I advise. "Knock yourself out."

Sam rolls her eyes. "So," she says, "what's next on The List?"

"I don't know." I pull the crumpled sheet out of my pocket, run my eyes to the bottom of the page. "You want to help me find a cat?"

Who knew *The Penny-Saver* was such a useful publication? It helped me find a place to take Helen on our date to the circus, which led us to the carnival, which led us to the single best kiss of my life atop the Ferris wheel, and now it's helping me find a cat.

"Which one should we check out first?" I ask Sam, looking over the listings.

"*First?* What do you think, we're going to drive all over Danbury like we're house-hunting or something, interviewing various feline applicants?"

"I'll take that as a 'we're just going to one place and take whatever they have'?"

"Precisely. Here's one. *Free, six adorable kittens in need of good home.*"

"But I don't need six. I only need one."

"What are you, stupid? We look at the six and pick out the one you like best. How hard can it be?"

"But it says 'good home,' not 'homes.' Clearly whoever placed the ad is looking to have all the kittens adopted at once."

"Oh, for Christ sake, Johnny, just get in the truck and drive."

• • •

In fact, it turns out to be very hard. Or maybe 'hard' isn't the right way to put it. Maybe 'not what the ad led me to expect.' I phoned ahead from the truck so they'd know we were coming, but when we arrive a little girl answers the door. She's wearing overalls with a light blue T-shirt underneath, her dirty blond hair in two pigtails on either side of her head. She's maybe six, eight, ten. Who really knows with little kids? It's not like they come with a badge or something.

"Wait here," she says grimly as we stand on the stoop, then she shuts the door in our faces.

"You ever think about having kids?" I ask Sam.

"Not as a rule."

"Me neither, but, I don't know. They're kind of cool, like little people or something."

A minute later the little girl comes back with a basket and she steps outside, shutting the door behind her. Inside the basket, two kittens are curled up asleep. One is all black and nicely masculine looking. The other is a powder puff of gray and white.

When you think about it, it's not much of a selection.

"Can we see the other four?" I ask.

"No," the little girl says.

"How come? The ad said you had six." Is she hiding them from us?

"The others are gone. You have to choose from these."

"Is there an adult we can talk to about this? Perhaps your mom or your dad?"

"No. I'm in charge of the cats. You have to choose from these."

She waves the basket closer to us, causing Sam to take a step back.

"They look so...cat-like," Sam says.

"Don't you like cats?" I say. "Alice says all women love cats."

"I like them in theory," Sam says.

"You can't have either of them," the little girl says, pulling the basket back. "I can't possibly let the kittens go to someone who won't love them properly."

"Oh no!" I say, feeling a weird sense of panic. Suddenly I *need* to have one of these kittens. I point to Sam with my thumb. "She doesn't live with me. She's just my friend, along for the ride. The kitten would be living with me." I make a decision to lay it on thick, forcing a super-bright smile. "I *love* kittens."

"What do you love about them?"

Geez, I wasn't expecting to be challenged like that.

"Well…" You know, when you've never owned a cat before, this stuff isn't so easy to come up with. "They're mysterious and, um, soft, and if you've got cold feet they'll sit on them for you. Stuff like that."

The little girl narrows her eyes at me. "Do you have references?"

"References?" What the—

"References. You know, papers, written recommendations…"

"No, he doesn't have anything like that," Sam says with no small degree of exasperation. "Who brings stuff like that to get a free kitten?"

The little girl casts an evil eye upon Sam, the cat hater.

"People who want pets should be properly prepared," she informs us. "And it shouldn't matter if it's free."

"Fine," Sam says. "I'm his letter of recommendation. I can vouch for him completely. He's gainfully employed, owns his own business in fact, and is more than capable of paying to support a kitten."

"But will he love it?" the little girl asks.

"Yes," Sam vows on my behalf. "He will love it."

"I guess that's OK then," the little girl says grudgingly. "Now go to the pet store and buy everything you need, then you can come back and pick out your kitten."

"Everything I need?"

"Yes. You know: cat food, cat toys, a scratching post, a litter box, a water dish and a food dish your new pet can be proud of. You didn't buy any of that stuff in advance, did you?"

"Well, no."

"I didn't think so," she says like she knew the answer to her question all along. She sighs a sad, weary sigh. "No one ever does." She heads back to the house, shaking her head at a world where people think they can just go get whatever they want without doing the proper preparation first.

I always thought that if and when I ever did make the commitment to get a pet, it'd be a dog, preferably a big one. And now here I am, about to get a cat, something I never in a million years pictured myself doing. I think it must be what it's like for people having kids. There you are, expecting a boy, and suddenly a girl pops out in the delivery room. It's not so much that it's a bad thing as that it's drastically different than what you were expecting, how you thought your life was going to turn out.

Now I picture that black cat and I'm thinking maybe this won't be so bad. It's not a dog, but I could live with that cat.

Despite that back at the little girl's house Sam revealed a previously unglimpsed aversion to cats, she proves very helpful at the pet store. I remember the basic stuff the little girl said to get—the food, the litter box, the special dishes for the food and water—but it's Sam who remembers about the scratching post and the cat toys, piling up a wide selection of the latter on the counter. Sam even thinks to get a collar with a nametag for in case the kitten gets lost.

"Good call," I say. "The little girl didn't say anything about that stuff but if we went back there without it, no doubt she'd send us to the pet store again."

I'm getting ready to pay when I see something behind the counter that grabs my attention.

"Can I get one of those too, please?" I ask the guy behind the counter.

"Which one you want?"

"Doesn't matter, just so long as it's sturdy."

The guy brings down the item and places it on the counter next to the rest of my stuff. "So you're getting a cat *and* a dog?" he says.

"No, just the cat."

"Then what do you want a leash for?"

"The cat. So I can take it for walks."

"People don't usually—"

"Don't even bother," Sam cuts him off. "He's probably got this whole thing pictured in his head: him walking down the street, his cool new sleek black cat on the leash strutting by his side, maybe the two of them popping into the neighborhood bar for an ice cold beer for him and a saucer of milk for his furry little friend."

Really? Am I that transparent?

The guy breaks out in a wide smile. "Man, that's the coolest thing I've ever heard. I never thought to do that with a cat before. Maybe I should get one."

"The Home Goods guy's going to get throw pillows because of you," Sam says, "now this guy's going to get a cat so he can take it to the bar because of you. You're like the Pied Piper of weirdness. Just what is it with you and guys?"

"I don't know. Are you ready to go back and see the Cat Cop?"

Back at the little girl's house, she goes through our items one by one as we stand on her lawn.

"Cat food, cat toys…" She looks at me. "I forgot to tell you to get a collar and nametag." Her look turns triumphant now. "I'm sure you didn't think—"

"Oh, yes we did." It's Sam's turn to look triumphant as she produces the items from the bag.

The girl, unruffled by being so flagrantly wrong about us, sticks her hand back in the bag. "What's this?" she asks, waving the leash at me like a narc who's just found a baggie in my glove compartment.

"It's for my neighbor," I lie quickly. I'm not sure why my immediate instinct is to lie. I just know somehow in my heart that if she knows the leash is for the cat she'll never let me take him.

"Your neighbor needs a leash?"

"For his dog. He asked me to get a leash for his dog. His broke."

"When did he ask?"

"Well, let's see, he knew we were coming here to look at kittens so he must have figured that if we saw one we liked we'd need to go to the pet store and get stuff, so, yeah, that's when he asked."

Geez, for someone who prides himself on his ability to think up loopholes for criminals on TV, I don't do so good when it's my own neck on the line.

The little girl studies me for a long moment, no doubt trying to find which part of my story to pounce on first, but there are so many possibilities for that, after a minute she appears to just give up.

"Fine," she says. "I'll go get your cat."

A minute later she's back with the gray and white puffball. She holds it out to me. I swear the thing must still be sleeping, the way it just hangs there in her hands.

"I'm sorry," I say as tactfully as possible, "but I thought I'd get the black cat."

"You didn't say anything about that before."

"I know, but—"

"You can't have the black cat."

"Are you sure there's not some adult I can—"

"No."

"Well, did you give the black cat away to someone else in the hour since we were here last?" Two can play at *this* interrogation game.

"That's none of your business. Do you want a cat or don't you? If you want a cat, if you want one of *my* cats, you have to take this one."

Oh, Christ. Do I want a kitten this badly? That thing is such a *girly* cat.

"You've already bought all the stuff," Sam says, as though reading my thoughts. "Might as well. It's not like I'm going to go through this with you again at any other houses."

"Fine," I tell the little girl. "I'll take it."

"Excellent selection," she says, placing the cat in my arms. "Oh, and one other thing."

"I don't keep guns in the house. The kitten will be safe."

"What?" She's puzzled, shakes it off. "No, the kitten's name. I forgot to tell you its name. It's Fluffy."

Fluffy?

"OK, um, that's good," I say. "But I was thinking I'd rename it to something"—*anything*—"else."

"You can't. If you won't agree to call it Fluffy, you'll have to give it back. How would you like it if you had one name for a while and then someone else just randomly changed it on you?"

"Yeah," Sam says, "how would you like it?"

"That already happened to me," I say, "when I went from Johnny to John, at least with certain people."

"I hardly think that's the same thing," Sam sniffs. Geez, now the two of them are in league together. What is it with women? No matter what their age…

"Do you swear?" the little girl asks.

"What?"

"Do you swear not to change Fluffy's name to anything else?"

"Yes, I swear," I say, figuring there was no harm in lying about my nonexistent male neighbor needing a leash for his dog so surely there's no harm in lying about this. Just let me get out of here with this cat.

"Pinky swear?" the little girl insists, holding out her pinky.

Shit. Now she wants to bind me to a solemn oath? A person can't lie in a solemn oath. Shit.

I hold out my pinky, entwine it with hers. "Pinky swear," I vow.

And now I am bound.

The Dinner Guest

"I can't believe how good you look—you look *amazing!*"

No, I did not just direct those words at Helen, although I'm sure when she does get here she'll look even more amazing. I directed them at Sam, who's stopped by on her way out for Lesbian Speed-Dating.

"I didn't know you could wear dresses," I say. "I thought it was against your religion or something."

"You don't think it's too much?" she asks, twirling in a circle as she holds the skirt of her dress out. The dress is sleeveless with skinny straps, close-fitting through the waist but with a flared skirt, the fabric something rich-looking like a satin or a silk, the color a vivid dark red. Sam's bare legs are already tan in preparation for the summer just around the corner and on her feet are high-heeled sandals with lots of straps. No wonder she had me paint her toenails dark red last night.

"Not too much at all," I say. "If you weren't my best friend and a lesbian, I'd do you."

"Thanks." She stops twirling, looks around. "You ready for the big date?"

"Ready as I'll ever be. Just putting on a few finishing touches."

Sam cocks her head. "Who's that you're listening to on the stereo?"

"Michael Bubble."

"I'm pretty sure his name isn't Bubble. It's Michael Bublé, pronounced boob-lay."

"Yeah, that guy. Alice told me to get him. She says the chicks love him, say he's the new Frank Sinatra."

"I don't know," she says. "I'm pretty sure the old Frank Sinatra was just fine without being renovated. Hey, are those real flowers on the dining room table?"

I look where she's looking. In the middle of the new dining room table, which is set with the dinnerware I bought earlier in the day at Pier 1 Imports, is the new crystal vase I also bought there. In the vase is a multicolored arrangement of long-stemmed flowers.

"Yeah, they're real. Alice's idea. Ponies, I think she called them."

"Peonies," Sam corrects. "Huh, that's a nice touch. I never would have thought to put fresh flowers in my place just because someone special's coming over. Oh, and look, you've even put a little green bow on Fluffy."

Fluffy's on the couch, sleeping, which is mostly all that Fluffy ever does. That, and go to the bathroom and eat. I'm told babies are like that too.

"Yeah, Fluffy's pretty excited about our big night," I say.

"So what did you finally decide to make for dinner?"

"Some shrimp dish. Aunt Alfresca gave me the recipe."

Sam sniffs the air. "I don't smell anything. Helen's due any time now and you haven't started cooking yet?"

"I figured I'd wait until she got here. I want it to be as fresh as possible."

"Have you ever made this recipe before?"

"No, but how hard can it be? Aunt Alfresca always says that any idiot can follow a recipe. She says if you can read you can cook."

"I can't believe how good you look—you look *amazing*!"

This time it really is Helen. She's not wearing a fancy dress like Sam had on. Really, there's nothing fancy about it at all—just white capris and a green and blue blouse in this floaty fabric. Still...

"I mean, of course I can believe how good you look," I go on, because I don't want her to think she doesn't always look good. "You always look good. I just meant—"

Stop yourself, Johnny. You're just a few words shy of being

a horse's ass.

But Helen doesn't seem to notice, just offers the bottle she's been holding in her hands.

"You didn't say what you were making," she says, "so I just brought a Malbec. This one's from Argentina."

"That's terrific. I love a Malbec."

I've never had a Malbec. I don't even know what one is although from the shape of the bottle I'm guessing it's wine. Hell, I don't even know where Argentina is right now, I'm so happy to be looking at Helen, so excited and nervous that she's here.

"Oh. You have a cat."

"You could call it that. Mostly it's just a furball that sleeps a lot. Do you want to pet him?"

"No, thanks. Maybe later. Does he have a name?"

"Fluffy."

"That's kind of a funny name for a boy cat."

"It is, isn't it?" I never really thought of that until she just pointed it out. Since getting Fluffy, mostly I've just thought how absurd it is for a man my age to have to call any cat that. But I did pinky swear. "And there's a funny story behind that name. But maybe I'll save that story for another time. After all, I have to retain some air of mystery, don't I?"

Now where the hell did that come from?

But Helen doesn't seem to notice my penchant for the occasional bizarre statement.

"Here," I say. "Let me put that wine in the kitchen and open it. It needs to breathe first, right?" I'm sure I've read that about wine before. Wine is unlike beer which you just open and, thank God, drink right away. "Then I'll take you on a quick tour of the place."

The quick tour—another suggestion from Alice. She says women love quick tours, that sometimes they like nothing better than going to a new person's home and looking around at all their stuff. Go figure.

• • •

The quick tour goes by fairly quickly since there's not a whole lot to show her. Alice said I should leave out the second-story portion of the tour, which would involve the master bedroom, second bedroom and upstairs bathroom, since showing Helen the master bedroom might be regarded as presumptuous. This leaves us with really just the main floor.

It's amazing how much you can do in a week if you set your mind to it. Since the party here for Big John's birthday, in addition to acquiring throw pillows and a cat, I've also repainted the whole place. I selected a different shade of green for each room—Helen's favorite color—so that now it's like eternal springtime in here all the time.

"Wow," Helen says, "all this green. It's like eternal springtime in here."

Exactly the effect I was striving for. Too bad I can't come right out and ask her, but I'm hoping she was impressed with the little shell-shaped soaps Alice told me to put in the little bathroom between the living room and dining room.

"So that's the whole place," I say. "Well, except for the upstairs and the basement."

"Is it a finished basement?"

"Sure. You want to see it?" I ask magnanimously. I've no longer got anything to hide.

Figuring the wine has breathed for long enough, I pour us each a glass—thank you, Pier 1 Imports, for giving me something with which to replace my old collection of NFL glassware, the only glassware I used to own—and lead her downstairs.

"A pool table," she says, running her hand along the baize.

I can't tell if she likes it or not.

"You play?" I ask.

She shrugs. "A bit."

I take a sip of the wine. Not bad for a drink that's not beer.

"Do you want to shoot a game before dinner?" I offer.

Another shrug. "I guess."

I still can't tell if she's enthusiastic or not as she begins to rack the balls. I do notice she racks them perfectly, just like I would do it.

"Would you like to break or should I?" I say.

There's that shrug again. "Either way is good."

Sam's a good shooter but hates to break, and I've noticed other women are often like this too, so I figure I'll do Helen a favor and do the honors so she doesn't scratch on the first shot.

The break is clean, sinking a solid and a stripe. Stripes are definitely the easier game with this spread, so I go for a solid, not wanting to run the table on her. But there's a lot of green on the seven ball and it caroms off the edge of the pocket.

Then Helen surprises me by also going for the more difficult game with solids, tapping in the seven I just missed. And then in a methodical blaze of pool shooting she sinks the other six remaining solids before double-banking the eight clean for the win.

To say I'm dumbstruck is to put it mildly. I don't know what to do with this new information about Helen.

"Wow," I say finally. "I guess you really do play a bit."

"All those older brothers." She shrugs again as she replaces the cue stick in the wall rack. "It was either learn or be laughed at all the time, but it's not exactly my favorite thing to do."

Suddenly I feel like I can't get a read on this woman. To do a thing so well, as well as she just shot that game, and yet I still can't tell whether she enjoyed herself or not, whether she even likes the game at all.

"I'll tell you one thing," I say, "if you're that good at something that's not your favorite thing to do, I'd love to be there to see you do something that is your favorite thing."

Immediately recognizing the oddness of what I've just said, rather than wait for another shrug, I offer, "Din-din? You ready?"

Upstairs, I leave Helen comfortably ensconced on the new living room sofa with Fluffy in the corner and Michael Bublé on the stereo while I go into the tiny kitchen to start the prep work for dinner. Alice told me to get a brass magazine rack for the living room to store magazines and newspapers so there should be plenty for Helen to entertain herself with in the way of reading material while I'm slicing and dicing. I thought to lay in a supply of gender-neutral periodicals, like *Fortune* and *Architectural Digest*, while taking my issues of *Sports Illustrated* and hiding it in the dryer in the laundry room. And of course I left the day's *New York Times* in the rack as well so she'll know I'm down with the paper of record. But even when you think you've thought of everything, there's always one thing left to trip you up…

I'm in the process of chopping parsley when Helen comes into the kitchen, extending a section of the *Times* toward me.

"What's this?" she asks.

Oh, shit. It's the Sports section and it's folded open to page four, a preview of tomorrow's Mets game. A person doesn't have to be a D.A. to deduce that if the Sports section is folded open, the person whose home in which the folded-open Sports section is currently residing must have been reading something in it.

When I don't immediately respond—I'm too busy doing that deer-in-the-headlights thing—D.A. Helen Troy proceeds casually with, "I thought that you said you weren't interested in sports at all? How come you're reading about the Mets?"

"I wasn't reading about the Mets," I say hurriedly. *Think fast, Johnny.* "I just try to be a really well-rounded person. While I'm mostly interested in the front section of the paper, I look over at least one thing in every section—you know, Business, Arts & Leisure, even Sunday Styles, just in case Mom jeans for men come back into style when I'm not looking—so naturally I have to look over at least one thing in Sports too. You know, to be really well-rounded."

"So what's the one thing you look over, if you say you're not interested in sports at all? I mean, you're not spending time reading whole articles on something you're completely uninterested in, are you?"

"No, of course not." *Think faster, Johnny!* "What crazy person would do such a thing? The one thing I look at in the Sports section is"—*think faster than you've ever thought in your life, Johnny!*—"is those cute little round things they put at the top of the articles."

"Excuse me? The cute little round things?"

"Yeah, here, let me show you." I take the paper from her. "See, here at the top of this article—what's this article about? Oh yeah, it looks like it's about the Mets. Do you see that little round thing?"

"Oh, you mean this blue circle thing that's got," she pauses for a second, "what I guess must be a Mets logo inside it?"

"Exactly. They do this for all the teams, no matter what the sport. In this case they're doing it for the Mets and, see there, there's another one in a different color. That must be the team the Mets are playing against. I can't quite make out what their logo stands for." Like I don't know who the Mets are playing tomorrow. Sheesh. The lies I am willing to tell.

"And that's all you look at the Sports section for? The cute little round things?"

"Well, sure. It helps me because at least then I'm familiar with all the team names, so that when I'm with the guys I can be sports-literate and not saying things like, 'Who are the Mets?' Plus, you gotta admit, those logos are cute, right?"

"Yes. Yes, they are, the way the paper does them. Also round."

"Exactly." She's getting it. I can't believe how relieved that makes me feel. "Now if you don't mind." I gesture at the chopping board—thank you, Pier 1 Imports. "I kind of want dinner to be a surprise when I'm finished."

Oh, it's a surprise all right.

It takes me a while to figure out where things went wrong. All I know at first is that as soon as I remove the lid from the top of the blender, an onion cloud wafts out, suffusing my entire condo.

"John?" Helen calls out, coughing a bit on the fumes. "Is everything OK in there? Fluffy woke up and he looks scared."

"Everything's fine!" I call back. "Everything's moving along just perfectly!" Everything is not just fine. Nothing is moving along perfectly, I think, as I cover my nose and mouth with a dishrag and grab the blender by the handle.

I take a colander and toss it in the sink and toss the pre-cooked shrimp into that. I can't serve the shrimp with this green sauce directly on it—it's probably lethal—but I can't just serve the shrimp plain over rice. What can I tell Helen? "Ooh, look, I made you pre-cooked shrimp with rice?" Maybe if I just pour the stuff in the blender over the shrimp but then drain the sauce away through the colander, the shrimp will pick up an interesting flavor without being toxic?

So I do that but as I'm looking at it in the colander with the sauce covering it now starting to drain, I realize this is no good either. If anything, the smell is getting worse. I open the window over the sink, tighten the dishrag on my nose and mouth, and turn on the cold water in the sink to wash the sauce off. Maybe this will—

"What's going on in here?" Helen says, walking into the kitchen. Immediately, she's struck by the onion cloud, causing her to take a step back. But she's a kind woman and after the initial olfactory assault, she forces herself to step toward me. "Can I help somehow?"

"I'm just trying to salvage dinner," I say. "But it looks like that's not going to happen."

"I'm sure it's fine," Helen says. Before I can stop her, she reaches into the colander, grabs a shrimp and pops it into her mouth. Immediately, both hands go to her mouth as though she's too polite and she's stopping herself from spitting the shrimp in my face.

"Is it that bad?" I ask.

Her eyes, peeking out over hands that make her look like a veiled woman, have pity in them as she nods yes.

"Here, let me see," I say, figuring I can't let her suffer this alone, whatever this is. I grab a rinsed shrimp, pop it bravely into my mouth, and...

"Oh my God!" I say after forcing myself to swallow. "That's the worst thing I've ever eaten in my life!"

"It wasn't that bad," Helen says.

"Oh no, it was, it really was." I hand her my dishrag so

she can protect her own nose and mouth. I deserve to suffer after this.

"What was that supposed to be anyway?"

"It's this special recipe." I hand her the recipe. "Well, maybe not so special. Aunt Alfresca gave it to me. She says anyone can cook, that if you can read you can cook."

Helen's looking at the recipe. "It looks fine. What did you put in that blender? Two scallions shouldn't have done all this."

"Two scallions? But it says green onions."

"Scallions are green onions."

"Oh. Oh!"

"John, what did you buy instead of scallions?"

"I couldn't decide which was right—a leek with all those long leaves attached or a big white onion that was showing some green on the edges, like maybe it wasn't wholly ripe yet—so I went with one of each."

"You do realize that two green onions, aka scallions, would be substantially smaller in size than that?"

"I do now."

"And then you did what the recipe says to do with those two smaller green onions?"

"Yes, I put the large white onion and the leek with all those long green leaves into the blender and hit puree."

She's out of questions to ask.

"I'm sorry," I say. "I wanted it to be special but I guess Aunt Alfresca's theory is wrong. I can read but I can't cook."

"When you look at it one way, this is pretty funny."

"Well, maybe if we were two people hearing about this as opposed to two people who are standing here in the middle of it."

"You were trying to impress me."

You don't know the half of it, I think.

"That's incredibly sweet."

Wait a second here. Is this onion-cloud incident working in my favor and earning me points?

"Yeah, well…" I'm not sure what to do with a woman who appreciates my charms. "Why don't I throw open a few more windows, order up a pizza and then while we're waiting for it to arrive, we can go for a walk, give the air in here a chance to clear?"

As we walk along the sidewalks of the condo in the orange-purple light of the dying day, I have one hand holding Helen's hand while with the other I hold Fluffy's leash.

"I've never seen anyone take a cat for a walk like this before," she says.

"People told me it couldn't be done," I say. "But I figured, what's the point in having a pet if you can't take it for a walk?"

"Was it difficult to get the cat not to mind the leash?"

"Nah. Well, maybe at first. But he likes it now. You can tell."

"How?"

"He's not hissing at me. Anytime a creature doesn't hiss at me, I figure we're doing OK. Who knows? Maybe it's love."

Helen doesn't say anything to this.

We just walk and for once I don't feel as though I need to fill the silence with talk, with *chatter*. She's here and she's her. I'm here and I'm me—well, at least the modified version of me I am when I'm with her. And Fluffy's, well…yeah. But it's good; wonderful, in fact. It's not ten-on-the-Richter scale excitement of the heart-pounding sort, like when your team wins the World Series or something; not that I have any recent memories of what that feels like. The Mets haven't won in twenty-four years. I wasn't even in double digits back then. And it's not all-through-your-major-arteries nerves, if there is such a thing, like that first night when I took her to the Barn Opera. This is just, I guess the word for it would be *companionable*. And right now companionable feels incredibly *nice*.

I don't want the perfect silence to end, but the pizza guy should be here soon and I did promise Helen dinner. If I'm lucky, someday I'll get another chance at this perfect silence.

• • •

Back home, the smell from the onion cloud has not dissipated one iota. Well, OK, maybe one iota, but certainly not two. And yet Helen doesn't seem to mind and suddenly I don't mind either. The pizza guy knocks pretty much the instant we're back inside. I pay him, take the box, and as I close the door on him and turn, Helen takes the box from me and places it on the table by the door—thank you, Pier 1 Imports. And then she's up on her toes, kissing me, and I'm leaning down, kissing her, and her lips are soft, still tasting of that Malbec, and I'm thinking I could get used to the taste of that wine, and then I'm not thinking at all, not worried about doing things wrong, not worried about doing things right, not worried about what I might get out of this or who I'll be afterward, who I'll be if it ever disappears on me.

For the first time since I've met her, articles of clothing are dropping like flies, and everything's fast and slow at the same time, Michael Bublé's still singing, Fluffy's purring, there's an onion smell over everything, thank God someone's got a condom, throw pillows are working out to my advantage, and what we're doing is no longer physical activity performed by isolated body parts. It's *adjectives*. Amazing. Gentle. Exhilarating. Beautiful. Lovely. Exquisite. Cataclysmic. Heartfelt. Zingy.

Finally, in the end, with the onion smell still persistently there, it is a *noun*. It is the true onset of something I've never felt before for a woman, not in a romantic way, never like this.

And that thing I'm feeling, that *noun*, I'm pretty sure it goes by the name *love*.

All-Star Game

Things progress with Helen for several weeks without a hitch and before I know it, we're in the middle of summer, it's July, it's time for the All-Star Game, only instead of watching with Sam and Big John and some of my other friends like I always do, Sam's going to a cookout with Lily, the third two-minute date she had on the night she went Lesbian Speed-Dating; after they each had thirty-seven other two-minute dates they looked around until they found one another again and have mostly been happily seeing each other ever since. As for me, I'm also going to a cookout.

At Helen's parents' house.

Where I'm to meet her parents for the first time plus her extended family.

Please allow me to convert to Judaism right now so that I can authentically say, *Oy vey*.

At least the weather's nice, I think, as I park on the street outside the house at the address Helen gave me. I'd park in the drive but it's packed with SUVs.

I'm barely out of the truck, checking my khaki shorts for creases, when Helen comes running over. Instead of looking like the woman in her thirties that she is, when she runs like that, hair gathered back into a ponytail, she looks like she could be sixteen.

"Ready to meet everybody?" she says, grabbing my hand.

"Hang on," I say, reaching my free hand into the truck and producing a bouquet of wildflowers.

"For me?" she says.

"For your mom," I say.

She smiles wide. "Nice touch."

Thank you, Alice.

Every person's life comes with its own cast of characters, like a movie or a book. God knows I've got a real cast of characters in mine.

Helen's cast, I learn, as she leads me around from person to person at the cookout, consists of the following:

Frank and Marlene Troy, the parents. Frank gives me a salute with a spatula from his position behind the barbecue grill. He's an imposing figure in his late sixties, tall enough to have played basketball in high school and still in really good shape. He does not seem to mind that he's wearing an apron that says "Kiss the cook." I neglect to kiss him, contenting myself with a firm handshake.

It was Aunt Alfresca who taught me the importance of a good grip. "Don't shake limply," she'd say. "No one wants to shake a baccala nor can you trust a man who shakes like that." A baccala is a salted cod and it's easy to understand why no one would want to shake one. I don't even know why anyone would want to eat one!

Marlene, happy to receive the flowers, looks like if you took a picture of Helen's face and used some kind of computer imaging to project what it will look like thirty some-odd years into the future. Not that I've met many of my girlfriends' mothers—in fact, the last time was so far in the past, I can't even remember it right now—but when you do it can be eerie, leaving you with the horrifying thought, "Oh my God, is this what I've got to look forward to?" But meeting Marlene isn't like that. Instead, it makes me feel: I hope I'm still around Helen in thirty-plus years, still there to see as each beautiful line etches into her face, still there to make her laugh at some stupid thing I said or smile over a bouquet of flowers so those lines crinkle.

I'd been dreading meeting Helen's brothers—five brothers to navigate at once!—but I'm glad that's next because it's keeping me from going totally sappy and getting tears in my eyes, which is what looking at Helen's mother and longing for the future's got me doing.

The brothers. Those five brothers.

I don't know why I'm so nervous about this. This should be the easiest part of the day. I mean, we are talking about me here, and I am not unaware of how groups of guys normally react to me. But of course I know why I'm so nervous. I'm so nervous because this is Helen's brothers we're talking about.

This time it actually matters.

Even though it can be intimidating to meet a whole group of people all at once, usually it's fairly straightforward. The people you're supposed to meet line up or they stand around you in a circle like they're the Colosseum and you're the Christian slave about to be eaten by lions. With the Troy family, it's not that easy. It's not easy because the brothers are all playing tag football on the lawn with various nieces and nephews, meaning Helen points each out to me, yells the brother's name across the lawn, something like, "Hey, X! This is John!" Then whichever brother it is yells, "Hey, John! Good to know you!" back and returns to playing.

In descending order, the brothers are: Frankie, the oldest in his mid-forties, followed by Sammy, Dougie, Jerry and the youngest, just a year older than Helen, Johnny.

"Good thing you go by John," Johnny calls to me. "Otherwise things could get confusing around here."

I wonder what Sam and Big John would have to say about all those names. With the Troy family, the whole E-sound thing is like a rampant epidemic.

The kids all have various names but none of them registers and neither do the names of the four wives I meet milling around the sidelines. Apparently Frankie's the only one without kids and who's never been married, although he is engaged, as Helen explains, introducing me to his intended, Mary Agnes.

"Catch!" Frankie calls, hurling a spiral at me.

Without thinking about what I'm doing, I catch it easily— "Nice catch," Helen says, eyeing me closely—and toss it back before I can stop myself, a perfect spiral.

"Nice throw," Frankie says. "Wanna get in on the game?"

Now Helen's really studying me closely.

I would like nothing more than to get in on that game. It's been years since I had an opportunity like this and it would feel so good, the ball in my hands, the summer air kissing my face as I run toward the end zone. It's my definition of home. This place, being with these people—despite the nerves I felt earlier, already this feels like home too. But...

"No, thanks," I say. "I don't really play. That catch and that throw—it was just beginner's luck."

Frankie's looking at me like he's not entirely buying it and I will admit: that was some nice catch and throw I just made. But in the end he just shrugs. "Suit yourself."

"Can I get you a beer?" Marlene offers, making her way over to us.

I look around the lawn, see that except for the kids, everyone who's drinking alcohol is drinking beer. Man, a beer would be perfect on a day like today. I'm about to say yes when I stop myself, look at Helen. "You drinking beer?" I ask, struggling to keep the hopeful note out of my voice.

"God no." She shakes her head, clearly horrified at the notion. "I'm drinking Prosecco. It's an Italian wine. White. Sparkling. It's perfect in the summer."

"My daughter the lawyer." Marlene rolls her eyes. "If not for her I could have gotten away with just buying beer and soda today."

"Prosecco sounds great," I say. "The perfect summer drink."

A person might not think a person could get such a quick buzz from something called Prosecco, but between the sparkling white Italian wine and the hot July sun...

By the time another woman shows up at the cookout, I'm pretty confused. This woman looks familiar, but I can't place her. Did I ever date her briefly? Pick her up at a bar, have sex with her and then when I called the next day to ask her out, she said no thanks?

"John," Helen says, "I'd like you to meet my best friend, Carla."

Shit, I hope I never dated her or slept with her. This could get awkward.

"Carla was with me that day at the Yankees game," Helen adds.

Phew. That's where I know her from. It's Rumpled Suit.

Now it's Carla's turn to look surprised as she shakes my hand, her grip like a baccala.

"This isn't the guy," she says.

What guy?

"The first time you went out with him," Carla goes on, "you told me it was one of the guys from the game and you described him to me. The one you described was one of the suits."

Of course. Carla must be talking about Monte Carlo. That time I was painting Helen's house and I saw her get in the car to go someplace with him. Helen must have told Carla about that and then when Helen went out on a date with me and kept going out with me, Carla must have thought she was always talking about the same guy. Of course, Helen doesn't even know I know that she went out with Monte Carlo.

"You're right," I say. "I was at the game, but I did not have a suit on."

"I know," Carla says. "You were the one with the hot dogs. And the beer."

"That's right," Helen says, turning to me with a question on her face. "I forgot about that part, you drinking beer that day. But you don't even like beer. You prefer wine, like me."

"That's true," I say, rushing to cover, "but just like I don't eat meat and yet I'll eat it at someone else's house or at the ballpark, because it's the thing to do, I drink beer the few times I'm at the ballpark because *that's* the thing to do."

"Riiiiiight," Carla says, and I can tell she doesn't believe me, nor does she particularly seem to like me as she scans the gathering, as though looking for someone more interesting to talk to.

I've been known to have that effect on most women.

The group that have been playing tag football disassemble—and may I say how proud of myself I am for thinking up a word like disassemble when I've got a Prosecco head—as the brothers head toward the sidelines in a herd, passing by us and stopping only long enough to grab burgers and dogs from the platter Helen's father has set up by the grill and more beers from the cooler.

"Hey, Hel," Frankie calls over. Hel—I've never heard anyone call her that before, probably because I never thought to. "The game's about to start. Aren't you coming?"

Helen looks at her oldest brother like he's slipped a screw. "Are you crazy? You know I'm not interested in that stuff."

"Right," Frankie says, "I forgot for a moment." He turns to me. "How about you, John. You gonna watch with us? Leave the women to talk out here about what Neanderthals we all are?"

How much do I want to say yes right now? Oh, not to the women-talking-about-us-being-Neanderthals part. The other part. The *baseball* part. And for more than one reason. I haven't missed an All-Star Game for as long as I can remember *and* I've already turned down an offer to play tag football and accepted sparkling white wine over beer—bad enough I'm drinking wine, but does it have to sparkle? If I refuse to watch the game on top of that, won't Helen's brothers think I'm a douche? And isn't part of the purpose of my being here today to get them to like me? But if I go with the guys, Helen might think I'm interested in that stuff, which of course I am, and then—

I take so long internally debating the pros and cons, that Frankie feels the need to prod me along by saying, "The All-Star Game?" As if I might not know what game they're all going to watch. *As if.* "You know," he adds, "baseball?"

Ouch.

"No, thanks," I say at last. "I'm not really interested in all that stuff either."

"Suit yourself." Frankie shrugs and jogs toward the house, Frank Senior falling in behind him.

Yes, that is what I'm doing. I'm suiting myself.

• • •

So as the Troy boys hang in the house, watching the game, only coming outside when they need more food or beer, I hang with the ladies, drinking my Prosecco. When they talk fashion, I agree that the new fall line of colors looks promising, particularly the emphasis on forest green. When they talk recipes, I share my disaster story about the shrimp and the green onions. The women all think this is hysterical, charming even. For a brief time, I even hold onto Helen's great-aunt's ball of yarn for her while she knits. Who knits outside in the summer?

When I start talking knowledgably about GH—a show I've become addicted to, I might add—the group of gals practically cream themselves.

There's also a lot of talk about the upcoming wedding between Mary Agnes and Frankie, just three months away.

"It's in October," Mary Agnes tells me. "It'll be on the seventh game of the World Series if it goes to seven games."

I comment not at all at this, inside thinking: What a sacrilege!

"Frankie was worried about the date at first," Mary Agnes goes on, "but that date is my lucky number and, besides, there's no way the Mets are going all the way this year."

Well, she's right about that.

And then it hits me: For her to say that, Helen's brothers must be Mets fans. Man, I wish I were with them right now. What great guys they all seem like to me. Instead, I'm out here with the ladies, who, against all odds, seem fairly impressed with me.

I wonder what the guys think of me?

They probably think I'm a douche.

In between all the ladylike chatter, Helen keeps popping in and out of the house, I'm guessing to offer the guys more refreshments or to get stuff for her mother.

Now it's my turn to pop. Who knows how many glasses of Prosecco I've had? It's definitely easier on the bladder than beer, but not by much.

I lean toward Mary Agnes, ask in a whisper, "Where do I go to—" *Do not say 'pee' in front of Helen's soon-to-be sister-in-law, Johnny,* I remind myself. "That is to say, where is the—"

Mary Agnes points toward a pair of sliding glass doors. "Through there's the family room where the boys are watching 'the big game'"—she says it just like that, using tolerant yet amused air quotes. "You'll find the little boys' room across the hall from that. Marlene reserves it for the brothers. The seat's never down in there."

"Thanks," I say.

I slide the glass door open. Immediately, I'm hit with the sound of a baseball game in progress and the sound of people watching the game yelling at the screen and the sight of...

Helen, perched on the arm of the plaid La-Z-Boy that Frank Senior is sitting in.

She practically leaps up, wiping her hands on her shorts as though to get rid of dirt even though I don't see any.

They were probably talking about me, the thought occurs. She was probably asking them what they think of me and they were telling her what a douche they think I am.

"We were just talking about plans for Frankie and Mary Agnes's wedding," she says, heading straight back outside again.

I so want to check the game out, see what's going on, but I can't risk showing any interest in sports, so I just keep my focus straight ahead as I point across the room at the door to the hall. "I'm just here to..."

I cross the room before I can say anything more stupid sounding. God, what a douche am I.

I'm through the door and on the other side of the hall when I hear something that stops me.

"That guy Hel brought to meet us," one of the brothers says. Since I can't see him and I don't know all their voices yet, except for Frankie's, I can't tell which one. Dougie? Sammy?

"I know what you're going to say," another brother says. "He's not exactly what I'd have picked out for her."

"You've got that right," yet another says. "He's not interested in sports, he's drinking sparkling wine."

"He even held Aunt Clara's ball of yarn," a fourth says. "I saw him."

"And yet," Frankie says, "and yet there's just something about that guy I really like. I can't put my finger on what it is, but there's something there."

"Exactly," Frank Senior says, belches. "I think he's a keeper, the first one she's ever brought home that is."

Thank you, Lord!

And now I can pee.

I'm feeling so good when I come out of the bathroom, in more ways than one, that as I pass back through the family room I let my guard down, just for a second.

Beltran's at bat and without thinking, out loud I say, "Yes! Beltran! Way to show them that all that pre-season nonsense was just that: nonsense."

"You know who Beltran is?" Frankie says, startled. "You don't like baseball and yet you know who Beltran is?"

"His name's right on the back of his uniform." I point at the screen, covering quickly. Good thing they're not Yankees fans. The Yankees don't wear their names on their uniforms, so how would I ever explain knowing who A-Rod or Jeter is? "Anyone can read that. It's right there."

"No no no." Now Frankie's turned a one-eighty in his chair to look at me. They've all turned one-eighties. "That stuff you said about pre-season. You wouldn't know that if you didn't know the game. So how come you're not watching with us?"

"Truth?" I say, and only as I'm talking do I realize it is the truth. "Normally I would want to watch, but I'd rather be with Helen. And anyway, even though I was barely alive when it happened, the free agency of the late seventies closed the coffin on any drama the All-Star Game might offer and the introduction of inter-league play of a few years ago nailed it shut."

"Did you hear that?" Sammy says. "'The free agency of the

late seventies'? 'Inter-league play'?"

"Oh, you do *so* know baseball," Dougie says.

"And did you see the way he threw that football earlier?" Johnny says.

Jerry doesn't say anything. I'm beginning to realize he's not much of a talker.

"I know, right?" Frankie says. "I told you there was something about him I liked. Some guys, you can just tell about."

"Exactly," Frank Senior says. "I told you he was a keeper."

I can't believe he just said that about me again. He even said it right in front of me!

But wait a second...

"Look," I say nervously, "you can't tell Helen about this."

"About what?" Frankie asks.

"Any of it," I say. "She can't know I know about Beltran or sports or any of it, let alone that I love it all."

"How come?" Frank Senior asks.

"Because the me that she likes isn't supposed to."

"You know that's kind of a crazy sentence?" Frankie says. "Like on a whole lot of different levels?"

"I know," I admit freely. "Be that as it may. And I know I'm asking a lot, too much really. It's your first time meeting me and I'm already asking you to lie to your sister for me." I turn to Frank Senior. "And your daughter."

He shrugs. "Well, it's not like you're asking us to lie about something you did with another woman. Now *that* we would have a problem with. But if all you want us to do is keep your interest in sports from her because for some strange reason you think it might put her off..." He shrugs again.

I *love* this man.

"Say no more," Frankie says. "Like Pop says, you're a keeper. I'm in."

"I'm in too," Sammy says.

"And me," Dougie says.

"And me," Johnny says.

Jerry just smiles, but I get the picture.

And the picture is that it looks like I'm in too.

. . .

"What was that all about?" Helen says when I come back outside. "You were in there for an awful long time."

"Just doing some male bonding," I say. "Nothing to worry about. I think your family likes me." I'm stunned. "I mean, they *really* like me."

"Why are you so surprised?" Helen smiles. "I'm not."

And then I become even more stunned as I look at the women in Helen's family and realize most of them seem to like me too.

"Hey, Aunt Clara," I say, "you got any foolproof recipes for shrimp?"

A few hours later, the game's over—I don't even know if the National or the American League won and I don't want to know; it's just the stupid All-Star Game after all. The Prosecco buzz has faded, the grill is shut down, marshmallows have been toasted and eaten, the fireflies are out and I'm realizing it's time I shove off before I wear out my welcome.

Helen walks me to my truck, her hand entwined with mine.

"Jerry asked me if we could watch his kids for a few hours on Thursday night while he and Susanne go see an R-rated film. You up for it? I'll tell him no if you'd rather not."

I can't believe Jerry actually talks to somebody, but what I really can't believe is the words coming out of my mouth when I say:

"Yeah, I'm up for it." I even smile when I say the words because I *am* up for it. Six months ago, if someone had asked me if I'd ever be up for babysitting someone else's kids, the answer would have been a resounding *no*. No, I have no experience. No, I don't think I'd be up for it. But six months ago, I didn't even have a cat. None of this had happened. Now anything seems possible. I'll bake cookies with the kids. I'll teach them how to play kickball. Surely playing kickball well won't expose me as a sports nut. Everybody plays kickball.

I'm about to kiss the girl when Frankie trots over.

"Hey, John, can I talk to you for a minute?"

"Alone?"

"Nah. I guess it's OK if Hel hears this too. Listen…" Frankie pauses, as though unsure how to begin.

Oh shit, I am so busted. He's going to tell Helen everything.

"Listen," Frankie begins again, "I know this is pretty unorthodox, but would you consider being Best Man at my wedding in October?"

"Your—"

"I know, I know, it's crazy, right? But when the other four got married, because I'm the oldest, they each asked me to be their Best Man. And I've been sweating this for months. Who to ask? If I ask one of them, the other three'll be all pissed and hurt. So I just figured, you and Hel do seem pretty close and you seem like the kind of guy who'd give a pretty good speech…" He turns to his sister. "Do you mind, Hel?"

"Don't look at me." She holds up her hands. "It's your wedding and it's entirely up to John."

This is strange, but certainly less strange than that complete stranger at Billy and Alice's wedding asking me if I'd be *his* Best Man.

"Sure, I'm up for it," I say.

"Great," Frankie says, backing away. "I'll get your number from Helen, give you a ring when it's time for tuxes and everything."

For the first time that day, I kiss the girl.

Suddenly I'm up for anything.

Anything *is* possible.

Dramatis Personae

It's August, and it's finally time for Helen to meet *my* cast of characters. If she can run this gauntlet without hating me...

It never occurred to me that August is the only month with no holidays or things to celebrate. Even June, lacking anything specific like Valentine's Day or Christmas, at least has significant dates to build a celebration around: end of school, graduation, Summer Solstice. Oh yeah. How could I forget? June's got Father's Day too—duh-me. But August? It's got nothing. Still, it's time for Helen to meet my people and I don't want to wait for September with its Labor Day, so I pick a date and invite everybody that matters to me and even a few who don't. True, I could do this one at a time, which would maybe be more manageable—dinner with Billy and Alice, dinner with Sam and Lily, dinner with Big John and Aunt Alfresca etcetera—but that would also be like subjecting Helen to the drip-drip of Chinese water torture. Better get it all over with once, like ripping off a Band-Aid. This means that Helen will be meeting the aforementioned six, plus Drew and Stacy, plus Steve Miller and Katie; of course she already knows Steve, but that's in a business context, not as my friend, which I guess he is now. It'll be like when I met her family: full-body immersion. If we can just get through this one day, I tell myself, we'll be in some kind of version of home free.

But before any of that can happen, I must brief everyone and swear them to secrecy.

"No sports talk," I tell Billy. "If Helen asks what you and Drew and I do when we get together, you say we discuss politics and *General Hospital*."

"I can do that," Billy says like he's psyching himself up for a big game.

"I may need some help with the GH stuff," Drew says. "Tell me why again that Nikolas's grandmother is so obsessed with passing Lucky and Liz's baby off as a Cassidine heir when there already is a real heir?"

"It barely makes sense to me," I say. "Just let Billy do all the talking."

I turn to Alice. "Please don't let on that the only reason I ever got a cat was because you told me to or that the magazine rack and pretty much everything else in this place of a decorative nature was recommended by you or that I used to have a chandelier with hula girls on it in my basement."

"I wouldn't dream of it," Alice says. "There's as much riding on this for me as there is for you."

"Sam," I say, "just be yourself."

"Done," she says.

"But don't tell her about those books we bought," I add.

"What books?" Lily asks.

OK, that's Sam's problem now.

"Steve," I say, "remember: I am not obsessed with loopholes. I know *nothing* about loopholes. The things I like are ice holes, sinkholes, peepholes and blowholes. I'm also big on saving the whales."

Steve scratches his head. "Gee, do you think you could write all that down for me? Is it OK to use crib notes for this thing?"

Katie punches her husband in the shoulder. Gee, I never would have pegged her as a shoulder puncher. "I'll take care of it," she assures me.

"Aunt Alfresca," I say, "I know it goes against every fiber in your being, but please try to refrain from making comments in Helen's presence that would indicate you think I'm a moron, imbecile, hopeless idiot, you get the picture."

"Come on," Big John says, "your aunt's a lovely woman."

A—

"You make it sound," he continues, "like your aunt's rude or something."

Is he kidding me? Aunt Alfresca's rude *and* something! I

always thought he and I were on the same page about this.

"You killed my sister," she says, "but I'll do it for your father."

"And, *everybody*," I say, palms down as I spread my arms wide to encompass the whole group, "no one is to call me Johnny. It's John. Dad, I swear to God if you forget…"

"I won't forget! I won't forget!"

OK, that's done.

Now all that's left is the residual nervousness.

Will they like Helen?

Of course they will.

Will she like them?

That remains to be seen.

At the cookout at Helen's parents' house last month, she trusted me enough to leave me alone with people occasionally, whenever she'd go into the family room to check on her brothers watching the game, and I realize I must extend the same courtesy to her here as well. I can't just stand at her elbow all day, because eventually she'll sense that I'm doing it because I'm nervous, anxious to tamp out any brushfires that may occur. I'll just have to let the brushfires flame as they may. But, I tell myself, it shouldn't be too bad. After all, I did brief these mokes.

So once the introductions have been made, I allow Helen the space to take it all in on her own terms. Me, I mingle, circling through the crowd as I offer people more drinks and etcetera, catching snippets of conversation as I circle.

"Actually," I hear Helen telling Drew, "you'll have to ask John what's up with Helena and the falsifying of that paternity test. I don't get to watch GH quite as frequently as he does."

More circling.

"John told me about the ice holes," I hear Helen telling Big John. "Are you still able to get out there together and fish?"

Oh shit. I never briefed Big John on this mythical past we supposedly shared, the one in which we went ice fishing together all the time in my youth.

Big John is silent so long before he answers, I wonder if

he's ever going to say anything at all, he's so busy rubbing his chin with one hand, a thoughtful expression on his face.

"You know," Big John says at last, "that's funny you should ask. On good days, like today"—and here he lifts his cane a bit, the wheelchair out in the car in case it turns into a bad day—"it gets a little slippery out on the ice with this thing. And on bad days, what with the added weight of the wheelchair, there's always the greater risk of falling through the ice. But sure, we still go ice fishing all the time. Every winter."

Bless you, Dad.

And then it hits me: If Helen and I are still together come winter—and we have to be; at the risk of sounding like Melanie Wilkes (Alice told me to watch *Gone with the Wind*, along with nine other movies she claimed were the top ten films women love), I'll just die if we're not—I'm going to have to take up ice fishing with Big John, if only to turn my lies into truths.

More circling, more circling, and things are going well, people are remembering their lines. Even Steve continues to do mostly OK. He's telling Helen a story from the second time I painted their dining room at Katie's request and he finishes up the anecdote with something Sam-like along the lines of, "Only Johnny." But then immediately he catches himself, turning the final E sound of my name into, "Eee, this is good shrimp." Just to make sure he's really sold it, he reiterates, "Only John—eee, this is good shrimp."

Helen no doubt thinks this is strange, that Steve is certainly strange. But since I've previously convinced her that her friendly adversary is a raging alcoholic, we're probably good to go.

'Course Drew, generally being the weakest link in any gathering of creatures that walk on two legs, nearly blows it when he clicks on the TV, saying, "Isn't it time for the Jets? Preseason, *baby*!"

Helen's eyes move directly to the big-screen TV while everyone else looks at Drew like he just dropped his pants and laid a huge turd on the carpet.

"You know we don't watch that stuff around here," Big John says, like the program on the TV is some snuff film as opposed to CBS Sports.

"It's OK," I say magnanimously, "I understand that some of you actually like football. For those of you who do, feel free to leave the game on while the rest of us mingle."

As the guys slowly drift toward the TV, like it has a magnet inside, and the girls head toward the kitchen, I think: Talk about your two birds with one stone. I've acquitted myself yet again as being a non-sports lover *and* I've managed to seem like a magnanimous host *plus* I can check out how Sanchez and the Jets are looking this year whenever I go to the living room to add more chips to the bowls and freshen everyone's drinks.

OK, make that three birds.

That is some stone.

I'm in the kitchen with the women and things are going pretty good. Alice seems really impressed with Helen. I mean, she *really* likes her. As I stand there with my arm around Helen while she and Alice jabber away, I'm thinking about the future, how maybe someday, maybe even soon, Billy and Alice and me and Helen can all do something together like dinner or a movie or maybe even dinner *and* a movie—the kind of simple couples' night out that couples all over the world enjoy.

I'm basking in my future-oriented glow when Aunt Alfresca grabs my elbow. "Can I talk to you for a second?" she says.

When has Aunt Alfresca ever asked permission to have a conversation?

This is unprecedented.

"Sure," I say. Then, "Wait a second, if this is about me killing your sister—"

"It's not about that. I'm over that. This is something else."

"Yeah, sure," I say again. "Where would you like to talk?"

"The basement?" she suggests. "Ever since you got rid of that old lamp"—and here she winks at me like we're in on this deception together, which I guess we are—"I like it down there so much better."

. . .

So we're down in the basement and now I'm getting really nervous. This is the longest Helen's been out of my sight all afternoon. I mean, sure, I let her mingle on her own, but except for trips to the bathroom, I could always see what she was doing, see what everyone *else* was doing in case someone slipped up. But now she's out of sight, I hope I'm not out of mind, and Aunt Alfresca is...

Stalling.

"These are some nice cue sticks you got here, Johnny," she says, fingering one of the sticks in the wall rack. "It's OK if I still call you Johnny when Helen isn't in the room, isn't it?"

Is she *threatening* me? Because that sounds like something a gangster in a movie might say, a gangster who's got the goods on the hero and is hoping to blackmail him.

When I don't immediately say anything, Aunt Alfresca starts racking the balls. "Why don't we shoot a game?" she says.

But then when she's racking the balls, her hands shake and she doesn't put the balls in the right position, which is totally fucked up because Aunt Alfresca was the one who taught *me* how to rack and shoot. And that's when I realize...

"Aunt Alfresca, are you *nervous*?"

She gives up on trying to get the balls racked properly, letting the rack go entirely.

"Fine," she says, "you wormed it out of me. Your father and me are getting married."

"The pheasant died," Big John says.

"The pheasant died?" I say. "That's your big reason for marrying Aunt Alfresca—the pheasant died? What does that even mean?"

I'm still down in the basement only now it's Big John who's down here with me. After I went all pole-axed following the delivery of Aunt Alfresca's news, she went to get him and then left us alone.

Big John sighs. "Let me tell you a story," he says.

"The story of why you and Mom's sister are getting married?"

"We'll circle around to that. See, it all started when I began sitting out on my back porch every evening. When you have trouble getting around like I do now, sometimes all there is for you is to just sit and watch nature. Anyway, I began noticing these two pheasants. Every evening just around sundown, the same thing, this boy and girl pheasant walking across the back lawn side by side. I watched them for months. Well, not constantly. Obviously I did other things with my life. But then one evening I'm out there, waiting to watch them take their nightly stroll, only this time, it's only one pheasant, the male. I realized then that the female must have died and now he was all alone in the world. For a few more nights he crossed that lawn alone. And then one night, he wasn't there anymore. I waited a long time but he never came back. It was then I realized that he'd died too. The poor guy must have died of a broken heart. Without his mate to live for anymore..." Big John's voice trails off.

"That's all very touching," I say. "I mean, *really* touching. But what does any of this have to do with you and Aunt Alfresca?"

"I don't want to be alone anymore, Johnny."

"OK, I get that. The pheasant and everything. But... *Aunt Alfresca?*"

"I know, right? I guess it would be a surprise to you. But your aunt and I have had... *feelings* for each other for years. Really, she's just like your mother, only mean."

"I thought you said earlier that she was, and I quote, a lovely woman."

"Yeah, well..."

"So, when were you and she thinking of getting married?"

"She says she wants January." He sighs. "I've got my issues with that, like what if there's a blizzard and no one shows up? But she's got her heart set on it. She says January is the perfect month to get married—new beginnings and all that, plus no one else wants that month so you've got your pick of reception halls."

"If this has been going on for years, then why wait until now to tell me?"

"Oh, that. We were waiting for the kid to grow up. And then, you know, the pheasant died." Big John pauses. "Don't be alone all your life, Johnny. It's not bad, certainly not the worst thing that can happen to a man, but it also kind of sucks." He pauses again. "Helen's a keeper. Don't louse it up."

Those words echo later in the evening as I'm bidding my guests goodbye one by one. Oh, not the "Don't louse it up" part. I'm pretty adept at running that self-recriminatory loop in my own sorry brain. But the other?

"Helen's a keeper," Sam whispers in my ear on her way out.

"Helen's a keeper," Lily whispers, even though she barely knows me let alone Helen.

"Helen's a keeper," even Alice whispers.

As I close the door on the last guest, I turn to Helen and realize that every single one of them is right. Helen *is* a keeper. Still, marriage? I know I've thought about it for a long time, but for these past months since meeting her, I've just been focused on making the next date work and the next. But really, marriage?

Then it hits me.

I'm thirty-three years old and my dad's going to remarry before I even marry once.

I've got to move fast, step this puppy up.

Labor Day

The day after Labor Day it's back to work, which finds me hitting Leo's for an early caffeine fix before getting on the road proper. It's a few weeks since I've been in here because most nights now I sleep at Helen's or she sleeps at my place and we have coffee together instead.

"What's the good word, Leo?" I say when it's my turn to order.

"There isn't one," Leo says grimly.

This makes no sense. Leo's always got a good word for me plus a smile, which is sadly absent now.

"What's wrong?" I ask.

"It's The Little Lady."

"The Little Lady? What happened—did you two have a fight about you forgetting a significant date? But I thought your anniversary wasn't until November."

"We didn't have a fight," he says. He stops working on my coffee long enough to meet my eyes and that's when I see the tears. "She went and died on me."

"Leo!" I'm...I don't even know what I am right now. What do you say to a man, a *friend* who's lost his wife of over seventy years? "How?" is all I can think to say. "When?"

"Early last week. In her sleep. Good for her. Bad for me."

What do I say to him? "I can't even begin to imagine how hard this must be for you, but you'll get through it, Leo."

"No," he says, "I won't." There's not a shred of self-pity in his words. He's just stating the awful new fact of his life. "I've always liked to think of myself as an optimist, Johnny. Did you know I was in World War II?"

I shake my head. I've known Leo for years and yet for the first time I realize how little I know about his life. What do I know

226

about him? His coffee shop. The Little Lady. The fact that he's always been kind to me.

"It's true," he says. "The European Theatre, the Pacific Theatre, everything from Anzio to the Philippines, which was where I was on a boat when the war ended. I had a buddy, a series of buddies, each one equally sure that every day when they got up, that was the day they were going to die. Some did, some didn't. Me, I never thought like that once. Each day, no matter how bad it got, I was sure I'd survive and that when the war was over, the world would be a better place. I don't feel like that anymore. The world is no longer a good place, not for me."

"Leo." I don't care that customers are piling up behind me. I reach across the counter and put my arms around Leo.

He leans into my embrace and whispers fiercely in my ear, "I *knew* her. And she knew *me*. Whatever else happens, I'll never know another person like that, never again."

For the remainder of the week, I make a point of stopping by Leo's every morning, sometimes making a second stop on my way home in the afternoon. We don't talk anymore about what life is like now for Leo without The Little Lady. Oh, I would if he wanted that. But I let him lead the conversations, wherever he wants. Mostly, he wants to talk about the Mets. They're looking like they actually have a shot at the playoffs, something no one ever would have guessed back in the spring.

He doesn't seem like he's in a state of despair or depression. He doesn't even seem particularly unhappy. But somehow he doesn't seem like Leo anymore either.

Friday afternoon I stop by on my way home. We talk for a bit and as I'm leaving with a coffee I don't really need, Leo shouts, "Don't do anything I wouldn't do!"

That used to be his daily warning to me but I haven't heard it once since The Little Lady died.

"I wouldn't even dream of trying!" I call back, my standard response, feeling heartened by our old exchange.

He smiles, I smile back, and the door closes behind me.

• • •

The next morning is Saturday, no work, and even though Helen slept over the night before and is still in my bed, I leave her there to go have my coffee with Leo.

When I get to the shop, the lights are all out and a sign on the door says: "Closed due to death of the owner."

The Little Lady, a woman whose name I never even knew, was Leo's pheasant. And once she was gone, his heart just broke and then he died.

I'm thinking this again three days later as I watch Leo get lowered into the ground, Helen by my side, when it hits me:

I've spent years hoping to find *a* woman who would be able to tolerate being with me enough that she'd be willing to spend her life with me. There were moments when it seemed like just about any woman would do. But it never occurred to me until this moment that what I needed wasn't just *a* woman, not just *any* woman. What I needed was to find someone who would be The Little Lady to my Leo, *just one specific woman* who *I* wanted to spend my life with.

One.

Just one.

Helen *is* my pheasant. I want to spend my life with her, like Leo did with The Little Lady, until one of us is no more, the other dies of a broken heart, and we both return to the earth.

But then I think of the words Leo spoke.

"I *knew* her," Leo said. "And she knew *me*."

And I realize that, yes, I want to spend my life with Helen, but not like this, not if it means not being myself.

Frankie and Mary Agnes's wedding is coming up and between now and then there are all the pre-wedding things to get through: fittings for tuxes and gowns, showers, bachelor parties, rehearsal dinners and all the etcetera. I'll wait until after the wedding. Because if I tell her beforehand and she's disappointed—which, I'm guessing, she might be, since I've basically been living a lie right under her nose—it'll spoil the wedding party. I mean, can Frankie really have me be Best Man if his sister breaks it off with me? I'm thinking no. And I don't want to ruin their big day for Frankie and Mary Agnes. They seem like nice people. Pheasants, even.

So I'll wait.

But after the wedding?

I'll tell her who I really am. I'll say I'm fine with remembering all those significant dates if it makes her happy—they're significant to me too—and that I'm interested in everything she has to say. I don't even mind keeping the cat. But I'll also tell her that I like wearing a baseball cap, backwards, that I love sports, baseball and the Mets in particular, and that while I've gotten used to being called John, I vastly prefer Johnny. I've been Johnny my whole life. And if she can't accept me for who I really am? If really *knowing* me puts her off, makes her love me less?

Well, maybe we weren't meant to be pheasants together after all.

Delay of Game

I'll say one thing for the Troys: they sure know how to throw a wedding. No bizarre tux color combos for them. The men are all in classic black suits with white shirts and silver-gray ties while the bridesmaids are all in close-fitting ice-blue satin gowns with one-inch straps. When I see Helen in hers, what with her red hair, she looks amazing.

Yes, I've made it to the church on time, bringing Big John and Aunt Alfresca with me because when the Troys met them at some extended-family get-together, Mary Agnes added them to the list. But as I stand with all the bridesmaids in the vestibule, all those bridesmaids looking unaccountably nervous, there appears to be some kind of problem. Then Frankie comes out, claps his hand on my shoulder, as the rest of the brothers circle round.

"I'm sorry, man," he says. "I thought I could, but I realized I just can't do it."

"Marry Mary Agnes?" I've heard of pre-wedding jitters causing people to change their minds. But isn't he cutting it a little close?

"Not that," he says. "The World Series. Who would have ever guessed the Mets would make it all the way to the Series and that if they did, that it would go to seven days?"

You're telling me. I've been kicking myself about this all day. I've been waiting since 1986, waiting since I was nine years old for this day to come again, for twenty-four years I've been waiting for the magic to come back, for the Mets to have their big shot. How can I spend this day at a wedding? And yet I promised Frankie and Mary Agnes. Not to mention, what would Helen think if I blew off being her brother's Best Man in favor of watching what she'd only regard as just another stupid baseball game? She'd never forgive me. Our relationship would be over.

"I can't miss this game," Frankie says when I don't say anything.

"So what are you going to do?" I ask. "The wedding's supposed to start at the same time as the game."

"I called Mary Agnes on her cell. She says she understands completely. She told me to just watch the game and that we'd get married as soon as it's over. She doesn't want me to see her in her wedding dress until the proper time, so she'll watch the game in the Bride's Room. She did say that if the Mets play lousy, I'm not allowed to pout afterward."

That's certainly reasonable of her. But this is all so unconventional.

"But you've got a church full of people," I say. "What about the priest?"

"Oh, that." Frankie waves away my concerns. "Everyone wants to see this game. I mean, come on, it's the Mets. We could all be dead before this happens again. As for the priest, he was relieved when I told him. As a matter of fact, he got his housekeeper to bring over his big-screen TV and they're setting it up in the Community Room right now." Frankie consults his watch. "Shit, the game starts in two minutes." Realizing what he's just said and where he was when he said it, he looks up at the ceiling. "Oops, sorry, God." He starts heading toward a door, brothers in tow.

At the door he stops and turns. "John, Hel, you coming? Come on. It's the Mets. I've got a game to watch so I can get married."

I can't even begin to describe how badly I want to see this game. It's one of those so-bad-it-hurts things and even beyond that. But then I look down at Helen, see the sad look on her face—she's probably thrown by this sudden change of events, not understanding how someone could delay their own wedding over a stupid game.

"No, that's OK," Helen tells her brother. "You know we're

not interested in that stuff."

I take Helen's hand firmly in mine and it takes all that's in me to echo her words, "Yeah, Frankie, you know we're not interested in that stuff."

"So what shall we do for the next few hours?" I say once the others are gone.

"I don't know," Helen says. "I think there are some chairs in the hall outside the Community Room. Maybe we should just sit there in case, I don't know, someone needs us for something?"

"Sounds like a plan."

So that's what we do. We sit on folding chairs outside the Community Room holding hands while on the other side of the double doors everyone else is watching the game. Occasionally someone will come out for a cigarette break or whatever, but of course I can't ask what the score is, if there even is one yet. All I can do is hear the crowd reaction through the gap in the doors.

We've been sitting there for about fifteen minutes, not even speaking, when Helen abruptly gets to her feet.

"I'm going to go see how Mary Agnes is doing," she says. "I know Frankie said this was all OK with her, but it is their wedding day."

As soon as Helen's out of sight, I duck into the Community Room. I figure she'll be with Mary Agnes for at least five minutes so I manage to see two batters before heading for the door again. No score yet.

"Come on, Johnny," Big John calls out, forgetting he's not supposed to call me that in front of these people and briefly confusing everyone regarding who he's talking to because Helen's youngest brother goes by Johnny. "You don't want to miss this."

"It's OK, Dad," I say, "really."

I'm back on my seat in the hall by the time Helen returns.

"Mary Agnes OK?" I ask.

"She's fine. Still no score." Then she adds, "I only noticed because Mary Agnes was glued to the game. I guess it's keeping her mind off things."

Another fifteen minutes go by and Helen excuses herself, this time to the bathroom which I assume is down the hall and around the corner since that's where she heads. I'm tempted to duck into the Community Room again but don't dare risk it. Helen going to the bathroom shouldn't take her nearly as long as going to check on Mary Agnes. What if she returns and I'm not here or, worse, she catches me coming out of the Community Room?

So I just sit, wait for her return.

No sooner is she back than suddenly *I* have to go to the bathroom. I guess it's the power of suggestion. Talking about bathrooms has made me have to use one.

"Men's Room that way too?" I ask.

She nods and I'm off.

But two minutes later, as I'm exiting the Men's Room, I notice that right across the hall from the bathrooms is another set of double doors to the Community Room. I allow myself a quick peek—bottom of the second, Mets down by one; shit— before heading back to Helen.

A few minutes later, she excuses herself to go check on Mary Agnes again.

And so the afternoon progresses, with Helen periodically checking on Mary Agnes while I sneak peeks at the game and with multiple bathroom visits on both our parts. For me, I claim I had too much coffee that morning—nerves over giving the Best Man's toast later, even though I have that toast down pat. Helen, she doesn't give me a reason for her multiple bathroom visits. But she's a lady—she'd never explain nor should she have to.

Over the course of my various peeks, I see the score seesaw back and forth from Mets down by one to tied to up by one to tied and so forth.

About four in the afternoon, three hours after the game started, Helen excuses herself to go the bathroom yet again. But this time, she's gone so long, I begin to get fidgety, what with all the muffled shouting coming from the Community Room.

Suddenly, I've *got* to know what's going on with the game. It's the Mets in there and it sounds like they could actually be winning.

So I poke my head in, figuring I'll just take a quick glimpse at the screen. It's the bottom of the ninth, Mets are up, score tied four all, one on, two out, and Beltran's making his way to the plate. The stadium's rocking, the *room* is rocking. Beltran cocks his bat and everything falls silent. And then, into that silence, I hear a female voice shout, "Hit a home run, you overpaid cocksucker!"

I *know* that voice. My head snaps toward the back of the room and there's Helen—*my* Helen, my Helen who hates all sports and baseball in particular—eyes glued to the World Series like her life depends on it.

"Helen?" I say.

Her head swivels from the screen to me in the doorway. "John?" Like she can't believe I'm there. Then, "John," flat, like something's over with, died.

And it's while our eyes are still locked on each other that I dimly hear the crack of a bat.

But I don't look at the screen. I'm too dumbfounded.

An instant later I hear, "Mets win! Mets win!"

OK, I do look at the screen now and Helen does too, just long enough to see the instant replay of Beltran powering a monster two-run homer over the centerfield fence.

And then my eyes are back on Helen and hers are back on me.

The room is pandemonium now with everyone celebrating the return of the magic. But for some reason, I don't feel like celebrating.

I watch as Helen makes her way over to Frankie and somehow over the crowd I manage to hear her say to him, "Can you delay the wedding just a little longer? You've delayed it this long. I just need a half hour, an hour tops. There's something I need to show John."

• • •

I just sit in the passenger seat, along for the ride, not knowing where we're going or what to make of this new information.

Helen drives us to her house.

As we walk through, I'm thinking how I've made love to her in every room of this house but then she leads me to the door of a place I've never been in here before.

"The basement?" I say. "Excuse me, but your brother's supposed to be getting married and you want to finally show me your messy *basement*?"

"It's not really messy," she says, flicking the switch and gesturing with her hand. "Please. Go down."

So I precede her down the long flight of stairs only to discover...

Sports memorabilia. Everywhere I look. Signed balls from various sports. Framed posters of the Jets' Sanchez, the Mets' Beltran—I think vaguely that if you're going to hang a guy's picture in your home, the least you can do is not call him a cocksucker when he's trying to win the game—one of Wayne Gretzky and even an old one of Kareem Abdul-Jabbar when he played for the Lakers.

"What is all this?" I say.

"This is *me*, John," she says simply, sadly. "This is who I am."

I don't understand. "Why would you hide something like this about yourself?"

Helen sighs. "I'm thirty-three years old and I've never had much luck with men. I have a high-powered job. I'm a D.A. and I guess for the most part I come off as no-nonsense." I think how Helen looked the first time I saw her at that Yankees game. She did come off as being pretty no-nonsense. "Men always wind up thinking my competitiveness and my obsession with sports is too...*manly*."

Well, it was manly yelling "cocksucker" at the screen. Also kind of cool.

"I just thought, I don't know," she continues, "that maybe if I seemed more feminine, maybe if I hid my true interests and got things like floral throw pillows around here, that maybe I'd finally stand a chance." She sighs again, sadly again. "And I liked you so much, right away. And you said you weren't interested in sports…" Her voice trails off.

"But this is who I am," she says firmly. "I love the Jets and the Mets. I even call up this all-sports station called The Wave on a regular basis. It's like I'm obsessed with it."

I *knew* that female voice sounded familiar!

"Oh, and one more thing I have to confess," she says. "I've never watched *General Hospital*, that thing you call GH, in my life. Not even once."

Wow. How could I have been so wrong about everything?

"I've got a question," I say.

"I'll bet you've got more than one," she says. "But sure, shoot."

"Were you actually dating Monte Carlo at one point?"

She looks puzzled for a moment. Then: "I went out with him twice, but those weren't dates. He just had spare tickets to two Mets games. How could I refuse?"

That I can understand.

"We'd better head back," Helen says. "We've been away long enough."

As we drive back to the church in silence I'm thinking how Helen isn't who I thought she was.

Who is this woman sitting next to me? I wonder.

And then I wonder something else: Who am I?

World Series

All through the wedding ceremony, as I stand by Frankie's side, I'm puzzling out those twin questions: Who is Helen? And who am I? Clearly, neither of us is exactly the version of ourselves we presented to the other. I already know about Helen's deception. She has yet to learn about mine.

I understand why she did it, for the same reason I did it. We were both trying to be the person we thought the other wanted us to be, both living lies in the process.

But does any of that matter? I think now. Strip away those few surface things we changed, and the essence of each other separately, the essence of *us* together, it's still the same. We never would have come as far as we did together if the basis wasn't somehow solid, that basic connection that was there from the first moment.

I think about something Leo once said: "You learn what makes the other person happy and you just keep doing it." I thought that's what I was doing, but as it turns out, I wasn't really listening to Helen. If I had been, I'd have seen the signs: the way she shot pool; how good she was with all the games at the circus/carnival; the way she kept going inside presumably to check on her brothers while they watched the game at the cookout at her parents' house when none of the brothers' own wives actually bothered to do that; how she'd jump on anything remotely sports-related that I said, with hope in her eyes, just like I did with her; and those calls to The Wave, her being Sexy Caller. I definitely should have picked up on that last. But I didn't because I wasn't expecting to, because I was too busy looking in a different direction.

Big John was right, what he said that long-ago night at the

poker game, that no one knows what women want. Turns out, no one knows what men want either. No one knows how to get love or how to keep it.

Wait a second. That's not true. Leo knew.

Leo knew it didn't matter what foolish games we mortals play over love—things like keeping a present in the trunk three days running to appease someone who thinks she needs to be upset over significant dates; things like who loves sports and who loves GH and who loves both. Leo knew none of that stuff mattered so long as, somehow, you saw down into the essence of the other person and they saw you. And now I see Helen. Like I've never seen her before.

All that time, even when I was missing signs so big they could have been painted on the side of a barn, even when we both thought that being someone other than who we are was the way to make the other person happy, we were still somehow happy together.

And now?

I know what I need to do.

"A man's life is composed of circles," I begin the toast, the words so familiar to me I could recite them in my sleep. "First, there's the circle of the entire world, which a man keeps in contact with through reading the papers and watching the news. Or not." I pause, give my wry smile. "The world can be a pretty depressing place."

I pause again, wait for the laugh.

It comes.

"Then, if the man is like Frankie and me and he chooses to stay in the same town he grew up in all his life, there's that town." I make a slight alteration to the prepared text. "Frankie's town may not be the same as my town, so please let me interject on my own town's behalf: It may not be much but," I raise my glass a little higher, "go, Danbury!"

Some more laughter, with a few answering calls of "Go, Danbury!"—one each from Big John and Aunt Alfresca plus a few people I've never seen in my life who are trying to be supportive.

"Then comes the circle of a man's acquaintances: friends of friends, coworkers, the guy with the little hot dog cart outside the library who overcharges like crazy but makes the best dogs in town. Doesn't every town have one of those guys? What *is* that guy's secret?"

Only a polite chuckle for that one. I detest polite chuckles. When it comes to laughter, a person should be all in or all out. But then I hear one loud all-out laugh. I know that laugh. Looking down the length of the bridal party table, I see its source: Helen.

It takes me a moment to remember where I left off.

"And then comes a very small circle: the circle of a man's dearest friends and family." I tilt my glass at Big John in his wheelchair. "I love you, Dad."

I pause again, not waiting for the laugh this time—there won't be any laughter for the rest of this speech—but rather to get control of my emotions, the tear in my eye mirroring the tear in Big John's.

Tearing my gaze away from my father, I let my eyes sweep the entire audience.

"Now if you've been paying attention, you'll have noticed something. The circles I've been describing have been steadily decreasing in size while at the same time increasing in importance. And so now, finally, we come to the last circle, the smallest circle. If a man is extremely lucky, if he's the luckiest man in the world, he finds the right person to share his life with, to form that smallest circle of two with, and that is exactly what Frankie has done."

I know I should be raising my glass to Frankie and Mary Agnes at this point, but I can't bring myself to do it. Not yet.

"You know," I say, "I have a confession to make. That speech I just gave? It was my ninth time giving it, practically the same exact speech word for word."

I hear some vague grumbles from the crowd. I don't blame them. Who wants a used speech? I learned about that from Alice. Good old Alice. But still I go on, raising my voice over the grumbles.

"Despite the speech being a general crowd-pleaser, the words have never really meant much to me, not until today. But now I understand. Now I understand what it really means for a man to be extremely lucky, now I understand what it means to be the luckiest man in the world, now I understand what it means for a man to find the right person to share his life with, to form that smallest circle of two with. Because that is exactly what has happened to me."

I scan the crowd. "I promise in just a minute I'll get back to toasting Frankie and Mary Agnes and then we can finally drink our champagne, but first I need to say that, against all odds, I have found my right person."

I turn to Helen. "She likes the things I like and she's exactly like me," I say, "only prettier. But even if she weren't just like me, I'd love her anyway because I did before I even knew. Helen, will you marry me?"

My name is John Smith to some people but you can call me Johnny. I like my baseball cap on backwards and my beer cold. If you let me, I'll leave the seat up in the toilet. I prefer cats that are more like dogs and I don't like opera unless it's in a barn and I'm with the right person.

I've been known to leave my Christmas tree up until something good happens.

Geez, I hope Helen knows what she's getting herself into.

My name is Johnny Smith. I'm thirty-three years old and I'm finally getting married.

ISN'T IT BRO-MANTIC?: A JOHNNY SMITH NOVEL

What happens after Happily Ever After? That's what Johnny Smith is about to find out. Having wooed—and won!—the girl of his dreams in The Bro-Magnet, he is ready to take on married life. Finally, Johnny will be the groom. But right off the bat, during the honeymoon, things start to go wrong. And it only gets worse when the newlyweds return home to their new house in Connecticut. Different taste in pets, interior design, friends. Too much togetherness. Jealousy. Nothing is easy, given that neither Johnny nor his wife has ever even had a roommate since college. Can this couple, still so in love, share a home without driving each other crazy?

THE THIN PINK LINE: A JANE TAYLOR NOVEL

Jane Taylor is a slightly sociopathic Londoner who wants marriage and a baby in the worst way, and she's willing to go to over-the-top lengths to achieve her dream. When Jane thinks she's pregnant she tells everyone. When it turns out to be a false alarm, she assumes she'll just get pregnant, no one the wiser. But when that doesn't happen, well, of course she does what no one in her right mind would do: Jane decides to fake an entire pregnancy!

CROSSING THE LINE:
A JANE TAYLOR NOVEL

In the madcap sequel to the international hit comedy *The Thin Pink Line*, London editor Jane Taylor is at it again, only this time, there's a baby involved. Having—SPOILER ALERT!—found a baby on a church doorstep at the end of the previous book, Jane is forced to come clean with all the people in her world when it turns out that the baby is a different skin color than everyone had expected Jane's baby to be. As Jane fights to keep the baby, battling Social Services and taking on anyone who seeks to get in her path, what kind of mother will Jane prove to be?

Only one thing's for certain: no matter how much kinder and gentler she is now, she is still and will always be crazy Jane.